Follow

TESSA BAILEY

D1719789

Dedicated to happily ever afters.
Especially for dogs.

TABLE OF CONTENTS

CHAPTER ONE

Teresa

AIRPORTS.

Some people find them romantic. Others think they're a nasty business. I fall somewhere in the middle. Crowded from all sides by limousine drivers holding signs and loved ones cradling stuffed bears, I watch in fascination as a man and woman race toward one another. What they must be feeling is so foreign to me, I might as well be watching two manatees mating on the Discovery Channel.

The closest I've ever come to falling in love is sliding on the red Ferragamo pumps I'm wearing—and that isn't changing any time soon. Unless they release the same style in pink. Then we'll talk.

No, there is only one male alive on this planet who could get me to LAX on a busy Saturday afternoon, holding a fistful of balloons. My baby brother, Nicky. I can already picture his reaction when he exits baggage claim, duffel thrown over his shoulder, sunglasses perched on his nose to hide the inevitable hangover. He's going to pretend he doesn't know me, the adorable scumbag.

There's a tight pinch deep inside my chest. I've missed torturing Nicky. We both dealt with the death of our parents this year in different ways. He went for a visit to Staten Island to revisit his

1

roots—and, I'm guessing, ex-girlfriends.

Me? I hustled.

The money our parents left us isn't going to last forever. Nicky still has a couple years left until he finishes college, rent in Los Angeles isn't cheap and I have a weakness for Italian leather. My film school pipe dream is definitely last on the necessities list, which is good, because it's such a long shot, I refuse to even hope for an acceptance letter.

Breathing in through my nose and out through my mouth, I glance up to check the Arrivals screen. Nicky's flight landed forty minutes ago. On time. Baggage claim at LAX is notoriously snail-paced, but my brother should be out by now.

"Relax," I mutter, ignoring a look from the limo driver to my right. "He's coming home. He promised."

Nicky is all I've got. Our parents chiseled the word *family* on our souls, but they needn't have bothered. I was only three years old when he was born, but I've loved my brother from the moment I laid eyes on him. Even when he grew up, developed a chip on his shoulder and started behaving like a prick on occasion, that love only manifested deeper. He's my blood. And he belongs in Los Angeles with his often broke, overprotective sister. Not in New York.

Our parents moved us across the country nine years ago for a damn good reason. They're not here anymore. And that makes Nicky my responsibility.

Swallowing hard, my gaze travels to the clock again. Forty-five minutes. In a desperate attempt to make myself feel better, I replay the conversation I had with Nicky four weeks ago, when I dropped him off in this very spot.

Chill, Teresa. I'm just going to see some friends. I'll be back in time for school. You'll live without someone to boss around for a month.

You love it. She'd ruffled his dark, unkempt mop of hair. *Don't come back smelling like the old neighborhood. You know what I mean.*

I know you worry too much. His attention had strayed toward the security line. *All right, I'm out. Don't get used to having the toilet seat down.*

Nicky. We'd traded a heavy look. *Please. Be careful.*

When the phone rings in my pocket, playing the old classic "Lean on Me," my fingers go instantly numb. I let go of the balloons, watching them float to the ceiling. Intuition buzzes in my middle like a mosquito hitting a bug zapper. That's Nicky's ringtone. He's been hard to reach all month, flippant when I finally pinned him down to get his flight information. Where is he? I won't believe the worst yet. He's not stupid enough to get sucked into the very situation we left behind. No way.

But if that's true, why isn't he here yet?

The buzz stops, starts again, and I stumble backward— clumsy in my high heels for once—out of the crowd. For the first time, I notice the faces in that sea of loved ones have changed since arriving. Been replaced with new features.

Horror scales the insides of my throat, and finally, I start fumbling for my phone. Cursing my skinny jeans, I manage to pry the bright pink, squalling device from my pocket. It's Nicky. With the acrylic point of my index fingernail, I punch *talk* and press the cool glass to my ear. "You, uh…" I have to stop for a stuttered breath. "You tie one on last night and miss your plane, dickhead?" No answer. The airport starts to close in around me. "Typical, b-but that's fine. It's fine. I can go home and do laundry and watch *Game of Thrones* or whatever. Book another flight on the emergency credit card. I'll be here when you land—"

"You're rambling, Resa. You're always doing that when you get nervous."

His voice fills me with relief and escalating fear, all at once. If he's calm, he's not worried or pissed about missing his plane. "You've got some nerve sounding bored." I steel myself. "Where are you, Nicky?"

Silence.

"Tell me you're trying to sneak out of a girl's hotel room in Atlantic City." I start to pace, one high heel click for every ten pounds of my heart. "Hell, tell me you're in the tombs waiting to make bail. Anything."

A shaky sigh floats down the line. "I didn't come home knowing this would happen. Okay? I...everyone we used to know is wrapped up in the game now. I couldn't get away from it. It just sucked me in."

I fixate on the first thing he said. "New York isn't your home."

"Yes, it is. *And* it's yours, Resa." His hardened tone makes my free hand lift, press to my throat. "It was theirs, too. Mom and Dad's. We were living in Los Angeles, but we never really left Staten Island. You *can't*."

"You have school here. Friends." I clear the wobble from my voice. "I'm here. We're good together, aren't we?"

"Yeah, Resa. We were good. You've always made sure of it." A second later, his momentary warmth fades. Gone like a whistle in the breeze. *Were* good, he'd said. Past tense. "Go home. Watch *Thrones* and work on that application for film school. I'll come visit as soon as I get a chance."

"I already sent in the application," I say, sounding numb. Someone bumps my elbow and I don't even have the energy to flash them a middle finger.

"Good for you, sis." A pause. "I'm proud of you."

"I'm the big sister. *I'm* supposed to be the one who's proud." My mouth is dry as dust, making it impossible to swallow. I'm afraid to ask him my next question. Terrified I already know the answer. "You went to work for Silas Case. Didn't you?"

No response.

I find a pillar and use it for support, waving off a man who asks if I need help. "Dad is spinning in his grave right now, Nicky," I rasp. I'm seeing none of my surroundings. Just blurring colors and flashes of the past. "You know what he had to do to get out of that life? How dare you run straight back into it. How dare you throw away the new life he gave us."

"Me? *I'm* throwing it away?" My brother's voice deepens, so different from the boy I helped raise. The boy I have a bone-deep responsibility to protect at any cost. "Let's be real, Resa. You're not at the library at night, studying film craft. You're not doing extra work on some Hollywood lot, either, even though that's what you tell me. Neither of those things makes the kind of cash you bring home."

Lies spring to my lips, but I don't give them a voice. So my brother knows about my job. If not the specifics, then at least the illegal nature. I swallow the shame and focus on the matter at hand. "What I do, Nicky, is not in Silas Case's league. It's a million miles from it." Grasping for a new tactic, I soften my tone. "Don't you remember Dad when he worked for Silas? He was a ghost. Scared his job would get us killed. Mom was a wreck." He makes a wounded sound and I experience a flare of hope. "You'll have no life. It will be expendable. *Everyone* is expendable to that man. Nicky, please. Please. Get your shit and get on a plane." I can no longer keep the desperation out of my voice. "If you've already done something, don't say it. Don't tell me now. Just know that I'll be ready to move once you land. It's not too late."

His laughter is sad. *Scared.* So unlike my swaggering, gum-snapping, snort-chuckling brother. "I-I...think it's too late,

Resa."

There it is. There's my little brother. I can hear him beaming out through the cracks, making a plea for help. The way he spoke to me before was just a tactic. A strategy. He's twenty years old, but with those five words, he's gone back to being the kid who cried for three days when he found out Santa wasn't real. My brother. The only family I have left.

The nearby ticket counter comes into focus. "I'm coming to get you."

"*No!*" His shout hurts my ear. "It's not like how I remember it when we were kids, all right? When it was just strange men coming over to speak with Dad. Or reading about shit that happened overnight in Staten Island and wondering if Dad and his friends were involved. I'm in it. It's real. We're not kids with only half a clue anymore. That means—"

"No sympathy. I understand the risk."

"Then stay the hell in Los Angeles."

"Nicky, when people give me an order, what do I do?"

His curse is creative. "The opposite."

"Correct." Having a course of action gets me jogging for the airport exit. "I'm going to take care of this. Try and have a smidgen of faith in me."

"I should've lied." Misery oozes down the line. "Fuck. I shouldn't have called you at all."

Picking up speed at the crosswalk, I brush off the hurt. "You know why you *did* call me with the truth, little bro?"

"Why?"

"Because you need me. That's why. Because we're family. We don't just embarrass each other in public, we have one another's backs. It's part of the deal." I reach the parking lot and hit the alarm on my keychain, a little trick I use to locate my car faster. "Hang tight. I'm going to take care of everything. And maybe someday I'll forgive you for sending me to LAX on a Saturday for fuck all."

"I love you, Resa. Dammit. I'm sorry I messed up." His voice cracks on the last word, telling me I was right. My little brother is scared. Which is only good for one thing. Making me *angry*—and about four thousand times as determined to go to New York and pluck my brother out of Silas Case's blood-covered hands.

"Hang tight, kiddo." When I reach my car, I notice a group of Marines in uniform checking me out, so I throw them a pinky wave. "And don't tell anyone I'm coming. I like to make an entrance."

CHAPTER TWO

Teresa

IT'S NOT THAT I don't love Staten Island.

Okay, fine. I don't *love* Staten Island. But it has nothing to do with aesthetics. Working-class heroes take pride in their homes, lawns and businesses. It's got charm. It's got swagger. But if you live here, you better own a pair of brass balls, because as far as the rest of New York City is concerned, you're the bastard stepchild borough. No one is going to stick up for Staten Island except you. Which brings me to yet another truth about this place.

Shit does *not* change.

Standing across the street from Tommaso's, I'm leaning against a brick wall of the deli where I bought my first and last pack of Parliaments, before my mother caught and grounded me for a month. My black hoodie is zipped up and pulled down low over my face. There's an *AM New York* in my hands, but I'm not reading a single word. No, I'm watching Silas Case follow the same damn routine he followed when I was a child and used to ride bikes on this block. He's unlocking the door to the restaurant—a place he doesn't even own—and pacing inside to make an espresso. His first of many throughout the day, while men slip in through the back door to drop off envelopes. Tribute to the boss.

Here. Hold my eyeroll.

I suppose there have been subtle changes. Silas definitely has a lot more white hair, more molasses gooing up his step. If I were filming this scene, I would open with a nice establishing shot. Get the whole old-school, business-lined block in, before switching over to a low-angle shot of Silas. Close-up on the shuffling steps of his shiny wingtips. His wrinkled hands as he unlocks the door. A suspicious look over his shoulder toward the hooded figure across the street.

He disregards them with a grunt, though, because this is his neighborhood. And no one fucks with Silas Case around here.

In picturing the various camera angles, I realize my eyes have drifted shut, yearning tickling my belly. My mind drifts to the application to The Film Institute I dropped into the mailbox last week, my hopes and dreams sealed tight inside yellow manila.

Probably won't happen.

Definitely won't happen.

Focus on the task ahead. This isn't a movie. This is real life. The man who just slipped inside Tommaso's isn't an innocent, doddering old relic. He's a dangerous felon who could ruin my brother's life. Throw him into the dire circumstances my parents fought to keep us from. If this were a movie, though, I know exactly how it would end. My brother and I sitting beside one another on an airplane, a feminine voice coming over the PA system to announce we're headed to Los Angeles. Click. Our seatbelts connect. Fade to white.

"Quiet on the set," I murmur, unzipping my hoodie and tucking it beneath my arm. The absence of my sweatshirt leaves me in a tank top that's as tight as a second layer of skin. I immediately feel more in control with my body as a weapon. Not that I intend to unleash it on Silas Case. God, no. It's more of a battlefield tactic—one that rarely fails me.

My inner confidence is less substantial than quicksand, but who's going to notice when the outline of my demi cup is much more interesting? "And we're rolling..." Once I'm across the street, I toss the newspaper into a dented, green trashcan and walk into Tommaso's unannounced.

A gun barrel winks back at me in the darkness. "Who the fuck?"

Pause.

In my attempts to break into the entertainment industry, I've had several shitty bit parts as an actress, so I've been around a lot of fake guns. But I've only seen a *real* gun on a single occasion.

My father came home late one night, which wasn't unusual. He didn't notice me sitting in the shadows in the living room as he discarded his shoes in a plastic garbage bag, then carefully slid a gun from a shoulder holster, stowing it in the bag, along with his shoes. Loafers my mother had bought him for Christmas. As long as I live, I will never forget his expression when he turned and saw me. Devastation. Why hadn't I just stayed in bed?

That night, we drove together to the edge of a river, filled the bag with rocks and let the current take it away. The very next day, my father approached Silas Case and demanded to be let out of the oath he'd taken.

That same boss points a weapon at me now. And it's *not* a movie prop.

Get the upper hand back. Don't let him see your fear.

"Teresa Valentini." Hoping to hide the fact that I'm trembling, I jerk my chin toward the sputtering espresso machine. "I like a lemon twist with mine."

"Valentini." Silas doesn't blink, but there's recognition in his tone. "You been out of this neighborhood so long you forget how to have some goddamn respect?"

I raise my eyebrows, hopefully giving no indication that I'm on the verge of peeing my pants. "You're the one pointing a gun at an unarmed female."

"I didn't stay alive this long by taking chances." He dips the gun, indicating my waist, the sweatshirt tucked under my arm. "Prove it."

Thankful I left my trusty stun gun back at the Motel 6 I checked into, I lift my hands in the air and let the hoodie drop. I turn in a circle, rolling my eyes when he makes an appreciative sound. It doesn't even make me want to cringe. Oh no, this is familiar ground, having my body serve as a distraction. Same way I do at work, I lean into that lecher behavior and show Silas it doesn't affect me whatsoever. I lift up my shirt, giving him a better view of my back waistband. When I'm facing him again, I even give my tits a nice little shake. "No gun. No wire. What do you say? Can we be friends now?"

His coffee-stained eyes narrow, humor curling one end of his mouth. "I remember you now. Couldn't have been older than fourteen when your father left like a thief in the night."

"Correction: he *stopped* being a thief in the night when we left. And he'd paid his dues."

"Oh yeah?" His gaze slithers down my thighs, but I refuse to flinch. "What do you know about your father's time with me, little girl?"

Smoothly as possible, I cover my misstep. "Only that we were all unhappy. And that he came to you and worked something out. A way that allowed us to leave in peace." I take a long pull of oxygen. "I'm here to do the same for my brother."

"No."

That single word is like being backhanded, but I command myself to maintain my poker face. I'm immediately resentful that he stole the upper hand I earned by shaking my tits, though. His smile tells me he loved doing it, too. "He can't be that valuable to you after four weeks." A thought occurs. "Or are you still salty about my father leaving?"

"Your brother is indispensable, just like the rest of these baby birds that want to be gangsters."

"So it *is* about my father?" I take a couple experimental steps into the restaurant, orbiting this man I'm hating more by the minute. "And my brother isn't a baby bird."

"Oh no? He's some hidden gem, but he needs his five-foot-nothing sister to come wipe his ass?" He winks at me. "Not that I mind the scenery."

I flutter my eyelashes. "As far as you're concerned, this scenery is government land. And I'm the president."

His laugh catches him off guard. After a few seconds, he lets the gun drop, and my insides unclench. "Let's go sit down. I like to drink my espresso hot."

I make a sweeping gesture toward the dining room. "Age before beauty."

My feet sink into the plush, outdated, ruby-red carpet as I follow Silas toward a two-seater table. He heaves a breath—and his belly—to get into the booth side of the table. Then he sets about rearranging himself. Straightening his collar, his coat. Twisting his ring. Organizing his spoon and espresso within reach. Those sharp movements remind me he's not some harmless grandfather. Didn't he almost blow my head off when I walked in here?

"All right. Let's continue." Staten Island is packed into his voice like sardines. "Is this about your father?" He pinches his fingers together in front of his face. "Poco." *A little.* "These kids...they think working for me is like a job at fucking Starbucks. They get bored and decide they want out. I can't allow that. Not without a penalty. You let one out, they all start itching to fly the coop."

My first thought is: this isn't as bad as I was expecting. My second one is: don't be naïve. There's a shoe waiting to drop somewhere and it's not as cute as the wedge heel ankle boots I'm wearing. "So what's the penalty? Money?"

A smile stretches across his face. "I got money, sweetheart."

"A job, then."

He leans back and sips his espresso. Seconds tick by as he studies me, thoughts cranking behind eyes that have probably seen more than their fair share of gruesome sights. "You should already be dead," he says, finally.

The hair on my arm stands up, bile rising in my throat. "My brother didn't tell me anything. Only that he can't come home to Los Angeles. I filled in the blanks."

No answer as he absorbs that.

"Look, this isn't going to mean anything to you, but..." Heat burns behind my eyelids. "My parents are gone now. Died within four days of one another. Dad first. Then Mom. He's the only blood I have left."

"Why wouldn't that mean anything to me?"

"I-I don't know." I'm humiliated when moisture obscures my vision, so I toss my hair back in order to look up at the ceiling. "If the penalty is a job...*I'll* do it. Once it's over, we're both off the hook."

He inclines his head. "Do you have the Instagram?"

"I'm sorry, what?"

"The Instagram." I watch from way out in left field as Silas tugs eyeglasses out of his pocket and peers down at the screen of his cell phone. "One of these squares opens it..."

Whoa. What is with the topic change?

Recognizing the pink icon across the table, I reach across the table and punch the app with my index finger. "Uh." Ducking my head, I check his pupils for dilation. "Should I call a nurse?"

"Here it is."

"Here *what* is?"

"My son. Will." Silas faces the screen in my direction. "Looks like he's in Texas now. Last week it was Louisiana." The lines around his mouth tighten. "He's driving across the country with his dog."

"That sounds slobbery." Leaning in, I get a good look at Will, and okay. Hell. My ovaries sit up and pant against my will. He's what the ladies at my job refer to as *foine*. Yummy in a dangerous kind of way. A harsh, unshaven jaw that looks like it would leave rug burns on the insides of a woman's thighs. His eyes are hidden by dark sunglasses, but the creases between his heavy, black brows tell me they're hard. Discerning. In the picture, Will is leaning back against an old, orange convertible, with a giant—I mean, freaking *enormous*—dog sitting on the hood, tongue lolling out the side of its mouth. Will's arms are crossed and I can't help but zero in on those corded forearms, the breadth of his chest. God. *Damn.*

He's a *beast* in the sack. I don't even need a test drive to make that judgment.

I don't test drive *at all* anymore. Men are fun to look at on Instagram. They can lift heavy things. The human race needs their man juice to procreate. But this vibrator-packing girl is just window shopping, thank you very much. That dog might be looking at Will with hero worship in its eyes, but within a month, that burly and apparently *loaded* male human would be making demands on my time and patience without giving anything in return. Except, maybe, an occasional half-hearted lay. Just like the rest of his brethren.

I might only be twenty-three, but I've been burned by enough men to know they share a common gene. They can't see past their own needs and if those needs—physical, emotional and food-ical—aren't being satisfied non-stop, they check out and start looking for the next girl who can provide instant gratification. Or an ego boost. I have *zero* time for it. Why am I thinking about this at all?

Sitting back in my chair, I start to ask why we've gone off the topic, when a thought occurs. "Wait a minute. I don't remember you having a son."

"My wife could never conceive." He inclines his head. "My girlfriend did, though."

"There it is. Lovely." Impatience cranks in my middle. "What does your son have to do with my brother?"

"Will is the job I'm giving you."

Without permission, my abdomen knits up tight, as if in anticipation of coming into real-life contact with Will. Silly, neglected hormones. "I don't follow."

Silas Case laces his fingers together, placing them carefully on the table. He seems to be choosing his words. "Will manages Caruso Capital Management—a revered hedge fund—and he's only thirty-two." That takes me off guard. After looking at Will's picture, I didn't expect him to work behind a desk. More like beneath a vintage car or in a football uniform. My musings are interrupted when Silas Case continues. "He's throwing away everything he's worked for in order to drive around the country with his fucking dog."

"Why?"

He snorts. "There is no acceptable reason. I don't care if the dog *is* dying."

My heart lurches. "The dog is…dying?"

Silas tilts his head. "Don't go soft on me now. I'm handing you a chance for your brother to walk away free and clear. And I'm giving you the chance because you don't flinch and I like that. It's rare these days."

"Touching," I say, trying to sound bored. Truth is, though, I'm still stuck on that massive pooch meeting his maker. Despite its size, the dog looks young. "So what's the actual mission, captain, so I can decide if I choose to accept?"

"This has gone on long enough." Silas's fist comes down hard on the table, splashing espresso on the white tablecloth. Another reminder that the man sitting across from me is a cold-blooded mafia boss. A tyrant who has ruled this neighborhood since before I was born. "I take responsibility for what I did. But it's no excuse to let his business fail."

"What did you do?"

His black eyes turn glacial. "None of your business." Battling a fierce urge to look away, I nod once and he continues. "Let's see what it takes to make you flinch, shall we?"

Trepidation sneaks into my gut, but I shrug. "Have at it."

Silas's attention falls to my breasts, lingering there long enough to make my arms tingle with the need to cross. "There are only three things in life that drive a man. Power, money. And women. Will has those first two bases covered, but even unlimited cash and clout couldn't keep him from this ridiculous escapade." He refocuses on my face. "That leaves women."

What the hell is he getting at? "Seems to me if he's rich and powerful, women come as part of the deal."

"Sure. But I'm talking about a *specific* woman. The kind the makes a man change his plans. Rearrange everything." He cocks an eyebrow. "You strutted in here looking like a centerfold and stared straight down the barrel of my gun. There's something about you. I don't change my plans for nobody, but my son isn't like me."

My pulse picks up. "What are you asking?"

"I won't be the reason he throws it all away. I need him to succeed." He smoothes a wrinkle in the tablecloth, very, very carefully. "Find Will. Convince him to give up this ridiculous escapade and go home. Back to his company." His gaze ticks to mine. "I think we both know what I mean by *convince* him."

I'm not so sure I hide my true feelings this time around. How can I when my skin is crawling with spiky-legged ants? Silas wants me to sleep with Will. Wants me to feign interest and give my body to a stranger, with the hope he grows attached to me—enough to bring him home. There's no question about that.

My system feels jolted, top to bottom. I've used my body as a shiny object and form of distraction since I started filling out a C-cup. But *I've* chosen to use it as a weapon—a harmless one that I've never deployed for the wrong reasons. Having this man call out *my* secret and ask me to put my money where my mouth is? I might as well be sitting here with no clothes on. No artful makeup or pricey shoes. Nothing.

Just Teresa. A girl who works a dead-end job and has no chance at film school.

So I do what comes naturally and default to indifference. No way is he going to know he stripped off a layer of my skin. Especially when my brother's freedom is my goal. I'll agree to anything he wants and adjust later. "Convince him. Right." I swallow. "So, I'm just supposed to believe this is all about you wanting the best for him?"

"Yeah," he snaps, daring me to question him. "Is that so hard to believe?"

His motives don't matter. He's giving me an out. I can't give him a chance to change his mind. "So, let's recap. I...encourage Will to go back to his fancy-pants life in New York City. You let my brother off scot-free?"

"You've got a week."

I reach deep for some bravado. "If I can get it done sooner, how about you throw in airfare?" He's clearly not impressed with the suggestion or my charming eyebrow waggle, so I push back my chair and stand, ready to split before he takes back the offer. Now that I've had time to recover from Silas's request, I'm mostly back in control. Convince a man to do something? I've had a harder time opening a jar of pickles.

After all, Silas didn't specify that I had to sleep with Will. He only implied it. There's a way to meet the crime boss's demands without selling my soul.

Isn't there?

I'll be conning Will no matter what happens.

Remembering the dog's expression of rapture, guilt climbs my neck like a ladder, but I shake it off. I can handle any amount of guilt to help my brother. "If I'm doing this, it's going to be done right. I need a few days to plan and make my cover story credible. The week starts when I get to Texas."

His mouth is flat, but he agrees. "Sure."

"Any further instructions?"

"Under no circumstances can Will know I sent you. Other than that? No." His gaze travels downward, lingering on my thighs. Between them. "You seem like an adventurous girl. I'll leave the dirty details to you."

Acid climbs my throat. Unable to get out of there fast enough, I swagger toward the exit, but Silas's voice brings me up short. "Oh, and Teresa, don't be alarmed if I send someone to keep an eye on you." He winks at me. "Just to keep you honest."

Smiling through my alarm, I finally make it out the door.

Texas, here I come.

CHAPTER THREE

Will

MY DEFINITION OF a bad day has changed. Drastically.

In a different lifetime, a bad day used to mean a trip to the emergency room with a busted eye, so I could get stitched up. Or watching the Giants get spanked.

In this lifetime, a bad day means losing forty million dollars on a bad trade.

To be fair, the latter doesn't happen too often, but when it does…it's almost like it's happening to someone else. Another man. Same when it comes to triumphs or hell, even uneventful days in the office. I'm always looking back on that other lifetime, wondering where that asshole with the busted lip went.

I draw a long breath in through my nose and let it out, staring out over the field. Neither one of those men seem to be here now.

Which one will I eventually return to?

A slimy snout presses into the palm of my hand, distracting me.

The tightness in my chest eases when I look down at my dog. His body vibrates with the leftover excitement of running in the field we pulled over to inspect, just outside of Dallas.

"Back already, huh?" I rub the top of Southpaw's head with

my knuckles. "Shit. Why are you wet? *Again.*"

My Great Dane responds by yawning, showing off the ridges on the roof of his mouth. He flops onto his side and rolls over, his four legs looking like highway mile markers pointed straight up at the blue sky. The mud splashed all over his white belly will be transferred to my leather car seat when we hit the road again. That's fine by me, though. Leather can be replaced, but Southpaw can't.

This is his vacation. I'm just the chauffeur.

See, bad days were always surmountable before. I could fix them. Or enough time would pass that I gradually forgot they existed. There's no moving on from a day when you find out your entire damn life is a lie—and your dog is dying—within the space of twenty-four hours. There's no way to change those things.

So I changed my priorities instead.

Southpaw makes a *snarf* sound and writhes on his back in the grass.

"What's that mean? You hungry?" His tongue unfolds and dangles out the corner of his mouth in response. "Yeah. When are you *not* hungry, you big-ass beast? Let's go. Hop in."

Southpaw animates in a flurry of fur, trotting toward my Chevelle when just a month ago, he would have streaked at a hundred miles an hour. I clear my throat hard to keep a lump from forming and school my features. Call me crazy if you want, but that dog picks up on everything. And he's truly my dog, because he's not a fan of pity. Or cats.

We've been on this road trip for one month as of today. Started in New York and made our way down to Florida, before cutting west. We don't have rules or plans. When we find somewhere we like, we stay until we get sick of it. In other words, until Southpaw drags my suitcase out from beneath the bed and sits on it until I get the hint and start packing.

Dallas has been keeping us entertained for a few days, but as we pull into the parking lot of the Drifter Motel and Southpaw gives a sigh, I'm pretty sure we'll be gone by tomorrow. Dogs have no attention span these days.

"Come on," I say, throwing the car into park. "Better clean you up or no respectable eating establishment will let us through the door."

Speaking of respectable establishments, this motel doesn't really fall into that category. The stucco is peeling, half the vacancy sign needs replacement bulbs, and guests consist of broke musicians and men of questionable morals. It's not that I can't afford something nicer—I can write a check and buy a damn hotel if I so choose—but even if a five-star hotel was willing to let a horse-sized dog sleep in their fancy sheets, they're not happy about it. My overly sensitive dog loves people, so I'd rather have him surrounded by people who'll love him back.

Case in point, someone puts their hand out for a sniff every two steps on our way to the room. Out front, a couple is getting romantic in between sips from a brown paper bag. Music blares out from two different rooms. One plays metal, Spanish opera belts through a fuzzy speaker in the other. Cigarette smoke, old and new, lingers in the air, along with the smell of lemon cleaning product and sweat.

"Home sweet home," I mutter, reaching down to pat Southpaw on the head. He head-butts my thigh in response. Sliding the key from my pocket, I dip it into the metal reader and push the door open. "I know. You love it. They don't mind you tracking in—"

Tits.

There are tits in my room.

Really fucking nice ones.

I'm so distracted by their unexpected appearance—any red-blooded man with working testicles would be—that I don't take in their owner right away. And all the *other* equally amazing shit that's going on. The sexy brunette has one foot propped on my bed, her hands paused on her calf where she's been applying lotion, before I so rudely interrupted her by walking into my own room.

A gruff bark from Southpaw prompts me to double check the door. But I do it fast—we're in the right place—because as I mentioned, there's a really fucking nice pair of tits in my room. Sue me for wanting to memorize the shape and color of her tight, rosy nipples before she screams and covers herself.

Which she doesn't exactly seem inclined to do.

"Can we help you?"

Up until now, a big waterfall of dark hair has been hiding the woman's face from me. But at my greeting, she tosses that thick mane back...and reveals features that accomplish the impossible. It nudges her tits into second place for most incredible body part in the room.

Hearing male voices approach in the hallway, I kick the door shut, surprised by the fact that I already don't want anyone else looking at her. "You going to tell me why you're in my room, woman? Or just stand there looking hot?"

When her red-stained lips spread into a smile, I once again marvel over the fact that she's got *zero* plans to cover herself. No complaints from this corner. I'm just acutely aware that she was waiting for me to react to her nudity so she could take my measure. Based on that smile and her squaring shoulders, that's exactly what she's done. I've logged nine thousand hours in the boardroom, so I know all about sizing up a potential ally or adversary. Reading people is my business. *I'm* usually the unreadable one—and I don't like how easily she managed it.

Leave it to a pair of knockout tits to throw a man off his game.

"You must be mistaken." In the saddest event in my recent memory, she produces a bra and snaps it into place, before strutting slowly around the bed. Legs. For. Days. My groin tightens like a motherfucker, which is saying something considering I've had wood since walking through the door. She's showcasing those thighs with a black strip of material some might call shorts, but they're more like underwear. Or two fabric samples stapled together. As if I'm not having a hard enough time keeping my eyes off that sweet little V between her legs, she slides a card key from the front of her shorts and waves it at me. "This is my room."

"Then they double-booked it." My tone is challenging. She thinks she's got the upper hand? Let's see if she can keep it. "I've been sleeping in that bed for three days."

Her throaty hum turns up the ache in my dick to full volume. "Comfortably, I hope." Leisurely, she cocks a hip and scans the room with pursed lips. "Where's all your stuff? If I'd walked in and seen your jeans on the floor, this peep show could have been avoided."

I shake my head hard. "Now that would have been a shame."

Color fills her cheeks, which seems to…annoy her? "Maybe your credit card got declined and this was their way of breaking up with you."

I can't quite keep the amusement from my voice. "That's definitely not it."

Another sexy purr. "Well, let's solve the riddle, shall we?" She tosses me a wink on her way to the bedside table, where she picks up the phone and hits a button. Waits a few beats. "Hello, this is Teresa Smith." *Smith, my ass.* "I just checked into room one-oh-seven, but the room's rightful owner just showed. I feel a little bit like Goldilocks. Was it double-booked, by any chance?"

Southpaw drops down on the ground at my feet, so I crouch down to rub his belly. Not to get an even better view of Teresa Smith's tush, which of course is just as mesmerizing as the rest of her. High, firm and looking to get slapped.

My life is lived within the walls of my offices, so most of the women I come into contact with are my employees. I'm only interested in their ability to bring me a winning play. On the rare occasions I get out and have the opportunity to meet women who aren't on my payroll, none of them make my pulse trip over itself like this one. I'm kind of stunned by the force of my attraction. It's potent and she calls to it more with every second that ticks by.

"Ahh," Teresa says, nodding over her shoulder at me. "I see. No, that's fine. Thank you for your help." After dropping the phone into the cradle, she starts gathering things off the bedside table I didn't notice on the way in. A cell phone, a pair of earrings, some loose change. "They gave me the wrong room. I'm next door."

Giving Southpaw a final pat on the stomach, I rise. "You're going to put a shirt on before you head into the hallway."

"Was that a question or—"

I shake my head.

Temper flashes in her eyes, but it doesn't reach her tongue. "Sure." Teresa saunters closer, all graceful-hipped and sultry-eyed. "You want to help me out with that shirt idea?" She bends down to scrub a hand over Southpaw's head and the dog pants with rapture. If she notices the lump on his front, right paw, she gives no indication. Laughing softly, she steps over him carefully, bringing us inches apart. With a low sound of interest, she lays her hands on my pecs, rubbing them in a slow circle, finding my top button with her fingers. Unhooking it. "I'd hate to go digging through my luggage when you've got a perfectly nice shirt right here."

"Only thing is, I'm wearing it," I rasp. *Fuck*. Up close, she's nothing less than extraordinary. She barely reaches my shoulders, but the little woman packs a punch. Her eyes are gray-green. Is that even a color? Her skin is just a hint sunburned, but the red sits on top of a golden glow, making her look rosy. Ripe. Everywhere. My cock is all but growling for freedom behind my zipper, wanting contact with that skin. Wanting to conquer it.

She flicks open the second button. "Can't I wrap myself in it for a while?"

I catch her wrist before she can undo the third. Southpaw yelps inside his throat, but I *shh* him. "Who are you?"

There's a line between her brows, those gray-greens racing all over my face. I'll be damned if there isn't buzzing static rippling back and forth between us, taking us both for a ride. "Teresa Smith," she murmurs. "At your service."

Just like before, I'd love to call bullshit on her last name. One thing at a time, though. "A strange man seeing you mostly naked doesn't bother you, Teresa?"

Me saying her name delivers some kind of jolt. I feel it travel through her arm and slide up into my shoulder. Around to the back of my neck. And I can tell the precise moment she decides to tell the truth, instead of going with some patented bullshit I'd see from a mile away. "Acting like something doesn't bother you is easier than admitting it does, right?"

There's a sharp pressure in my chest. What the hell is going on here? "Yeah." Reluctantly, I let go of her wrist, but only after I apply some pressure to her veins and watch her lids slide down. "Yeah. A hell of a lot easier."

Keeping her in front of me with a look, I open the rest of my shirt, drape it over her shoulders, then re-do the buttons. All the while, she watches me like *I'm* the mystery in the room. I should be smug, shouldn't I? Girl shows up topless and does her damnedest to turn me into a sputtering jackass. She didn't quite succeed, even though having her look me over, neck to belt buckle, is giving my dick the consistency of iron. So how come all I want to do is tug her close and run my thumb along her bottom lip? To ask her what else bothers her that she doesn't find easy to admit.

Jesus. If someone told me this morning a woman existed who could make me feel protective, jealous, horny, challenged and curious in the space of five minutes, I would have laughed until my fucking face turned blue.

"How about you return that shirt later when we have dinner?"

"I have plans."

My hands do their own thing, curling in the shirt and dragging her closer. "Break them," I breathe against her mouth. "I want to…talk to you."

Her laughter puffs out. "Yeah, I can feel how badly you need to *talk*."

"Come on now. You've been strutting around naked looking hotter than fuck. You'd be offended right now if my dick wasn't hard."

Humor twinkles in her eyes. "Good point."

"Dinner, woman."

Turning her head, she presses those soft lips against my ear. Breathes in and out. "I'll think about it."

Before I can formulate a response, she sidesteps me, taking the handle of a rolling suitcase, which has the strap of a laptop case wrapped around it. Without missing a beat, she glides toward the door. I should let her go, right? She's in the room beside mine. And I've *just* made her acquaintance, but I already know she's a woman who makes up her damn mind only when good and ready.

I can't simply close the door and let her simmer for a few hours, though, because those male voices I heard earlier? Their owners are posted up right outside my door, passing a joint back and forth. Maybe it's due to the marijuana or they're just plain stupid, but they don't even see me. Or they can't manage to take their stunned eyes off Teresa's bare legs long enough to acknowledge my presence.

"Damn," says Moron Number One. "Hey there, pretty thing."

And never count out Moron Number Two from chiming in. Moron number twos can never help it. "I'd ask to get inside your pants, but you're not wearing any."

A paint splatter of black obscures my vision, heat sinking into my veins. Especially when Teresa takes a backward step, her eyes searching for me over her shoulder. Behind me, Southpaw starts to growl, but I'm already on the same page. It has been a while since *this* man, the one I used to be, was invited to come out and play, but it's like riding a bike. The immediate transformation supports the theory that I've been pretending to be someone else for too damn long. Brushing past Teresa in the doorframe, muscle memory and disgust bring my right fist down in the center of Moron Number One's face. He hits the floor and stays down, so maybe he's not as stupid as I originally thought.

Moron Number Two, however, is just as moronic as his first impression gave. He telegraphs his punch in stoner slow motion—it takes so long I could make a fucking sandwich—so I sidestep and let him stumble against the far wall, before spinning him around and pinning my forearm against his jugular. "A woman walks out of *my* room, wearing *my* shirt, you don't speak to her. You don't even look at her. You got that?" He lets out a strangled *yeah, man*. "Matter of fact, you're not getting a second chance. Pick up your asshole friend and get the hell out. I don't want to see you back here again."

When I let Moron Number Two go and he scrambles to collect his buddy, I glance over at Teresa and I'm surprised to find Southpaw guarding her, lips peeled back to show off his teeth. Has he ever done that for anyone but me? Granted, I'm a complete loner so he's only got me most of the time, but still. It makes me study her harder. Makes my gut kick.

She looks back at me with a sardonic tilt to her lips. "All right, all right. I'll go to dinner with you." After giving Southpaw a scratch behind the ear, she saunters past me toward her room. "You can stop showing off now."

By the time her door clicks shut, I'm laughing.

CHAPTER FOUR

Teresa

L ISTENING FOR WILL to reenter his room after the hallway altercation, I finally hear the door snick shut. Footsteps traveling down the hallway, man and dog. After meeting him, I have no doubt he's going to double check my story with motel reception, but I'm safe. They're disorganized enough to think they truly made a mistake and definitely won't suspect I simply climbed the first-floor balcony and jimmied the flimsy lock.

Entering the bathroom, I barely recognize myself in the mirror, my neck flushed from the encounter with Will. I grip the sink edge and blow out a shaky breath, attempting to get myself under control. It doesn't work. My hips sway forward and press against the cheap imitation marble, my head falling back on my shoulders. Without consent, my butt muscles flex, grinding me closer—and wow. Nothing to see here, I'm just humping the sink. *Christ.*

I'll admit that after Silas showed me Will Caruso on Instagram, I scrolled through his feed…all the way to the end. Purely for research purposes, of course. And yeah, he is potent on a tiny digital screen, but nothing compares to real life. Nothing comes close. For one thing, I can smell him. Can smell nature hugging him closely, laced through with undertones of menthol aftershave.

Part of me was wondering if Will's vamoose from New York was some rich boy emo quest to discover himself. After spending a few minutes around him and Southpaw—seeing the way they react to one another—I have to admit it's the real deal. Whatever happened between him and Silas might have contributed, but as his Instagram account implies, he's on the road to give Southpaw a treasure trove of final memories. A man showing genuine affection for something other than himself must be the reason I'm so damn attracted.

Good thing we're incompatible.

I'm not talking about physically. Because, hello, I'm grinding against a sink and if someone ran into my nipples, they would impale themselves. I don't think I've ever been this hot for a real-life man, have I? The closest I've come in recent memory is seeing *Magic Mike XXL* in theaters after two mango margaritas.

We're incompatible for three reasons. One? He's a man, which definitely doesn't work in his favor. Two? I'm here under false pretenses. Three? Silas *expects* me to sleep with Will.

I can't give that evil man the satisfaction.

In another world, if Will and I had a chance meeting in a bar, I would let my libido get some exercise and strut away without looking back. But my goal is getting Will back to New York, right? As I've discovered too many times before, as soon as sex ceases to be the big, mysterious driving force between a man and woman, he starts to lose interest. I have to *keep* that interest.

And that means sex is a no-no.

Easy peasy, right?

I fan my heated cheeks.

The most important thing I noticed about Will during our first meeting is this: he's as sharp as a samurai sword—and not the prop kind. I don't have long to accomplish this mission before he smells something rotten in Denmark. As every reality show villain in history says, I'm not here to make friends. I need to remember that next time I'm faced with all that keen intelligence and scarred, rugged muscle in one huge, animal-loving package.

Don't. Don't think of his package. Or the way he came to my defense and then acted so freaking cool about it. Smiling as I passed. Instead of crushing a beer can on his forehead like most guys after the tiniest squabble.

I fan myself harder, but the added wind doesn't help. Admitting defeat, I drop my right hand, sliding it into the front of my shorts. As soon as my middle finger grazes my clit, I cinch my tights around my hand on a moan. Eyelids drooping, I remember how his thick shoulders rolled as he removed his shirt, that muscle popping in his jaw. And that dusting of black hair decorating his stomach. Not the abdomen of a man who flexes and preens all day in the gym, but goes extra hard on the weights when he needs to burn energy. Making him rock solid beneath a tight layer of rough, no frills, glorious bulk—

My cell phone buzzes on the sink. A frustrated whine breaks past my lips at the interruption, but when I look down and see my brother's name, I whip my hand out of my shorts faster than drug stores discount heart-shaped candy after Valentine's Day.

"Shit. What…uhh…" I run my hand under the tap and dry it on a threadbare towel before answering. "Nicky. Hey!"

Congratulations, that sounded totally natural.

"Hey, Resa." Traffic competes in the background amid honks and humming engines. "You go back to LA?"

"No." Aware of the thin walls, I shut the bathroom door and sit down on the closed toilet. I'm also aware that Nicky's phone line isn't a smart way to communicate now that he's running with Silas Case—it could easily be monitored—so I search for a way to keep things vague. "I had to take a little vacation. To handle everything."

"A vacation."

"Yeah." Not having total control of my brother's safety makes my right leg jiggle. Why did he have to go to New York in the first place? I should have worked harder to keep him from leaving. *God.* When my parents left us, I swore to myself I'd be his rock. Turns out I'm less rock, more slippery slope. *Fix it.* "Just…lay low for a while, all right? Real low. I'll be coming to get you very soon."

"How soon?" His tone is part impatience, part nerves. "I know you're probably doing everything you can. And this is my fucking fault. But…nothing has changed. I'm still working. He called me personally and reminded me to show up as usual. No exceptions. He's never done that, you know?"

Dammit. I come to my feet without realizing it and start to pace. "There's nothing to worry about. That was probably just to put pressure on me—"

"*Pressure* on you? Resa, that's never good coming from this man." I can practically see Nicky snatching the ball cap off his head and jamming it back on. "I can't believe I dragged you into this."

I take a deep breath to combat the pressure in my throat. "Nicky, do everything you can to stay clear of trouble until I get back. I'm working on it as we speak." Heat blooms behind my eyes, my arms shaking with the need to hug my little brother. The irresponsible *shithead.* I'm too far away to hold him, but there's no way I'm ending this call with him sounding so scared. "Hey. Remember that summer I tried to recreate *E.T.* shot for shot with my first camcorder?"

"How could I forget?" He snorts. "You wrapped me in a sheet and made me be E.T. when I wanted to be out playing ball."

"Right." The memory of him sitting on the bathroom sink

while I colored his index finger with bright red Sharpie makes my throat hurt. "I showed that recording to your first girlfriend, remember? Consider this payback."

"I would never. But that was pretty fucked up."

My laughter is halting. "Yeah, it was."

There's a long pause. "I'm more worried for you than me, Resa. Whatever you're doing, be careful."

I wave a hand, even though he can't see me. I can see myself in the mirror, though, and there's no mistaking the conflict in my eyes. "Trust me. I already got this half in the bag."

An hour later, I have one foot propped on the bed while I lace up my chocolate-colored gladiator sandals, quietly thanking Lilly Pulitzer for the added reminder that I'm here to win. Losing could cost my brother everything.

A knock at the door brings my head up.

This is a job. Eyes open. Take it seriously.

And since Silas issued me an indirect warning, I'm giving him the mental bird by remembering one small but important fact.

He said I need to get Will back to New York.

He didn't say anything about keeping him there.

Will

PAUSING IN THE act of refilling Southpaw's food bowl, I pick up my ringing phone. "Mom," I answer. "Everything okay?"

"Sure, sure. Just watching my programs." In the background I can hear the little dings signaling Vanna White to turn the letters on *Wheel of Fortune*. Such a familiar scene. One I haven't visited since shit hit the fan in New York and I left town but remember like the back of my hand. "I just wanted to see how the road trip was going."

I think of the woman on the other side of the wall. "You could say it's getting interesting."

"Oh. Well, that's…nice to hear." I straighten at her obvious disappointment. "Have you talked to anyone?"

There it is. Never fails. At least it took her a full thirty seconds this time to ask. "Who would I have talked to?"

Ding. Ding. More letters being turned. "Your father, maybe?"

Biting down on my tongue, I resist the urge to say *he's not my father*. He is, though. Denying it is pointless. "No, I haven't heard from him, Mom. I never did. He showed up the same time every year, no calls in between."

Her laughter is light, dismissive of the truth. "But I thought things could be different now. Since there are no more secrets."

"Those secrets are why I want nothing to do with him." I pinch the bridge of my nose. "I don't understand why it isn't the same for you."

"He's a man. All men make mistakes." Her voice wobbles when she adds, "He shared so much with us over the years. Shouldn't we forgive and forget?"

Ironically, this is one of the major reasons I'll *never* forgive the bastard. My mother is too trusting by nature and he took advantage of that. As far as I'm concerned, he still is taking advantage, leaving her to wonder if he'll ever come back, now that we know his true identity. The alternative is having him break off their odd relationship, though, and I don't know if she could handle that, either. "Listen to me carefully, Mom. He's a criminal. He's not the good man you thought he was—and you need to stay away."

I leave out the part about me warning Silas to stay away from *her*, in our one and only phone call, before I left New York. Not that I have a lot of faith in him listening.

"I'm a grown woman, Will. I decide how to spend my time."

Knowing from experience there's nothing I can do to make her budge, I take a breath and move on. For now. "I don't want to argue with you." I clear my throat. "Are you okay for money?"

"Yes, yes," she rushes to say, sounding equally regretful over us trading words. "It's really not polite to talk about finances over the phone, though."

"You just summed up what I do for a living." When she laughs, I can't help but smile. "I'll call soon, Mom. Take care."

"You too, Will." Silence stretches. "I'm...you take care. Bye now."

We hang up.

My mother being enamored with Silas is nothing new. It's something I've been around my whole life. Her effusive praise and excuse making. I know what he really is, though. I'll be here for my mother when she realizes it, too.

Minutes later, when Teresa opens the door to her room, the phone call is forgotten. I don't know if I'm disappointed or relieved she's wearing more clothes this time. Hell, it's possible she's just as edible in that little flimsy, floaty outfit as she was mostly naked. I've had over an hour to digest our first encounter, however. Long enough to realize she likes knocking me off balance with her looks. The question is, why does she *want* me off balance?

She slides a hand up the doorframe, and the hem flutters higher up her thigh, that smooth skin begging for a man's hands. Mine.

"Hi," she murmurs. "Ready to go?"

Fucking right I am. Just say the word. "In a minute." I prop my own forearm on the frame and step closer. "I'm taking you in."

A touch of irritation highlights the green in her eyes. But since I'm a gambling man, I'll bet she's annoyed because I throw *her* off balance. Not just because I'm a presumptuous cockhead. After a short stare-down, she shakes back that thick mane of hair, revealing the sweet slope of her neck. "Well, gosh. Don't let me stop you."

I smile.

She narrows her eyes.

Look, I'm the first to admit I like putting everyone on notice that I'm not an easy customer, whether it's the mailman or the hotel clerk I interrogated earlier. Teresa's story about the room mix-up checks out as much as possible in this shit-show establishment, but I'm still wary as hell. Today wouldn't be the first time a rival hedge fund played dirty, trying to find some ammunition against me. I've never been part of the blue blood boys club and they don't like my wild card image. Don't like that they can't find a formula for my stock plays. They can't match my level, so they prod for weaknesses.

My only weakness in their eyes is a working-class upbringing. A reputation for settling disputes with my fists, instead of lawyers.

Growing up in Jersey City, being the biggest guy made me a target for every punk in the damn neighborhood. So I learned early how to be prepared. How to fight. Intimidate. Battles are backhanded in the New York financial market, though. They're not the kind of fights I grew up participating in and they often get personal. However, both types of battles require determination. And my determination to succeed meant nothing was going to hold me back when it came to putting my fund on top.

Landing on the *Forbes* list next to men I've never heard of wouldn't have meant a damn to me if it hadn't been for my father's influence, though.

Resentment curls in my stomach. I use the term father loosely. While I was growing up, he visited me exactly once a year, on my birthday. Yet his name was synonymous with Jesus Christ in our house. My mother never stopped singing the God-man's praises. After all, he was the one keeping the lights on. Paying for us to eat. Live.

Over the last few years, I've settled into a less volatile way of life, having learned the hard way that investors don't give their money to a fund run by a hothead. My new lease on life hasn't stopped those rivals from attempting to undermine me, though. On two occasions, competitors have sent a belligerent, insulting drunk to my table during dinner meetings, hoping I would take a swing and make a public scene.

There has never been a *woman* used as bait, though.

If Teresa was, in fact, sent by a rival, what purpose would it serve? I'm not in the habit of whispering market values in between sweet nothings. Fuck, I don't even know what a sweet nothing sounds like. But I'm having a hard time buying this dynamite girl showing up in my room, in a shitty Dallas motel, with no shirt. If someone was hoping to make me look like an unstable fund owner, now would be the ideal time. Investors are already skittish over my extended leave of absence from New York. Kicking me while I'm down could be a nail in the coffin. With Southpaw's and my movements documented on Instagram, it wouldn't be difficult to find me, either.

So it would be wise of me to stay away from Teresa, right?

See, caution really isn't my style. I'll get to the truth one way or another. In the meantime, I'm almost curious to see what she's got in store. If she has been coached, I'll see through it right away and she'll get nothing of value out of me. I'll have no choice but to walk away if she's lying to me—lies are kind of a recurring theme in my life lately and I'm finished being on the receiving end. That being said, caution means staying in my room knowing this knockout exists on the other side of the wall. And that simply isn't happening. I don't have to remind myself to keep my wits about me, either, because they never take a vacation.

"Are you finished taking me in yet?"

Not by a damn sight. My suspicions do nothing to stop me from being turned on. She looks like a sin I want to commit. Frequently. "You can't put a feast in front of a man and expect him not to gorge himself."

She tilts her head. "There's not going to be any gorging tonight, sweetheart."

"No?"

"Nope."

"I bet you call all the boys *sweetheart.*"

Her laugh catches her off guard. She jerks a little, before dropping her hand from the doorframe. "Actually I call them more trouble than they're worth. That doesn't bode well for you."

This is another reason I didn't do the cautious thing and stay away. It doesn't hurt that she's sexy as a motherfucker and twice as fascinating. But if she wanted to get me in a compromising position or attempt to get insider secrets out of me, would she be wasting time by playing hard to get? "I won't deny I can be trouble."

She brushes a hand against her pocket, probably checking for the room key, before stepping out. The door shuts behind her, the move bringing us up close and personal. A breath apart. "What kind of trouble?"

"I'll tell you." I settle a hand on her hip, easing her back against the door, watching her lips for protests. "Now that your door is closed, do you feel more secure that I won't try and back you into the room?" Our hips meet and she whimpers, low and needy at the evidence of what she's inspired. "I can kiss you without doing that. I'm kind of a prick, but I won't take more than you offer me."

"I wasn't worried you'd back me in." She's staring at my mouth, too, her voice verging on breathless, and her interest makes my ball sack ache. "If you were that type of man, you had your opportunity earlier."

Those protective instincts that fired to life earlier ride back in on a wave of irritation. She shouldn't be so trusting. Even of me. "And if I'd changed my mind? Or decided dinner was too much trouble?"

Green-gray flash up at me—and at the same time, cool metal presses to my neck. "I live in Los Angeles. Both times, I've had my stun gun." A flutter of lashes. "Sweetheart."

Surprise filters in as I turn my head slightly, getting a good look at the object she's holding. It looks like a flashlight, but the sharp points and divots along the surface tells me it doubles as something more hardcore. "Good girl."

Her chin comes up. "Good girl? That's it?" A wrinkle forms between her eyebrows. "Most guys would have called me a crazy bitch or something equally offensive by now."

"You sound disappointed."

"Not disappointed. Just…"

"Contrite over lumping me in with most guys?"

"Not even close."

Heat licks at my veins, my groin. Where the hell has this girl been hiding? The honest truth is, if she confessed to being a plant right here and now, I'd still be interested. While that's a hard pill to swallow, I think walking away would prove more difficult. Pressing her into the door, I lean in to absorb her rushing exhale. "Are you going to use that stun gun on me if I kiss your sexy little mouth?"

There's conflict and lust battling in her eyes. She doesn't want to enjoy the way I talk to her, but she does. A lot. And if that gentle rock of her hips is any indication, she likes being plastered to me even more. "N-no. I won't use it."

"Put it away." I brush our lips together, and *Jesus Christ*, she's so soft. So giving. There's a vibration inside her that matches my own, only I can't remember ever being aware of mine before. "You're about to get excited and I don't want your finger on the trigger."

Her head falls back in unspoken invitation and I accept, raking my tongue up the silky skin of her throat. The stun gun is lowered to her side. That tight body molds to mine, writhing against my waiting cock, even as she says, "Confident, are we?"

"If I wasn't, woman, you'd have already chewed me up and spit me out."

"I still might," she breathes, her eyes bright with excitement. With challenge. That response sets off a corresponding pound of need so loud, it almost drowns out what she says next. "You're not the only one who's trouble."

Fuck. I'm so worked up, I'm beginning to sweat, just from *talking* to her. If this was a jerk-off fantasy, I'd rip off that short skirt and bang her to kingdom come, right here in the hallway. This is real life, though. She's vetoed my motion to gorge—for now—and I don't second-guess women with stun guns.

So I drop my head and fuck her mouth, instead. It's meant to be slow and thorough, but the second our tongues twine together and she whimpers, my restraint fizzles out like a torch dropped into the ocean. I've witnessed how assertive she is, but she submits to me, face turned up, arms slack, mouth *mine*. It's a deadbolt clicking into place. Because God knows, I'm as dominant a man as they come. Yet I've never experienced this raw a level of satisfaction being the aggressor before. My senses are trying to find an anchor and can't, being driven crazy by this mysterious woman who holds a stun gun to my neck one minute and gives me carte blanche with her sweet mouth the next.

I allow us to break for air, before we collide back together, one of her thighs lifting to hug my hips. If I wrap the other one around me, I'm not sure my cock will forgive me when we stop, so even though I catch that leg and keep it tight and elevated, I focus my hunger on her mouth. The texture, the way she matches my rhythm. Our lips open wide, my tongue slides in, finds hers for a lick, retreats out, followed by incredible slanting suction. *Shit.* Shit, no one has ever tasted this good.

Teresa moans into my mouth, her palms slapping my shoulders, and I realize we haven't come up for breath in a while. It's so bad my lungs are burning and I didn't even notice. I'm having trouble thinking around her. "Look, woman," I pant, rubbing our damp lips together. "I can't help it if you taste better than oxygen."

There's a catch in her breath, confusion joining the arousal in her eyes. "If that wasn't gorging, we have different definitions of the word."

I wink at her. "Mine is better." Feeling her retreat a little, I push some loose strands of hair from her face. "We don't have to compare notes tonight."

Her exhale is shaky. "That's more than enough euphemisms on an empty stomach."

We share a quiet laugh, our gazes connecting. Holding.

If you're here under some false pretense, Teresa, just tell me.

I almost say the words out loud but manage to keep them to myself. There might even be some small part of me that doesn't want to know just yet. "I'll go grab Southpaw and we'll head out."

Teresa nods once and I steady her before stepping away. Just before I open the door for Southpaw, I look back to find her staring into space, a frown marring her pretty features. When she realizes I'm watching her, she meets my gaze head on, her expression half bemused, half serious...and I can feel a barrier forming that wasn't there a moment ago.

I've known this woman less than a day.

But I'm going to knock that barrier down.

CHAPTER FIVE

Teresa

WAY TO KEEP your eyes on the prize, idiot.

What happened to *This is a job. Eyes open. Take it seriously?*

It got scrambled up by earthy man smell and hairy, corded forearms. And that mouth. Mother of God, that mouth. I can't even imagine how many women need to be kissed to achieve that expert level of skill. I don't want to know, either, because it makes me want to smack him, which is scary in itself. I've dated players who might as well have mounted their notched bedposts on their mantles and I never gave a flying squirrel about their pasts. Yet I'm jealous over a guy I'm supposed to be conning?

Paging common sense. Come in, common sense.

We're crossing the twilight-draped parking lot, heading for the tavern. There is a dozen or so motorcycles parked outside, Queens of the Stone Age blaring from its dark depths, smokers congregated in a circle near the entrance. Will wanted to take me to a nicer place downtown—maybe an outdoor café where Southpaw can cool his heels while we eat—but what little common sense remains in my hollow head told me that was a bad idea, so I suggested the tavern. I need a quick escape route to my room, where I can lock myself in the bathroom if he comes on to me again. And he will.

Sex—or at least, the promise of it—is going to be part of this job. I kind of encouraged that idea by introducing my nipples to Will before telling him my name, didn't I? Resisting the pull for more, for *all*, wasn't supposed to be so difficult, though. I never expected to feel this level of attraction for Will. Nor did I expect these currents running between us to be so...personal. I can't really describe the way we look at one another, because I've never had anyone look at me like Will does. Like he's dying to get to the bottom of me. Metaphorically *and* physically.

Who was the girl who went all limp and needy in the face of his aggression? I don't know her. I'm not interested in meeting her, either. Especially now, when there is so much at stake. How my brother lives his *life*. Maybe his life in general. So maybe that kiss was a good thing. A warning shot. If I let him physically overwhelm me, mistakes could be made. I could slip up and say something that would clue him in to why I'm really here—and that kind of mistake would lead to Will getting in touch with Silas. I won't be in New York to protect Nicky from the fallout if I fail Silas. Not to mention, a mistake could screw up Will's relationship with his father even more than it already seems to be. Which would put a big ugly target on my back.

When I look at Will, I need to remember that he's just a man. He might be smarter than the average bear and sexier than hell, but his species is genetically predisposed to disappoint. Or get bored. Or bounce just when things look optimistic. I've been there, done that, and this stupid flutter he gives me in my stomach isn't going to distract me from the task at hand.

Will tosses a chewed-up tennis ball up in the air for Southpaw. He leaps for it, landing on the asphalt with a happy grunt. He charges Will, ducking down to head-butt his owner's thigh, then drops the slobber ball between his boots. "You want to give it a whirl?" Will asks, holding up the dripping green object. "I can give you a tetanus shot later."

"Ha. Um…" I start to decline. Not because I don't *want* to throw the ball, but because I'm finding it hard to even *look* at Southpaw. I'm not supposed to know he's got a date with death, but I do. And my cold, dead heart apparently isn't quite as cold and dead as I thought, because I want to cradle his big, dirty head and sing Angel by Sarah McLachlan at the top of my lungs. I swallow hard and paste a smile on my face. "Sure."

Will lobs me the ball. Southpaw bounds toward me, his nails clicking on the ground, tongue lolling out. If it weren't impossible, I would swear his expression says, *let's see what you got, lady.* So I fake him out. He turns in a circle, yips and returns with a look of utter outrage.

"Sorry, couldn't help it, big guy." After a quick, contrite scratch of his head with my free hand, I toss the slobber sphere up, up—and it bounces off a beat-up Buick, setting off the car alarm. Southpaw still makes the catch, trotting back toward me and a laughing Will looking all smug, as if to say, *what now, humans?*

"I think that's our cue to leave." Will's arm snakes around my waist, tugging me toward the tavern, his breath warm in my ear. "We'll work on your throw, baby."

A traitorous pulse starts thrumming between my legs. "I was just testing his versatility. He passed."

"Sure." Will holds open the door to the tavern, leaving only enough room for me to squeeze past, Southpaw at my heels. My breasts rub along Will's chest, setting off the jerking flex of his jaw. "Stay close to me in this place."

I raise an eyebrow. "You're not giving me much of a choice."

His smile is the furthest thing from repentant as he takes a firm hold of my hand, leading me deeper into the loud, rowdy establishment. On the way to an open spot at the bar, I give fate the side eye. I'm *definitely* not looking for a man. But leave it to fate to throw one into my path who digs my attitude and stun gun, when nothing can come from it. Not even a fun, guilt-free diversion.

Will slides out a wobbly stool—the only one available—and tests its sturdiness. Or at least, that's what I think he's doing, until I see his eyes. Directed at the men around us, they're full of dark warning. He passes on some kind of caveman *don't even fucking think about approaching her* signal to each of them, one by one, and I've never been more aware of getting wet in my entire life. It's like someone pressed a warm washcloth to the juncture of my thighs and rubbed side to side. By the time he slaps the split leather seat, indicating I should climb on, I'm flushed head to toe.

As soon as I'm seated, legs crossed, Southpaw takes up residence between me and the closest male customer. Will and I reach down to pet him at the same time and our hands collide. We share an intimate look over my shoulder and I think he's going to kiss me, but instead, he pushes aside my hair, leans in and breathes against the back of my neck. The warm washcloth feeling intensifies, my most intimate muscles squeezing hard. Harder than ever.

"I wondered if it was a fluke. Southpaw being protective over you earlier in the hallway." His thumb traces up my nape slowly, all five of his fingers burying in my hair. Tugging gently. "Not a fluke, though. He likes you."

Your dog is a bad judge of character. "He's protective, huh?" He tugs my hair again and it turns my voice to a rasp. "Like father, like son."

His low, rumbling laugh breaks goosebumps out down my arms. "Yeah. It's unusual on both counts."

"Is it?"

Another tug, this time a touch harder. Enough to bring my head back, our gazes colliding. "Yeah."

"Apparently you both like to mark your territory, too," I say, turning in my seat to face him. His hand drops from my hair and no longer having it there, I can't deny a kick of disappointment.

As if me making the accusation out loud allows him to drop pretense, his eyes go hard and rake over me. At the end of their journey, his head drops, that skilled kisser's mouth pressing to my ear. "Those legs could start a fucking riot, woman. A man who doesn't lay claim to them...and all the sweetness you've got attached...isn't worth a damn minute of your time."

His smoky drawl has turned my nipples to certified spikes. "Are we going to have an actual conversation or spend the whole night...gorging?"

"What are you doing in Texas?"

I'm so startled by his abrupt question that it takes me a beat to realize throwing me off was his intention. At least partly. His wide, powerful body is still exuding a monster dose of lust. We're practically nose to nose, both of us breathing heavy, and I get the distinct impression he's scrutinizing every blink, every lick of my lips. I'm finally meeting the millionaire hedge fund manager. Unofficially, of course.

I have a story all ready to go about visiting a friend on the east coast. About wanting to see the country along the way. But when I open my mouth, guilt catches me off guard and I find myself sticking much closer to the truth than I intended.

"I needed to get out of Los Angeles for a while." Taking a sip of my freshly delivered beer, I choose every word carefully. "I make decent money at my job, but there's some...danger involved. It was making me claustrophobic. Scared, too, I guess." His thumb strokes my neck, like he can't help but comfort me even though his narrowed eyes are zeroed in on me, weighing, analyzing. "Anyway, my friend in New York invited me to visit and I jumped at the chance. Figured I'd see the good old US of A while she gets the couch ready for me."

"New York."

Making my expression fathomless, I nod. "Yeah. Never been to the Big Apple. I'm excited."

Quietly, he reaches past me to retrieve his beer, taking a deep pull, before setting the half-empty glass back on the bar. "Tell me about this dangerous job in Los Angeles."

"I'd rather not."

"Why did you mention it, then? You had to know I'd bite."

The conversation is moving too fast, so I uncross and recross my legs, drawing molten eyes toward the action. "Aw, you don't bite *too* hard, I hope."

"The hardest. And you'll love it." He tips my chin up with two big fingers. "Let's hear about the job."

I wasn't lying when I said my job was dangerous. And it's the craziest thing, but I want to tell Will about the den. How I've wanted to escape it for a long time, but the money was too good. Too *needed*. It's all true. And I've had no one to confide my fears and frustrations in. Even before Nicky went on his trip to New York, I never spoke to him about my job, lest he worry. What's the harm in talking to Will about my job, when it has no bearing on my mission? "I…"

His fingers are still lifting my chin. "Teresa."

"A gambling parlor. An illegal one." Weight topples from my shoulders. "I'm a hostess of sorts. Trading money for chips, watching for collusion and reporting it to the boss. Soothing damaged egos with free drinks. Managing the books. Sometimes I deal if we're short-handed."

A series of beats pass. "That's not what I was expecting." Distaste twists his mouth, his fingers dropping from my chin. "I don't like it."

His tone tells me he's just made the understatement of the year. Having him on my side is…nice, though. I graduated with my accounting degree around the same time my parents passed, so I've been carrying this burden alone. The burden of knowing I ended up in an illegal profession, despite my father's efforts to give us all a clean life. Despite the fact that I yearn for something different.

I refuse to let Nicky fall into the same trap I've fallen into.

Girls who make deals with gangsters don't end up in film school.

Noticing Will's scrutiny, I default back to a flirtatious smile. "Blah. I don't like my job neither." With another sip of beer, I keep going, hearing catcalls and shuffling chips in my head. "New York for a while just seemed like a good idea."

"How long are you planning to stay there?"

I shrug. "Not sure. Long enough to figure out what's next." Not liking the weight of the lies on my tongue, I straighten my spine, letting him see what his attention has done to my body. My breasts. "What about you? Are you headed east, too?"

Will's muscles tighten, his hands seeming to move on their own as they settle on my thighs, kneading. "No." His unreadable gaze lifts to mine. "I'm going in the opposite direction."

CHAPTER SIX

Will

THREE THINGS AREN'T sitting right about Teresa's story.

One, she isn't being completely truthful with me. And after the lies that just came to light about my youth—coupled with the fact that she might be headline bait—that should make me want to walk away. I don't put up with lies anymore. Yet here I am, my palms chafing the hem of her skirt up and back along smooth thighs, growling at the way her lips part on uneven breaths. Here I am wanting to get her beneath me in the dark, wrists pinned over her head so I can dominate the full truth out of her.

There's an instinct growling deep in my belly, reminding me of what clicked into place back in the hallway outside her room. During that kiss I can't for the life of me stop thinking about. She doesn't seem to hold any part of herself back when we're touching. If I drove my cock deep between her legs and threatened to withhold her pleasure unless she revealed herself, would she thrash around and claw me until finally coming clean? Would she pout and moan and try to fuck herself on me from below with little writhes of her sweet ass?

What's your real last name, baby? Tell me and I'll bang you so long and hard, you'll forget the answer. Good girl. Doesn't that feel so good? Grab the headboard. Good. Now, why are you here? Tell the man who's got your pussy so full you can't think straight. I'll take care of everything. You'll have nothing to be scared of.

Goddamn. It's an addictive possibility…and one I'm surprised to be considering. I'm an aggressive man, but this level of intensity is exerted only in the boardroom. I've never had a connection with a woman that would make me push this hard if I thought she was lying to me. Especially now, after discovering my upbringing was founded on one massive fabrication, I would cut my losses and walk away from someone I suspected of being deceitful. But my gut is telling me there's too much to gain here, headline bait or not.

There's…*her.* The woman looking back at me like she can't decide whether she'd like me to fuck her or fuck off. She's got me by the balls, this one. She had me the second I walked into my room and she flipped her hair back.

Second thing not sitting right about Teresa's story? She wasn't lying about her job being stressful. Unsafe. I heard the anxiety in her voice, witnessed the strain. It made me want to fly to her hometown and knock heads together. Whether she's here to screw me or not, there's no way she's going back there. Period. But if she's really from Los Angeles, how is she connected to my competitors in New York?

Lastly and most troubling, Teresa is going east. Southpaw and I are on our way west. My reaction to this is split. Panic over her slipping away on one side. On the other, I'm hopeful. If she really means to move on in the opposite direction, there's a chance this meeting is just one sexy coincidence.

"When are you leaving Dallas?" I ask her.

"Tomorrow morning." Her fingers lazily toy with one of my shirt buttons, as if she didn't just slap us with a deadline. "So, what's your story? What are you guys doing in Dallas, besides destroying innocent tennis balls?"

"Exploring." I take a doggy snack out of my pocket and drop it into Southpaw's waiting mouth, unable to stop my grin when he licks his snout, begging me with desperate eyes for another. Maybe it's the dark atmosphere or the fact that Teresa just let herself be vulnerable in front of me a moment ago, but I find myself ripping off a Band-Aid. One I've never ripped off in front of another person. "The first few years of his life...I didn't necessarily take him for granted, but I worked long hours, so he saw more of the dog walker than me. I'm trying to make up for it now."

She runs assessing eyes over my faded jeans and lack of a shave. "You pay someone to walk your dog?"

"Used to." I pick up my beer and take a swig, watching her features for any form of recognition. "I pay a lot of people."

"Do you." Her fingers travel south to one of my lower buttons. An invitation for my hands to move higher up her thighs? I'm powerless not to take it. Setting my beer back down, I grip her mid-thigh until she gasps, then circle my thumbs on that soft inner flesh and watch her cleavage shudder, her complexion transforming to burnished rose gold. "What d-do you pay them for?"

"Working at my company."

"Are you being purposely mysterious?"

I lean in and capture her mouth in a hard kiss. "Are you?"

She breathes heavy a moment. "It's called flirting. And if you don't want to tell me about your profession, star sign and idea of a perfect date, that's fine by me. We're both moving on tomorrow, anyway."

"You'd just get on a bus and go?" Can't help it, I hook my hands beneath her knees and yank her to the edge of the seat so I can feel her pussy against me. Have her mouth near mine. "You'd leave, just like that?"

"I'm sorry..." Her voice is a scrap of nothing. "Was there another option?"

Maybe, just maybe, she's the real deal. My job—hell, my *life*—has turned me into a paranoid motherfucker who assumes the worst in everyone. It's possible, isn't it? With her delicious breath pelting my mouth and her hot cunt pulsing against the fly of my jeans, I want like hell for that to be true. "I've got a hedge fund in New York. A large one. I'm usually in a suit and tie. And I hate it."

That last part wasn't meant to slip out, but it seems to be the bit that makes her smile. "That's too bad. I love a well-dressed man."

Jealousy crackles in my belly. "You love a man dressed exactly like me, baby. And nothing else. How does that sound?"

"Tricky." She hits me with a guileless look. "What if you decide to wear socks with sandals?"

It's unbelievable. I go from wanting to pile-drive every man in the place, to having the insane urge to laugh. No one has ever made me feel like I'm swinging from vine to vine before, each better than the last. "You're something special, woman, you know that?"

The rhetorical question was intended to be a compliment, but it makes the corners of her mouth dip, creates an almost imperceptible distance in her gaze. She stops playing with the buttons of my shirt, opting to mess with her hair instead. I'm about to request she put her hands back on me where they belong, when she asks, "So, we kind of got off the subject." Her expression warms as she looks down at the dog. "You don't take Southpaw for granted anymore?"

"No. I don't." Sharpness prods my jugular, remembering what led to the change. That one fucked-up day full of life-changing news. "Little over a month ago, I'd just found out something. A family secret that had been kept from me." Again, I'm surprised that I continue to confess to Teresa, especially when I should have my damn guard up, but I can't seem to help it when her attention soothes me. "Southpaw had an appointment the same day with the vet. My assistant was scheduled to take him, but I needed to get out of the office and clear my head. So I took him instead."

I sense Teresa holding her breath, but I can't seem to recount all the ugly details yet—at least not out loud. But I hold her attention for a long beat and watch moisture pool in her eyes.

"Did you ever have a moment where everything feels bigger than whatever bullshit you're hung up on?"

She blinks at the ceiling and comes back to me with dry eyes. "No. Sometimes I think I'm chasing that moment, though." Her soft laugh is halting. "And looking for it in all the wrong places."

My fingers find her chin, lifting her face to bathe it in the dull bar lights. "You saying I'm one of those wrong places?"

"Maybe I'm a wrong place for you," she whispers, so low I can barely hear her. "Have you considered that?"

"Yeah. And I can't quite buy it."

The bartender appears to our left, throwing his meaty forearms on the bar. "You folks ready for another round?"

Teresa takes her chin away and faces the man, her hands restless at her waist. "Yeah. Sure." He starts to walk away, but she stops him. "Oh! Any way we could get a bowl of water for the dog?"

Oh, now she's done it.

This woman isn't getting away just yet.

Oblivious to the fact that she just sealed her immediate fate, she turns back to me, tucking some stray hair behind one ear. "So the thing that was more important than your bullshit...it was Southpaw?"

I've never put into words what I'm doing on this trip, apart from a bare bones explanation on the Instagram account where I've been documenting our stops, so I have to think about what I'm going to say. Everything I say to this woman seems to matter. "Forty years from now, I'm not going to remember the best investments I made or my most lucrative short. But I'll remember this trip. I'm more satisfied watching him chase a squirrel or swim in a lake than I ever was shifting the market."

The bartender sets down a new beer and I drain half of it.

"This dog…he was trying to be a constant in my life and I was too busy gambling on numbers some analyst pulled out of thin air. Coming home late. Letting someone else walk him." Resentment sinks into my stomach, remembering why I ever landed behind a desk in the first place. Why I was so driven to be there. "I'm not going to miss the next good thing that comes along. I'm not going to take the good things for granted ever again."

Christ, am I actually self-conscious? Yeah. I think I am. As I tug my phone out of my pocket and pull up my Instagram account, handing it over to Teresa, I realize I've either been recognized on the road by followers or communicated through two-word replies. But I've never actually had to *show* anyone the product of the last month in person. "That's, uh…turns out, making those memories for him is what's more important than my bullshit." I exhale. "He's sick."

There's no more explanation required. I can see she knows what I'm telling her and I'm relieved when she doesn't ask for details. She wants to. But instead, she simply breathes with me for a few moments, then says, "I'm so sorry."

Her eyes drop to Southpaw, before dragging back to my cell phone screen, her fingers scrolling and hovering—but not actually tapping on—the pictures. "Good for you, Will. Doing this for him." Her scratchy voice seems to startle her. She clears it. "Most people don't realize something like that until it's too late. You didn't even have to be visited in the middle of the night by three apparitions."

I take my offered phone back, the right corner of my mouth twitching. "Are you making fun of me for taking my dog on a vacation?"

Her spine snaps straight, making her tits jiggle and my palms itch to steady them. "No. I'm the furthest thing from making fun of you. I'm envious." Her mouth opens and shuts, right knee bouncing. "I'm, um...proud of you, too. Isn't that ridiculous when we just met?"

Something warm and unfamiliar sweeps through me as I stow my phone. High school, college, my career. All of it was done to make my absent father proud of me. To make myself worthy in his eyes, when he didn't deserve that consideration. And that feeling of worthiness never came, either. Any pride I'd earned from him stopped having meaning, too, when shit hit the fan. So maybe my methods of reaching the top were effective, but I wasn't at the top of the right place. I've never felt more right than I do with Teresa starting up at me—granted, looking a little shell-shocked—and telling me she's proud. "Nothing about this is ridiculous."

I lean in and kiss her mouth, long and thorough enough to have her ass scooting closer to me on the seat, her pussy settling in against my junk, but I stop at the sound of her stomach growling. My laughter blends with hers, low and damp.

"Whoops," she breathes at my lips. "Guess I'm hungry."

"Guess we both are." After signaling for menus, I bring our foreheads back together, drag my thumbs up the insides of her spread thighs. "Spend the night with me, woman. Let me feed you dinner. Then I'll feed you that cock you can't stop rubbing your pussy on."

Her head falls back on her shoulders, before she straightens, using my shoulders for balance. "Oh, Will." She searches my face, her eyelids drooping with lust. "Not a fucking chance."

CHAPTER SEVEN

Teresa

NOT A FUCKING CHANCE.

If I was directing this scene, it would be followed by a record scratch. Maybe a sigh from Southpaw and some *ohhhs* from our neighbors at the bar.

To Will's ever-growing credit, though, he throws back his head and laughs. Not the kind of laugh a man makes to hide his humiliation or worse, transfer embarrassment to the woman. No, it's pure enjoyment. It's appreciation of me. And against my will, I'm absolutely transfixed. The deep, rolling thunder sound brings to mind musky cologne, flannel sheets and worn-in leather. I just turned down his proposition for sex and he's not butt-hurt about it at all. *God*, that's attractive.

It's making me wish I could just say yes. Maybe that's his master plan?

That theory doesn't hold water, because he's not the one with the plan. I am.

I'm the wrench in his leisurely *no* plans vacation.

Saying yes and spending the night with Will would be exactly what Silas wants, but even that isn't enough to deter me anymore. Doing so *would* bungle my strategy, though. I'll never lure Will back to New York if I sleep with him. If I'm going to use this attraction to maneuver Will halfway across the country, I need to dangle myself like a carrot. And in the meantime, try not to be tempted by *his* carrot. His very thick, flesh-colored carrot.

Yes, I'm avoiding getting beneath Will because of a strategy. It has nothing to do with the fact that I…kind of like him. In a way that is exclusive to how he manipulates my lady regions. Don't be an idiot, Teresa. There's only one of two ways this ends. I disappear as soon as I fulfill my end of the bargain with Silas. Or Will figures out he's been played somehow and hates me.

I'll take disappearing for $400, Alex.

My phone buzzes in my pocket, dragging me out of my clouded head. Will is occupied with the menu, but I'm still careful to keep the screen turned away as I open a text message from my brother—and find a picture of him and Silas. They're standing side by side, a grinning Silas's arm thrown around my brother's shoulders.

Nicky isn't smiling. Was he forced to take this picture? Was he forced to *send* it?

"Teresa?"

I try to speak, but my heart is blocking the path. "Um. Yeah?" I finally manage.

Concern draws Will's brows together. "Do you know what you want yet?"

"Oh. Yes." Realizing the menu has been sitting on the bar to my left for long minutes, I barely glance at it before murmuring a burger order to the weary bartender. Will orders the same, while I command myself to pull it together. This is what bad men like Silas do. They apply pressure until good men, like my father, almost buckle under the strain. But I have a week. A whole week. I can't let the picture unnerve me, like it was designed to do.

"Everything okay?"

"Uh huh. Totally fine," I respond, smiling. "I want to know more about where you've stopped since leaving New York, though. Tell the truth, you and Southpaw are really a duo of bank robbers on the lam."

My joke succeeds in sidetracking Will—I think—as he tells me more about Southpaw as we eat. How the dog likes to sleep on the bathroom floor because of the cool tile—which leads to an affronted look when Will needs to handle his business in the middle of the night. How there's a spot on Southpaw's belly that—when scratched—turns his right, back paw into a lethal weapon. And how the dog howls through the opening riff of "Baba O'Riley" by The Who.

While Will talks, Southpaw laps from his bowl of water, but mostly stares up at his owner with heart eyes. When the bartender comes back to take away our empty plates, I realize I haven't tasted a single bite. Have I been looking at Will the same way as Southpaw, looped into every sincere word that comes out of his mouth? My heart pounds out a staccato rhythm in my chest, dread flooding me when I think how this could end.

I need to regroup. To get my head back in the game. The beer definitely isn't doing me any favors, either. Ever since I told him we wouldn't be sleeping together, he's stayed close but hasn't touched me. A way of letting me know he heard me loud and clear. But every second I spend in this bar, wrapped with him in a dark cloud of intimacy, the more I want to loop my fingers in his belt buckle and tug him back into the V of my legs.

Will jerks a thumb at the bartender. "You want another drink?"

"No." I push back the stool and stand, brushing imaginary crumbs off my skirt. "I think it's a good idea if I head back."

I dig two twenties out of my skirt pocket and start to hand them over, but he stays my hand. "I got this, Teresa." His thumb strums the pulse at my wrist. "Wait for me to pay and I'll walk you back."

It's only been thirty minutes since the last time he touched me, but my body reacts to that little brush of his thumb like a desert after a storm, soaking in the wild tingling sensation it sets off. "No expectations?"

All cool and loose, he plucks the wallet from his front pocket and takes out a foursome of bills, tossing them on the bar without taking his eyes off me. "Can we agree on one kiss?"

"Are you using your hedge fund negotiation skills on me?" I wet my lips, drawing his dark interest. "That doesn't seem fair."

"This hard-on I've got for you isn't fair." He adjusts the tented denim at his lap. "I'm going to handle it like a man, but a fresh memory of your mouth will help get me finished faster."

I can't stop a whimpering laugh from escaping. "Are you telling me you plan to jerk off when this date is over?"

"Soon as I'm inside the door." He steps closer, wrapping me in earthiness and beer and man. "And I've got some news for you, baby. You've never been on a date that didn't send the guy home to jerk off like a horny high school kid afterwards."

Those words, plus imagining Will's flexed forearm and gritted teeth while he rubs one out, makes muscles I only discovered today squeeze between my thighs. Before he can press that advantage and pull me under the surface, I breeze past him toward the exit. Carrot. You're a carrot. "I'll take that as a compliment."

"Good. That's how I meant it."

Will's long strides mean he keeps up easily, reaching the door in time to hold it open for me. As we pass through—Southpaw's silky hair grazing the outside of my knee—he lays a firm hand just below my waist, that warning look back in his eyes as we pass a group of men outside. Most of them sport cowboy hats, but one has a white baseball cap, the brim pulled low over his eyes as he nurses a cigar. The men smirk at Will but keep their interest in me to one, abbreviated glance…and it's obvious they all think we're going back to his room to have sex. Five minutes from now, they'll assume I'm naked beneath Will, my nails leaving bloody, half-moon indents on his thrusting ass.

With a rush of forbidden excitement, my go-to fantasy sneaks in and spikes my pulse. The men think he picked me up over in the bar. Because that's what happens in places like this. Men go out searching for women to give them release. Sometimes they even…pay them. Do those men think he's paying me? My three-beer buzz does me no favors, a low thrum of heat stealing through my middle.

"Here we are."

My face heats over being caught even imagining such things. We're at my door and I have no recollection of entering the motel. *Come on, Teresa. Stop letting this guy get to you so bad.* "Right." I fish for the key card in my pocket, but cease all movement when Will brushes his fingertips down my arm, then trails them back up. Slow. And all the while, he invades my space, eliminating inches at such a leisurely pace that I'm panting by the time our mouths are a breath apart.

"What are you going to do when I close this door behind you, Teresa?" He grazes my bottom lip with his teeth, making me gasp. "You going to get undressed in front of the air conditioner, thinking it might cool you down after teasing my cock for over an hour in the bar? It won't. I give you five minutes before you're face down in bed, riding your own fingers."

My knees threaten to buckle. "That's my business."

"Make it *mine.*"

Mayday. Mayday. "Will—"

He stops my admonishment with a drugging kiss, his tongue stroking in and out of my mouth. His hands grip my elbows, lifting me up on my toes in desperate degrees, meshing our bodies, our lips, until I'm moaning, letting him have rough intercourse with my mouth. Just when I'm on the verge of giving in and begging him to take me up against the door, he steps back, eyes glittering, wiping away the moisture on his mouth with a wrist swipe. "I'll be out on the balcony. If you're going to finger yourself in my honor, I want to listen."

I stand there like a gaping fish as Will opens the door to my room and nudges me inside, closing it behind me. The *In Case of a Fire* map stares back at me so long, it starts to blur, need ravaging me from the inside out, making my skin feel like it's going up in a blaze. This is safe, isn't it? Going out on the balcony and getting rid of this ache to the sound of Will's scratchy baritone? Technically, we wouldn't be having sex. We wouldn't even be touching each other, leaving all carrots untouched and continuing to dangle.

Enough thinking. I kick off my sandals and move through the pitch-black motel room, not even stopping to turn on a light. When I slide my door open, an appreciative male growl greets me from the other side of the thin wall, which separates my balcony from Will's. We're on the same floor as the lobby, so there's no drop. I could hop over the safety bar and land in the scrappy field running behind the motel without hurting myself. It also means either of us could join the other on their balcony, but some part of me knows Will won't try it. I'm positive he won't.

This is safe. This won't wreck my plan.

Plan? How long has it been since I even remembered I had one?

"Come over to the wall, Teresa."

The command sends a tremble running through me, and that tremble increases as I obey, reaching the barrier and resting my forehead against the coarse stucco. "I'm here," I say. "Can anyone else hear us?"

"Everyone in this place is out getting drunk. It's just us." I'm not a trusting person. Growing up I was taught to sleep with one eye open. Yet I believe Will when he says no one will hear us. That we're alone on the backside of the motel in the dead fall of night. "You still wearing that skirt, baby?"

My eyes close on their own. "Yes."

"You know it would only take me a second to shred that pretty thing in my hands, don't you?" On the other side of the wall, I hear his zipper come down, a grating curse. "Were you aware of it all night, with your sweet ass balanced on the edge of that stool? I damn well was. One rip and you'd be in nothing but a tight, little thong, huh? One that wouldn't need more than a yank to one side so I could lick that golden pussy."

Oh my God. Have I ever been spoken to like this? I mean, there's dirty chatter. And then there's Will's Fantasyland of Fuck Talk.

"Going to need you to focus and answer me, woman."

His guttural speech jolts my eyes open. "Are you...?"

"Jacking my cock, thinking about your thighs wrapped around my goddamn head? Yeah." His heavy breathing reaches me, and I bunch the hem of my skirt in my hands, dragging it up to my waist. What did he ask me again? Was I aware he could rip off my skirt on a whim? "I was aware. Your hands look..."

"Look what, baby?"

"Like they could do anything they want."

His answering groan makes me tremble. I'm shaking and sweating, skirt pulled up, on a balcony in Texas, and it's like a tornado picked me up and dropped me here.

"If you're speaking in full sentences, your fingers aren't inside your panties yet, Teresa. What are you waiting for?"

That's a really good question. I think I'm scared. Scared that Will talking me through a solo session is going to be better than any sex I've ever had and I'll be ruined for life. *Coward*, whispers a voice in my head, and my spine straightens.

Biting my bottom lip, I let my right hand release my skirt and massage my feminine flesh through the front of my thong, air bursting out of my mouth in halting starts and stops. "*Mmm.*" Needing more, I stuff my fingers inside my panties, leading with my middle one and hitting the jackpot with that sacred bundle of nerves. "Ohh."

"There's a good girl." I can hear the wet sounds of Will's hand choking up and down the length of his erection. *Swap, swap, swap.* Judging from the amount of time each stroke takes, he's long. So long and hard. *Jesus.* "Slide two fingers around your clit, stroke them up and back. Can you do that for me?"

"Yes," I say, putting my middle and forefinger into a tight peace sign and rubbing the sensitive sides of my clit, setting of chain reaction of lust inside me, concentrated below my belly button. "God, oh God, *so good.* I-is this what you would do to me?"

There's no time to wish the unexpected question back, because he answers right away. "Damn right, but my tongue would be working the middle. I'd knuckle the sides of that little pink clit, while I suck the top nice and light."

Holy shit. Moving my fingers faster between my legs, I grind my forehead against the partition. "Nice and light doesn't sound like you."

"Consider it an apology for how hard I'd be getting ready to fuck you."

I don't recognize the moan that comes out of me. I've never, ever sounded so abandoned or desperate in my entire life. "How hard?"

The squelching sounds coming from the other side of the wall grow louder, faster, along with his breathing. "How hard do you want it?"

"So hard…" My voice trembles. "Like you can't help it."

A vile curse interrupts his rumbling groan. "I get you now, woman. You want to get me so fucking turned on, I can't control myself? That's what you're going to get." There's a loud crack above me, as if he's just head-butted the wall. "I'll spit on that pussy and raw dog it from behind. That what you like, baby?"

Apparently. Every single nerve ending in my body converges at once, meeting in my middle. There's only a hint of warning—some sparks behind my eyes—before I explode into fragments. I fall forward against the wall, stunned by the impact and magnitude of my climax, thighs spasming and clenching around my hand. "Will. *Will.* It's…I'm…oh *God.*"

He growls. "You coming?"

Hello understatement. "Y-yes."

"This isn't over. Keep moving your fingers until I'm done."

"Yes, Will."

Who is this woman obeying commands? I've never been her…outside of my very private thoughts. She feels so addictive, though. So right. The sound of his voice is like a warm, transcendent calling that beckons me a little closer every time I do as I'm asked. Welcoming me. "What would you do for me, Teresa? If you were on my side of the wall?"

And I think this is why. Why I can allow myself to be commanded by Will. Because there's a balance. There's a respect and choices, even while he's dominating me. My God, we're not even touching and I'm on my knees, head tipped back like a sexual servant. Wait. When did I get on my knees? "I'd give you my mouth."

A rough intake of breath. "Christ. If you're on your knees over there, I'm going to blow, baby. You like knowing how easy you manage that?"

"*Yes,*" I whimper, palming my breast in one hand, rubbing my clit with the other. "I-I like hearing you moan."

"Yeah, I'll bet you do. Bet you love making my cock ache." Another bash against the wall. "Should have known you were a tease when you were walking around my room with your sexy tits jiggling around."

"Not a tease," I choke out. "I'm…"

"*Tell me.*"

Can I voice my most private desires out loud? No. No way. Right? Only…it feels like I can. Feels like I could say anything and it would only make him hotter. And that's my reason for living right this very moment. I want him to climax on the other side of this wall so bad, it's a full-blown obsession. It's a good thing my legs are too weak to carry me or I might try and climb over it, just so I can watch his big body shudder, watch his powerful hand stroke his straining, red flesh.

"Tell me what's in that head, dammit."

"I want you to use me," I blurt, using two fingers to massage myself in quick circles, my blood heating at the very act of making the admission out loud. "Sometimes. Just…just while we're touching, I don't want to be Teresa to you. I want to be the girl you picked out for a quickie. Because you *need* release so bad. Now. You're so hot and hungry, you just throw me down and…and—"

"You want to be my plaything, Teresa?"

"Yes." How did he do it? How did he vocalize the need inside me in a single word? "Sometimes, yes. I want that. Maybe I even want…"

"Yeah?"

"Want you to buy me," I blurt. "S-sometimes. I don't know—"

His growl cuts me off. "I'll know when you need that, baby.

I'll know when to look you in the eye and fuck you slow, until we're both dripping in sweat and you're moaning for God." His tone is growing choppy, the wet flesh sounds hitting a rapid tempo that echoes my pulse. "And I'll know when to cover your mouth to muffle your screams while I ride that tight pussy like I paid ten grand for it."

"*Yes,*" I gasp, pushing two fingers into my heat, my head dizzy with spiraling, tangible lust. My flesh spasms in a quick, shaky pattern. *Squeezesqueezesqueeze.* "Use me to make yourself come, Will."

"Get your tits out. Going to come on them." His voice breaks into a harsh, guttural groan, something from the depths of a cave, and although it makes me want to keep touching myself—I've never been this sensitive *in my life*—I want to serve him even more. Yes, serve. I'll examine that later. "They out, woman?"

I slide my fingers from inside myself with a whimper and wrench my shirt up and over my braless breasts, not surprised to find my nipples hard as diamonds. "Yes, they're out. Waiting for you." My voice has fallen to a throaty purr and it makes me feel sexual. Alive. Feminine. "Make me wear you."

The enthusiasm in his release makes my chin drop, my eyes flutter shut. My God, I never knew male moaning was my thing, but the barked curse and his subsequent *fuck yeaaahhhh that's a good girl* are almost enough to give me another orgasm. It's desperate, grunting, flesh-slapping glory, and I could have kneeled there for a week and soaked it up, picturing his come landing on the wall while he thinks of my breasts.

For long moments, there's only the sound of us trying to regain our breath, music from the tavern trilling in the distance. I can't believe it. My body is replete and satisfied in a way I've never experienced. Will is capable of making me like this without laying a finger on me? That doesn't seem fair. In fact…it's kind of terrifying. I'm conning this man and he just forced me to recognize things about myself out loud that I never imagined leaving the confines of my mind. Without judging me at all.

I'm returning the favor by lying to him.

Swallowing hard, I stagger to my feet. "Good night, Will."

A heavy beat passes. When he speaks, it's as though he's rasping right against my ear. "I *will* see you in the morning, Teresa."

There's no mistaking the promise in those words.

Too bad I already made my promises, and they have to be kept.

CHAPTER EIGHT

Will

I BOLT UPRIGHT in bed, my arm coming up to shield my eyes from the Texas sunlight pouring in through the sliding glass door. It's not unusual for me to wake up stressed out, so I follow my practiced routine of breathing through my nose, counting backwards from ten and waiting for my eyesight to adjust.

Yeah. Regaining consciousness in a funnel cloud is standard fare. I'm financially responsible for eight hundred employees, ninety-three accredited investors, Southpaw and two thriving charities.

My mother, too. We were fed the same line of bullshit for years. The difference being when I found out the truth, I wanted nothing more to do with the man. Her phone call yesterday confirmed she still wants the opposite. My father no longer supports her, however, thank God. I've set her up financially and even made her an investor in Caruso Capital Management. I hate the tension between my mother and me since the truth came out, but at least I know she wants for nothing.

Until I took Southpaw and drove the hell out of Manhattan with resentment and betrayal burning in my gut, every day of my life was about the bottom line. Still is, considering my accountant is still cutting checks in my absence. How else would everyone else afford to live? Songwriters can wax poetic about love fueling the world, but that's bullshit. Hate it or love it, money is what makes the world spin. It's what people need from me. Lots of it.

Apart from supporting my mother and Southpaw, I never wanted this kind of responsibility. Growing up, I wanted to be a boxer. Put in the time, too, training before and after school. Weekends. Hell, even in my spare time, I was landing in fights, so I'd chalk that up as practice, too. That lifestyle didn't fly with my father—and therefore my mother was against it as well.

Before high school, my father's yearly visits on my birthday were the best present I could ask for. I'd circle the date with a red marker and rehearse our conversations in front of the mirror, dressing in my best shirt when the day finally arrived. Those visits took on a more serious bent when I became a freshman in high school, however. My passing grades were no longer good enough, and his disappointment hobbled me, as did my mother's red-faced embarrassment where she stood behind his chair at the kitchen table.

One afternoon, Silas took me for a walk around my neighborhood, his big hand clapping down on my shoulder and pulling me to a stop across from the park. Four men around my father's age sat congregated around a stone table, passing a lighter amongst each other to light their cigarettes. I recognized the guys from the boxing gym. They usually hung out in the gallery shadow boxing, hooting and whistling when someone landed a good punch in the ring.

"You see those men, Will?"

"Yeah, Dad."

"They spent ten years living. And now they're going to spend the next fifty rehashing a single decade. Over and over. Because who's going to remember their best years if they don't, huh?" He'd jostled my shoulder. "You know the answer to that? No one. No one is going to remember them."

I knew where he was going with the lecture, so I shrugged. "I'm not going to end up like that. I'm good. People are going to remember me."

"Oh yeah?" He pointed across the street. "Black jacket fought in the Golden Gloves before you were born. I saw him myself in the Garden. One hit. That's all it took and now he can barely remember his address. That isn't the life your mother and I want for you, son."

My mouth tried to smile over being called son, but I kept my features sharp, confident. Like my father. "What future do you want for me?"

He'd taken me by the shoulders and turned me to face him. "No son of mine is going to skate by with C's on his report card. You understand me? That kind of shit is going to land you in the park, yammering on about how you threw a good right hook once upon a fucking time." I hid my devastation, even though he tried to shake it out of me. "Don't you want to take care of your loved ones someday? Like I do?"

"Yes, sir."

"Good. You make good grades and focus on college. Make something out of yourself, like I did, or you'll end up in the park with these losers." In my peripheral vision, I could sense that the men had overheard, their conversation having stopped. My face heated in response, but Silas continued, not sparing them a thought. "I like a man who can defend himself. You got your temper from me and that's fine. A little fighting never hurt nobody. But next time I come here, I want to see A's. Or maybe I'll start skipping visits. Putting my time where it's respected."

My chin came up like I'd been cold-cocked, denial rippling through me head to toe. "I respect you, Dad. I won't let you down."

That respect hadn't lasted. Not once the truth came out a

month ago. But it was too late, my life had already been molded into my father's ideal. As predicted, my penchant for getting into scrapes never went away, but I still became a suit and tie-wearing motherfucker with a legion of people breathing down my neck for results. Fortunately, I know how to deliver, but the stress never goes away.

Except for yesterday. Hell if I thought of a single damn thing besides Teresa from the moment she showed up in my room, to last night, when her husky voice gave me the most brutally intense sexual peak of my life—

Teresa.

I drop my hand from my eyes, drilling the bedside clock with a look. Eight a.m.? When is the last time I slept to a normal hour? Of course I wake up later than my customary five thirty on a morning when I need to be on my toes.

"Southpaw," I call, throwing my legs over the side of the bed. A minute passes while I drag on jeans and finger comb my hair, already thinking of my sexy, take-no-prisoners brunette who can't help but be sweet, too. Damn, I can't wait to get my *actual* hands on her. "Where you at, boy? Walk? Let's go for a walk."

My movements freeze when Southpaw doesn't trot out of the bathroom.

Cold slithers into my blood.

"Southpaw."

Forgetting to breathe, I brace myself and approach the small, tiled room, praying like I haven't in years. *Please. Not yet. We're supposed to have longer.* But he's not inside. Relief is immediate and drastic. I double over, bracing hands on my knees, black spots swimming in front of my vision.

Confusion starts to trickle in a moment later. He wasn't in the bedroom when I woke up. Definitely not in the bed, because on the rare occasions he crawls into bed with me, he takes up the whole damn mattress. I would have noticed him.

As I walk out of the bathroom, my gaze is drawn to the sliding glass door. It's open. Did I leave it open last night? It's entirely possible, since I floated inside on a cloud of sexual satisfaction. And more than a little preoccupied with the withdrawal I sensed from Teresa on the other side of the wall.

Not bothering to put on a shirt, I head for the balcony and step out into the sunlight, pausing mid-step at what I see. First thing I notice is Teresa in cowboy boots and a red sundress, throwing the tennis ball for Southpaw out in the field. Second thing I notice is the camera she's holding. A small one. A GoPro, I think?

Each time she tosses the ball for Southpaw, she holds up the device, smiling to herself over whatever she sees on the screen. She captures a new angle with every throw, pacing right and crouching down.

Taking my attention off Teresa looking so relaxed and in her element isn't easy, so it takes me a few minutes to notice her suitcase. It's lying on its side in the grass, a purse set down on top of it. As if she was getting ready to leave.

For the second time since waking up, I'm cold. Freezing, right there in the hot sun. Commanding myself to get my bearings and handle the situation, I watch Teresa laugh as Southpaw leaps into the air, catching the green fuzz ball between his teeth and wrestling with it, shaking his head side to side.

"Good boy. Such a good *boy*," Teresa praises as Southpaw prances back, definitely showing off for my hot—mysterious— LA girl. "Okay, go long." She juggles the GoPro, trading it for the tennis ball in her right hand. "Let's see what you got."

Of course, she's got an arm on her, too. Like I need one more reason to want to fuck her stupid. *I want you to use me*, she said last night. If she gives me an opening, I'll be more than happy to oblige. "Morning," I say, my voice like gravel. When she whirls around, I nod at her suitcase. "Going somewhere?"

She rubs her dirty hands together. "This place isn't a destination. It's just a stop on the way to somewhere else." Her demeanor changes as I approach, her cheeks turning pink like she's thinking about the dirty things I said to her last night. The kind of dirty things I'd like to say to her again, but with her ankles up around her ears. "You knew I was on my way to New York," she mutters, fussing with her hair. "Stop staring."

"Can't. You're already too goddamn beautiful. Then you had to go and play fetch with my dog." Her deepening flush might as well be a stroke of my dick. "Don't suppose I could convince you to let me drag you into bed. Might fuck up that pretty dress stripping you to the skin, but you won't have the power of speech to complain when I'm done with you."

Her breath leaves in a rush. "Let me ask you a question, Will. Can you really back up all that shit you're talking?"

"Please try me, woman."

The air between us thickens along with a certain part of my anatomy, although I don't really expect her to agree. Which is a new one for me. Been a while since I indulged in a woman, but I remember them being pretty damn agreeable. Not Teresa. And even more unusual? I'm just as anxious to find out how her mind works as I am to see what it'll take to get her naked. "Maybe next time," she whispers, hair blowing across her mouth. "Like I said, I'm headed east."

Southpaw skids to a halt between us, barking happily and turning in a circle. I don't break eye contact with Teresa as I scratch his head. Talking about her departure is putting me in a bad mood—not that my cock has received the memo—but if we need to play games to make her understand I'm not ready to let her go, then I'll bite. "How are you getting to your next stop?

The bus?"

"That's right. There's a bus leaving for Nashville at nine fifteen."

I'm still not one hundred percent convinced Teresa isn't here at the behest of a rival fund, but damn if that theory isn't being discounted by the second. She couldn't be more eager to leave me standing here like a punk.

Unless that's the idea.

Southpaw starts doing figure eights through her legs, as if he's a teacup poodle and not a Great Dane. Mid-laugh, she starts to lose her balance and I lunge forward, catching her just before she can fall into the grass. From the cradle of my arms, her green-gray eyes catch the sunlight, a smile curls her lips and *oh fuck*. I am not prepared for the fresh onslaught of possessiveness that plows into my chest. It takes me a few breaths to turn the dial on it to manageable. All the while, she watches me with a vulnerable expression, like she doesn't know whether to run or wrap herself around me.

This is her. Right here. I might have doubts about her motives for being in Dallas, but this is the real her looking at me. My gut wouldn't be this sure otherwise.

"Nashville is next for you, huh?" I settle Teresa on her feet and gather her hair in a fist to keep the wind from blocking her face from me. "There's a national park on the way. Ouachita. Southpaw would enjoy it."

I can see the jumping at the base of her neck. "You're...offering to drive me?" Decision made, I nod. "But you're on your way west."

"We're not on a timetable, so it won't hurt to backtrack a little," I say, pulling up a mental version of the map in my glove compartment. "Break up the trip to Nashville into two days. We can stay in Arkansas tonight, check out the park tomorrow morning, then decide what comes next."

I already know I'm going to want more of you.

She searches my face. "Do you always go to these lengths to sleep with a woman?"

"Never." I step closer, bringing her tits up against my stomach. She closes her eyes and licks her lips, making me groan. "Do you always tell the kind of secrets you told me last night?"

The wind blows the seconds by. "Never."

"Good. They're mine now." I lean in and catch her bottom lip between my teeth, tugging it gently before letting go, giving the spot a soothing kiss. "And I want more of them."

Is it panic that flares in her eyes? Or indignation? Maybe a little of both. "You can't just demand secrets from me."

"I can if I'm willing to give you some in return." I tip my head at the GoPro clutched in her hand. "Maybe we can start with how much you love that camera."

If possible, she seems jumpier about my interest in the camera than she was about giving up actual secrets. With our noses an inch apart, I think she's going to mouth off some more and try to put me in my place, but her shoulders sag instead. "Will, I..."

Tell me, baby. Tell me why you're here so we can straighten this shit out and move on. "What?"

She steps back, putting a couple of feet in-between us. "I'm guessing your Chevelle doesn't have a navigator." With a wink and a toss of her hair, she starts back toward the motel, Southpaw on her heels. "If I'm going to be in charge of directions, I need coffee first."

"We're in full agreement there," I murmur, a weight sinking in my stomach. Moving to join her, I reach her suitcase and purse first, picking them up. "I'll go put these in the trunk."

Teresa sways a little, fingers flexing at her sides. Like she wants to snatch the items out of my hands but can't. "Such a gentleman."

"When the occasion calls for it." I give a quick whistle. "Mind keeping an eye on Southpaw while I'm at the car? You can wait in my room. Won't take me more than fifteen minutes to shower and pack when I come back."

"Sure." She saunters backward toward my balcony, a too-bright smile on her face. "See you in a minute."

"Not if I see you first."

I think a corner of her mouth dips, but she turns away before I can be sure, hopping with fluid grace over the balcony bars. Southpaw follows. Teresa turns and gives me one last look and disappears into my room.

For a few beats, I stand there in the empty field, knowing what I'm about to do is a betrayal of trust. She's left me no choice, though. I've got a growing interest in a woman who could be deceiving me. If that's the case, I have to protect myself.

And possibly *Teresa.* For the first time, it occurs to me that whoever sent Teresa could have some kind of leverage that's forcing her to compromise me against her will. If that's the case, the sooner I find out the better so their heads can roll and she can be free of any duress she's under.

Standing beside my open trunk two minutes later, I pause for a beat before taking Teresa's wallet out of her purse. First thing I see is a picture of an older couple, both of whom share Teresa's default mischievous expression. The woman leans into the man, a bouquet of flowers resting in her arms. Her parents.

I bypass a gym membership and a couple credit cards, landing on a rectangular receipt from a shipping company with a tracking number. I unfold it and make note of the recipient address. The Film Institute. That doesn't answer any pressing questions about Teresa's motives or identity, but I'm damn well interested, so I tuck that nugget of information away for later and continue on to her driver's license. I'm already positive her last name isn't going to be Smith, but a sharp jab catches me in the throat nonetheless.

Teresa Valentini. LA address.

Grateful she didn't lie about her first name and zip code, I screenshot the identification with my phone and forward it to one of the numbers on my speed dial. As soon as the message goes through, I hit *call* on the same number.

"Yeah, it's Caruso. I just sent you something."

"Received," says the brisk, faceless voice on the other end. "What do you need to know about her?"

"Everything. Specifically, if she has any ties to QLR Management or Century Investments," I say, listing several other cutthroat New York funds in direct competition with mine. "Run her information against everyone on their payroll. And mine. Update me as soon as possible."

"On it."

After snapping the trunk closed, I go through the front entrance of the motel, feeling guilty despite the reason I ordered a background check in the first place.

I'm guessing your Chevelle doesn't have a navigator, she'd said.

Too bad I never told her what kind of car I drive. Unless she went back to her room last night and took a *much* closer look at the Instagram account, she has no way of knowing the model. She's either a closet car enthusiast, interested enough to stalk me a little online—which I don't mind one bit—or she's done some homework.

I intend to find out.

CHAPTER NINE

Teresa

I'M PACING THE room, waiting for Will to return from stowing my luggage in the back of his car. Shouldn't he be back by now? I drop down on the bed, and Southpaw wastes no time putting his big head in my lap, burying his nose in my skirt. I sigh and cradle him to my stomach, feeling unworthy of the comfort.

A memory of last night's text message drifts in and I shake my head. No, I'm not unworthy. I'm a sister looking out for her brother. A reminder of why I'm in Texas in the first place is what I need. Especially right now when I can still feel Will's teeth tugging at my lips, his deep, coaxing voice inviting me to bed. And now he's driving me to Nashville. Lord. These two males—of different species—are making me feel like a traitor, when I'm actually doing Silas's bidding out of loyalty to Nicky.

Thankful I didn't leave my cell phone in my purse, I slide it out of my dress pocket and pull up a familiar video. One I've transferred every single time I've purchased a new phone. Eight-year-old Nicky dangling from a tree in our backyard wearing homemade angel wings and a halo. He recites his lines from the Christmas pageant I'm directing in the background while our parents and neighbors watch.

"Flap your wings," I can be heard whispering off-camera. *"Do*

it."

I have to go number two, he mouths back at me, holding up a pair of fingers and looking miserable.

Southpaw looks up at me when I snort-laugh, although the sound is much sadder than usual. This is why I'm here in Texas. Why I'm doing Silas's dirty work. My brother. I can't forget, no matter how deep Will and his dog pull me under their spell.

When my cell phone rings, it's so unexpected, I shoot up from the bed, juggling the device. I see the screen and my throat closes. It's Nicky.

No, no, no. As much as I want to hear my brother's voice, I can't take this call right now. Can't deal with my brother at all when I'm so on edge about Will walking away with my purse—which contains all my freaking information. Granted, we both knew I was bullshitting when I told Will my last name was Smith. Covering myself in Mysterious Girl Body Spray was part of the plan. But I'm not going to be a mystery for long if he looks inside my wallet.

Would he do that?

Oh yeah, he would. There was a tension running between us back in that field, Will daring me to call his bluff. So I did, letting him walk off with all my possessions and gambling on the hope that me and Nicky aren't connected to Silas Case anywhere on paper. We shouldn't be. Nicky has only been working for the man a short time and in lowest-man-on-the-totem-pole capacity.

There's a slight chance Will snooping in my purse will work in my favor. It's not like there's a Luring Will Back to New York checklist in there, complete with Post-it notes and diagrams. My wallet is only going to confirm the *truthful* things I told him. My name is Teresa and I live in Los Angeles. Three thousand miles from his dear old dad. I'm not a total amateur—I remember my father covering our tracks upon moving to California. I've created enough of a trail that I should be in the clear. *Should* be. I can only imagine the kind of tech whizzes Will employs.

Right. Okay. I need to remember the phase I went through after reading *The Secret*. Life is following *me*. The destiny is in *my* hands. I got this.

Will is going to walk back into this room, twice as enamored of me than before now that he's satisfied I haven't lied about my identity. We're going to drive east, which is exactly what needs to happen in order to snatch my brother from Silas's clutches. The plan is working. I just need to keep Will interested and moving in the right direction.

Toward New York.

Speaking of New York, my phone rings again. Weighing the risk against the relief of knowing my brother is alive and well, I stalk into the bathroom, flip on the rattling fan and answer. "Hey. Listen, I can't really talk right now. Are you okay?"

"Yeah, but…look, we're going to need a daily check-in. I'm fucking worried about you."

"I know. I'm sorry. Just…" I catch sight of my crazy eyes in the mirror and quickly look away, breathing in and out through my nose. "What's up? Are you all right?"

The slightest pause. "Yeah."

I stop pacing. "Why did you hesitate?"

He expels a breath. "You're a human lie detector, just like Mom." My heart lurches at the comparison and we're both quiet a moment. "I don't know if we should talk about this now. But we need to talk."

My pulse drums in my temples. "Has something changed?"

He doesn't answer. Which is an answer in itself.

I swallow hard. "Okay." *Think.* "Remember that place we used to go on Saturdays with Mom and Dad? When we were kids?"

"Yeah."

"I'll call you there at ten o'clock tonight. East coast time, okay? Be smart."

When we hang up a second later, I brace my hands on the sink and wrap myself in a layer of calm. I don't want to be calm. I want to laugh like a hyena because I'm in the middle of Texas attempting to seduce a man into following me home. And that man is too smart for games, so every move counts. Or my brother will get swallowed up by the lifestyle my parents fought to remove us from. This can't get any more risky or ridiculous, and I would like nothing more than to hand myself over to the oncoming panic attack. But I won't. I won't.

Okay, screw *The Secret*. What would Kathryn Bigelow do?

My head comes up. The famous director would sit back in her reserved chair and weigh the landscape calmly. She would know how to make every movement of her characters effective, in a way that moves the plot forward. There wouldn't be any succumbing to panic or self-doubt when the opposite was needed, that's for sure. So I won't succumb, either.

Will walks into the room on the other side of the bathroom door—and that's when I admit what's upsetting me the most. Every second I spend screwing with Will's life is a second spent guaranteeing his eventual resentment. Disdain, even. Have I been playing the what-if game in the back of my head? What if we met under different circumstances?

Useless thoughts, Teresa. Pointless.

If Silas's betrayal was enough to drive Will out of New York and away from his multi-million-dollar company, whatever his father did was bad. Bad enough that he's going to have zero mercy for the woman doing his bidding. Not to mention, I've only spent one day in Will's presence and I already know he's proud. Too proud to let me get away with lies.

"Teresa?"

"Yeah." I bend over and flip my hair back before taking a long breath and opening the door to reveal a concerned Will. Concerned is good. Eons better than betrayed. "Just checking my makeup. I'll get out of your way so you can shower."

On my way out, he snags me around the waist with a strong arm. "Hey."

There's a fluttering in my belly when I lift my chin and meet his eyes. "Hey, yourself."

He turns us in the doorframe, pulling me into his hard body at the same time. "I like coming into my room and finding you there." His hands slide down and cover my backside through my dress, kneading one side and then the other. One, two. One, two. Most men would have tasted a backhand by now for touching my ass without asking, but I only want Will to squeeze me there harder. "Wouldn't mind making a habit out of it. When we get to Arkansas, stay with me."

There's nothing phony about my stomach leaping. "Mmm. I don't know. What other habits do you have?" I look up at him through the veil of my lashes. "If I'm going to consider being your roommate..." I'm *not*. That would be stupid, right? "I should be aware of the ugly details."

"Sometimes I walk around naked. If that's going to be a problem for you, I can put on sweatpants." His slow grin makes my knees wobble. "Or you could join me."

"See that?" I shake my head. "You give a man one free show..."

"That show wasn't free, baby. It's costing me big time."

"Awww." I wink and shake myself free of his hold. "Sounds like you've got more to handle in the shower than a good shampoo job."

I feel his engine-rumble laugh everywhere, but when it fades, he's studying me. "What you told me last night through the wall...about me buying you. I want to make sure that's just something that gets you hot." He pauses, resting his tongue on that full lower lip. "If we're going to play around with it, I need to know it's a good thing for you. We're going to be on the same page."

Well, hell. It's true. Knees really can turn to jelly. The familiar impulse to be flippant is checked by the moment itself. By the naked honesty between us. Unable to believe I'm speaking about this without a wall to shield me, I try and remember where this call girl fascination began. "Um. So you remember a few years back, when that politician got caught meeting a girl on the sly in that fancy DC hotel? Everyone was so disgusted, and I-I mean, I *knew* the man was doing something wrong..."

His voice is raw. "But it made you hot."

Nodding, I blow out an uneven breath. "I guess there's something about a man's needs being so overwhelming that he can't even get through the day without..."

"Needing to fuck something sweet." He reaches out and strokes a thumb over my belly button, across to my hipbone. "Never had that problem before, but it's starting to become one."

"Learn to manage it," I breathe, just as his knuckle finds the V of my thighs, right over that needy spot, twisting with increasing pressure until I gasp.

He drags his open mouth across my shoulder, up the slope of my neck to stop at my ear. "See you in ten, woman."

Still reeling, I force myself out of the doorway and into the room. "Not if I see you first."

SITTING IN THE plush leather passenger seat of Will's Chevelle as we fly down the open highway should feel like something out of an erectile dysfunction commercial.

All that is missing is a long, paisley scarf tossed carelessly around my neck and some giant Jackie O sunglasses. With a high angle shot above the moving car, the material would snake out through the window, catching the wind. Viewers would follow that scarf into the car where Will and I would laugh merrily about our carefree lifestyle complete with bountiful boners.

It doesn't feel like an erection ad whatsoever, though. Will clearly has no issues in that department. And unlike watching those mandatory ads play in slow motion before a YouTube video starts, I'm immersed in real-time moments. Small towns whizz by with their fuzzy slogans painted on the sides of water towers, sunshine heats the leather beneath my thighs. In the backseat, Southpaw snores in a comforting drone.

I'm...*enjoying* myself. Will connects his iPhone and throws on a Miike Snow album, turned to the perfect volume. He doesn't sing or force conversation. No, he just throws one buff arm over the steering wheel and drives—while I try not to scrutinize him and figure out if he looked through my purse. There's a concentration line between his eyebrows but no tension in his jaw. His easy demeanor is almost enough to forget I'm playing a dangerous game. As if we're just some picnic-packing couple taking their dog to the park for some exercise.

A hysterical laugh tickles the sides of my throat, so I turn toward the window and muffle it with my shoulder. In the glass, Will's reflection sends me a curious look, before he goes back to watching the road behind a pair of black Ray-Bans.

It has been over a year since my last "relationship," and it was only a loose interpretation of the word, just like its predecessors. The men I attract tend to want a mommy more than a girlfriend. Multiple ones, on occasion. So what's happening right now? This spontaneous adventure to a national park? It never would have happened with those other guys, unless I was the one organizing it. And this girl was too busy, scrounging for paid acting gigs and working the gambling parlor. So dates tended to be of the Netflix and Chill variety, complete with whatever takeout I paid for *and* picked up.

I'm walking out on a shaky limb admitting this, but Will keeps proving to be the opposite of those past player and pity hounds. If last night on the balcony is any indication, deep down I've been hungering for a man to take physical control of me—without realizing I've been harboring the need. I always thought that secret, recurring fantasies of mine were so exciting simply because they were different from my real-life experience, but after last night I know the truth.

You want to be my plaything, Teresa?

A shudder passes through me, and Will flips off the air conditioner with a definitive click...and a twitch of his lips.

Crossing my arms over my hard nipples, I search for something to distract me from thinking about last night. Or from considering doing it again, without a wall dividing us this time.

Glancing out the passenger window, I jerk a little when I find a man passing in a black sedan—staring right at me. It's not unusual for drivers to look over at other motorists as they go past or anything, but...there's something familiar about him. Something about his white baseball cap and smirk triggers my memory, but I don't know why. Not at first. It takes me a few seconds to piece together where I've seen him before.

Was he standing in the group of men outside the tavern last night?

I try to shake off the suspicion and chalk it up to being stressed and overly paranoid, but the sedan stays no farther than a few car lengths back for a good twenty minutes before I lose sight of him. Still, Silas's words ring in my head, making the hair on my arms stand up.

Oh, and Teresa, don't be alarmed if I send someone to keep an eye on you.

"You're quiet over there," Will says.

I swallow and sit up straighter, praying to God my mind is playing tricks on me. "Um. When we go to Ouachita in the morning, will you leave Southpaw on the leash or just let him run around?"

Will checks the rearview, affection for his dog clear, and I encounter a surge of guilt for not telling him about the black sedan. That would lead to a full confession, though, and if I'm *not* crazy...if we're really being watched...a blow up between me and Will is exactly the kind of thing they'd report back to Silas. I can't allow that. Can't allow Nicky to suffer the consequences. "Most of the places we've visited require the leash," Will continues, sliding me a look. "But I tend to ignore that rule and pretend I didn't see the signs."

"You realize no one believes you."

"Because I seem so naturally competent?" He flashes his teeth at me in a devastating smile. "Thanks, baby."

"Hmm." Tingles. I have so many tingles. "What has been the best part of your trip so far?"

"You know the answer to that," Will responds, voice chafed by gravel. "But if you're asking my favorite part of the trip involving Southpaw...I'd have to say the people we've met. Online and in real life."

"Have you posted anything today?"

Without taking his attention off the road, he unhooks his phone from the USB cord, closes the music app and taps a different one. When he hands me the phone, the Instagram feed is familiar—I might have scrolled through it a few more times than I'd care to share—except for the two most recent pictures.

There's one of me in the field, red dress billowing in the wind as I throw the ball to Southpaw. It's a great shot, anchored by shadow and structure in all the right places, the dog caught in mid-leap. The field was a shit heap, but Will managed to make it look like a sunshine-soaked slice of Americana. It was only posted three hours ago, but the picture has already received over sixty thousand likes.

"Don't look at the comments."

Who's the cute girl?

Nice ass.

Aw, shit. Caruso got laid last night.

"Too late," I say.

He winces. "That bad, huh? I usually don't get a chance to read all of them, but I'm definitely going to hold off this time."

I shrug. "Just typical bro stuff."

"If it's disrespectful, you shouldn't consider it typical." A muscle ticks in his cheek. "I'll take it down."

"No, it's fine…" My face isn't showing in the shot, and I take a moment to be grateful over that fact. I created an Instagram account forever ago and never used it to do anything but drool over the Hemsworths, so even if he'd tagged me in the picture, zero people I know would see it and comment, right? There's no use running through what-ifs, though, because I'm just a faceless girl in a red dress. No harm no foul.

Still, I need to be more vigilant about Will taking pictures. I've been out of Staten Island for almost a decade, but someone could easily recognize me, comment, and connect me to Will's father as fast as it takes to hit *post*.

He watches me tap on the second new picture, which depicts Southpaw asleep in a tangle of towels on the bathroom floor, above the caption, *All play and no work makes Southpaw a happy boy.* "Our first stop out of New York was in Lewes, a small town in Delaware. He was still kind of confused by the sudden trip and I was still getting my bearings, too. Being a full-time dog dad." He shakes his head, laughing under his breath. "Anyway, I wanted to get him the biggest bone I could find, thinking maybe it would make him feel better. Went into a butcher shop and the owner's kid was working the counter. Peter was his name. He fell in love with Southpaw on the spot."

Will's smile dims a little. "Peter knew, without me telling him, that something was wrong. I'm still not sure if I wasn't hiding it very well. Or if the kid was just special. But he knew." My heart is in my throat as a few seconds tick past, Will staring through the windshield at the road. "I opened the Instagram account so Peter could follow along on the trip. It was just meant to be for him, but around the end of the first week, it kind of blew up. And I realized all those reasons I was on the trip— recognizing the important things—maybe people were doing that through me. So I just keep posting." In a clear attempt to lighten the mood, he raises his eyebrows at me. "Who am I to deprive everyone of the best dog in the world, right?"

"You're right, that would be selfish. And you're not selfish at all, are you, Will?" The words whisper right out of me without any encouragement or forethought. They startle me in their absolute clarity and sincerity. But startled or not, I can't stop myself from reaching across the car and laying a hand on Will's forearm. "My mother used to say, love is never a small thing. Even the tiniest hint of love is a forest fire. All those likes and follows…people sense when something is real and good. You and Southpaw are real and good."

Will's eyes are behind sunglasses, but the look he turns on me is no less potent. It's gratefulness wrapped in hope, baked in *I want to fuck you*. My hand flies off his arm like I've been burned, when all I really want is to leave it there to feel the inferno. Let it race over my skin.

An idea occurs to me and I voice it, unable to hold back in the midst of our snapping connection. "My GoPro is in my suitcase. I could attach it to Southpaw's collar when we get to the park. You could give everyone a dog's-eye view of his canine adventures." Hearing the excitement in my tone, I immediately try to reel back and play cool. "No pressure, just think about it."

"I don't have to think about it. Let's do it."

"Oh." I press my knuckles to my mouth, trying to mash my smile back down. "Okay."

Will's interest heats my left side. "Do you always carry a camera?"

"Not really, just…" Not liking the taste of yet another lie on my tongue, I shrug. "I carry it a lot, actually. You know how, like, when you walk down the street, you're only focused on yourself? How you're walking, the music you're listening to, the next intersection? I clip the camera to a hat or my purse sometimes, then watch the footage back later." Colors, sounds and laughter play on a reel in my head. "Even with a small angle adjustment, it's like you were in a whole other world without realizing it."

My words hang in the air a moment. Not long enough to make me want to snatch them back, but close. "I'm guessing you don't want to work in a gambling parlor the rest of your life," Will says softly.

"No."

"What *do* you want to do?"

A gradual pressure drops down on my lungs. Nicky is the only person who knows I applied to film school, but it's something we only talk about in passing. My parents were so proud when I graduated with my accounting degree, their newly safeguarded way of life provoking them to push me toward numbers. Accounting. Where paper cuts and carpal tunnel are the most extreme hazards. Having grown up in the same house as me, they'd been my indulgent audience more than once—usually during screenings of whatever high drama I'd shot with Barbie dolls and a camcorder that day. But any hints at attending film school had been met with flat smiles and pats on the head.

Filmmaking is already a male-dominated industry. Throw in the fact that my appearance prevents me from being taken seriously and I don't have so much as an independent short under my belt? I win the award for Most Likely to Be Laughed Out of the Building. When my parents died, I was devastated. Still am and always will be. But I would be lying if I didn't say their passing gave me the green light to take a wildly aimed shot at my dreams.

Just one.

But sending a sneaky application—that could *easily* be reject-ed—and talking about it out loud are two different things. My past boyfriends thought my GoPro and the videos I edited together on my laptop were cute, but didn't really "get it, hon." What are the chances an über-successful hedge fund manager won't pity me, even if he doesn't say it out loud?

God. You know what? This isn't me. I'm a ballsy, Italian leather-wearing, shit-talking, chip-counting man-eater. If this guy doesn't take me seriously, *he's* the idiot.

For the first time, my patented bolstering technique doesn't work. Might as well face it, I can't keep my mask in place as easily around this guy.

Before I can lose my nerve, it flies out. "I applied to film school."

He nods once. "Where?"

"The Film Institute." His matter-of-fact tone is easing the pressure on my chest already. "They have campuses in LA and New York. They're…the best."

"Sounds like there's a but," Will says after a moment. "Why is there a but?"

"*But* I won't get in." I smile and shrug off the disappointment those words carry along with them. "Don't worry, I'm not banking on being accepted. I have a degree in accounting." I pretend to check my eye makeup in the mirror. "I'm just another twenty-three-year-old taking her time learning to be a responsible adult. Pining for an unrealistic career is part of the fun, right?"

"Twenty-three." He gives a low whistle. "Fuck."

"Oh." I snap the mirror shut. "Have we hit a roadblock?"

"Nope. Just taking a second to acclimate." Laughing under his breath, he flexes those giant hands on the wheel. "Will you show me some of your work? I want to see it."

My stomach bottoms out. "Why?"

"So I can give you an opinion."

My laugh is high-pitched, making me cringe. "Who said I wanted one?"

"You realize it took you a full two minutes to even admit you applied? I'm guessing you don't tell a lot of people. So I can safely cut the number of people who've seen your work in half."

"Don't use psychology and math on me at the same time."

His gorgeous mouth ticks up at one end. "Don't you think I'm the kind of man that would give you an honest opinion?"

"Hell no. You're trying to sleep with me."

His laughter booms through the car, earning him a *snarf* from the backseat. "Good point." The look he sends me is one of mock sympathy. "Looks like we'll have to sleep together first, so you know I'm being truthful. Should I pull over?"

"Yes." Leaning back in the seat, I run both hands over my breasts, down to my stomach and thighs, triumphant when a growl rips from Will's throat. "But only because I want lunch," I say, fluttering my eyelashes.

"We'll see about that, woman." A beat of silence passes, and then he's reaching across the console to cup my chin. "It's not about my opinion. I want to see what you love. And you might be goddamn twenty-three, but nothing you wanted at any age could be unrealistic. One day with you and I'd take that to the bank. I just want to be the one who looks at your work and tells you that." His thumb brushes my bottom lip. "Think about it."

CHAPTER TEN

Will

I'VE LET MILLIONS of dollars ride on a hunch—and won—but it never satisfied me as much as Teresa telling me she applied to film school. It doesn't take a genius to see she doesn't confide in people easily. I like being that person. A lot.

The irony that she opened up about her private goals but lied to me about her last name definitely isn't lost on me. But these questions hanging over her head don't make me want her trust any less. Actually, *want* doesn't begin to cover it. I'm craving more of what's inside her head by the second. She's guarded and, hell, she could be here to try and screw me over, but I know in my bones there's more real here than fake. Right now, I'm interested in the real.

I've been a fighter and I've stood at the helm of Caruso Capital Management. Those two professions don't have a lot in common. Hell, I'm still trying to figure out which of them is where I was meant to belong, but they both require a man to trust his gut. My gut is driving me to give Teresa more of what she needs.

I want you to use me. Want you to buy me.

As I pull into the parking lot of a two-story brick building, my cock stretches and curves to my fly. She whimpered those words to me in the heat of the moment last night. But they weren't just dirty nothings, they were an admission, just like the one she made about film school. More proof she finds me worthy of her trust. The fact that she's placed that trust in me makes me feel guilty as shit for ordering the background check. *Dammit.*

I want to make up for doubting her, whether it's founded or not. If that doesn't tell me I've got a growing infatuation for this woman, nothing will. But there it is. I need to earn her secrets. And I want to blow her fucking mind so the idea of getting on a bus won't come so easily for her come tomorrow.

Broken Bow is a small town I've never heard of, but a billboard ten miles back claimed Boney's Brisket has the best Tex-Mex for a hundred miles. I've been in this part of the country long enough to know that every restaurant makes the same claim, so I'm not holding out a ton of hope. I'm more interested in what's going to happen before lunch.

I open the door for Southpaw and he takes off, as per usual, heading for the tree clearing behind Boney's. Teresa makes a little squeak and tries to lunge out the passenger side door after him, but I lay a hand on her arm and stop her.

"Don't worry. It's just his routine." My hand travels down to her wrist, so I can press a thumb to her pulse. It jumps. "Freaked me out a little the first time, too. But he always comes back. He'll be gone about twenty minutes."

Her thighs shift on the seat. She's trying not to look at my thumb on her wrist and failing, color spreading up her neck. "Should we go inside without him?"

"No."

Her pulse leaps again, continues to race. "So we just s-sit here and wait?"

When it comes to Teresa's hidden needs, we've only scratched the surface. But I remember what made her come the loudest last night, because I was paying damn close attention. When I told her I wanted to ride her pussy like I paid ten grand for the pleasure, she went off like a bottle rocket. *Yes*, she said. Yes.

I wouldn't gamble on something that could hurt her, but our conversation this morning took care of that concern. And the nipples trying to poke through the front of her dress tell me what I'm about to do is a solid bet.

Come on, baby. Trust me to give you what you need.

"I'd like you to get in the backseat."

Her laughter is uneven. "I-it's…we're in a parking lot."

I bring her wrist to my mouth and lick a path up the sensitive skin, straight to her elbow, and Jesus Christ, she tastes like watermelon and woman. If I had the freedom I need, I would lay her on a flat surface and go for broke between her legs, but only after tasting her in places she wouldn't expect. Her hips, the small of her back, behind her knees. "We're in the last spot, up against a wall. Only one person could discover us and they've probably just gone in for lunch. I like our odds."

"I don't know," she breathes, shaking her head. "I—"

My wallet lands in her lap. Her eyes shoot to mine and I see the flash of emotion she tries to subdue but can't. Excitement. There's irritation, too, but it's surface bullshit. The reaction she *thinks* she should be having, maybe.

"A lap dance. I'll let you keep on panties, but all your other clothes come off." I reach across the console and run a hand up her thigh, lifting her dress as if to judge the goods, but on the inside I'm groaning over the way her legs flex and part, just a hint. Involuntary? "You look expensive, baby, but I'm good for it."

She chokes on whatever she's trying to say, then falls silent. Her eyelids droop, and all the while, her tits shudder up and down. God above, I've never been so desperate to fulfill a need for another person. But my hands are fucking shaking with the impulse to drag her onto my lap, spread her thighs open and bang her tight little body up against the steering wheel. Yeah, I want to come. No doubt. But I'd damn well forgo getting my own rocks off to make her orgasm one extra time.

Fuck. What this woman *does* to me.

"How much?"

Her whisper is so low, I think it's the air conditioner I've left running. "All of it." I lift the hem of her dress even more, my jaw clenching when I see how tightly she's squeezing her legs together. Not enough to hide the pretty tiger striped thong cupping her pussy, though. No, I definitely see that. "You're going to be worth every red cent, aren't you?"

"Let's just say you'll be a repeat customer," she murmurs, pushing open the passenger door, dislodging my hand and stepping out of the car. The more she plays along with the illusion I've created, the more pink suffuses her skin, her eyes taking on a bedroom quality. I can't get out of the driver's side and into the backseat fast enough…and she waits. Waits for me to slide into the center of the rear bench seat, my legs splayed, hands at my side. Genuine impatience to see some skin ticking in my jaw. A man about to get a show.

"I don't have all day." Opening the wallet I brought with me, I take out a stack of bills and lay them into the door handle. "You came highly recommended. Let's see if you're as good as everyone says."

Teresa presses her lips together but can't quite trap the moan that escapes as she climbs into the backseat, walking toward me on her knees. I take a second to thank 1970s car manufacturers for all the room…and then my world is all Teresa. She rolls into my consciousness like succulent, summer storm clouds and demands every facet of my attention. Using my shoulders for balance, she straddles me slowly, her lower lip caught between her teeth. With her ass settled on me mid-thigh, we both seem to be holding our breath, waiting to see what she'll do next. Patience is not my strong suit, but I'm not rushing this. No, she might be discovering something about herself with my help and I'm savoring every second.

Her eyes lift to mine, trapping me in the sticky atmosphere blooming between us, her hands leaving my shoulders to settle on her beautiful pair of tits. She pushes them up, massaging them, turning her already low neckline into a complete joke. "Fuck." Whatever remaining blood I have left in my body rushes to my cock, swelling the flesh in a mind-bending rush of heat. "That's a pretty dress, but it's useless. You're spilling out of it." I reach beneath her dress and deliver a testing slap to her backside. "Give me what I'm paying for."

A shudder blows through her, those teeth clamping down so hard on her bottom lip, I expect to see blood. "A-are you going to take your clothes off, too?"

There's only a small thread of uncertainty in her voice, but I'm already moving. Cupping the sides of her face and kissing her, hard, long and steady. It's seeking and finding, confessing and smoothing. Most important of all, it's reassuring. After a moment of coaxing, she lets me feed my tongue into her mouth and it's like being gifted with the Crown fucking Jewels, except she doesn't taste like some inanimate object. She's wet and giving and...vulnerable. For me. It serves as a shot of protectiveness and adrenaline, straight to my bloodstream.

When I pull away, I keep her close enough to rest our foreheads together. "No matter what comes out of my mouth, I know you're Teresa. I respect you," I whisper against her panting lips. "You're going to work this little kink out on my lap so we know its flavor, woman. Understand?" She gasps into my kiss but is quick to participate, licking her tongue against mine. "Then I'm going to hold the door open for you on the way into that restaurant. Going to pull out your chair and dare anyone with a dick to look below your neck. I'm going to be the same man after you take off that dress for me."

She shakes her head. "Why do I believe you?"

"I'm guessing it's a gut feeling. Like the one I have about you." Her eyes race over my face like she's trying to solve a puzzle—and I can damn well relate. But there's a second bone-deep instinct telling me we're not ready to explore that part of what's going on in our heads yet. We're on our own unique path to get there and it involves one hurdle at a time. "To answer your question, no. My clothes stay on." I fall back against the seat and settle both hands on her spread thighs. "You're the one punching the clock."

One tick passes. Two. Until finally she grips the hem of her dress, hesitates for a split second, and pulls it off over her head. I vaguely register her tossing it aside in a red flash, but I'm too busy needing to fuck Teresa until she can't move after that. I've seen her bare thighs, seen her bouncy little tits. It has been voted on and decided that her face is the most spectacular part about her, mainly because it's so curious and suspicious and sly and charming and everything in between. But the whole package put together?

She's a gift from God.

I accept.

"From here on out, you're mine."

Her hands freeze on their way to my shoulders. "What?"

Pull back, man. She's not there yet. I *am*, though, apparently, and my impulse is to demand she get there, too. The unknown secrets between us force me to check myself, though. "I want you and this body of yours on retainer." I slide my hands up her thighs, stopping at her hips to pull her closer. "If I call, you show up. No questions asked. You spread your pretty thighs on the couch in my office and wait for me to unbuckle."

Right in front of my eyes, her nipples turn into even tighter peaks, her knees shaking on either side of my lap. "I-I—uh…" She sucks in shallow, back-to-back breaths. "What do I get in return?"

Intuition tells me she doesn't want to hear what I'd do in real life. That I'd fall like a starving man to my knees and eat her pussy, not giving a fuck if my employees heard her shrieking for mercy through the walls. No, right now she's hot to be used, just like she told me—and I need to be the one who gives her that. "You get to keep the boss happy, whether it's on your knees or on your back." I tip my head toward the stacked pile of cash. "And I make it so you start wishing I'd call twice a day, which I damn well might, because you've got a sweet, young pussy on you. Isn't that right?"

"Yes." I look down to find a dark shadow on the front of her panties, and knowing she's that damn wet makes me want to pound my chest. My dick is so full and aching, I'm about to break. To crack the fantasy in half. About to unzip my pants and tempt her to sit down on my cock with more of the filthy talk she so clearly loves. But she has something else in mind.

Both hands lift, fingers tangling in her long, dark hair. She looks me right in the eye as she slowly pops her hips left, right, left, right. If she's challenging me to maintain eye contact, I fail after about five seconds, desperate to memorize the jiggle of her tits, those rosy points turning my mouth to a fucking desert, making my hands clench where they've fallen on the seat. I don't know where to look, because she's a goddamn feast of golden, glowing skin and sex and jack-off fodder. Lust is coating me like sizzling oil, pooling in my lap.

I rake a hand down my open mouth, not surprised to find

I'm breathing like a bull during a rodeo…and I do it. I finally let myself look at her pussy. And the moan that rips from me is almost inhuman. "Ah, Christ. Those wet panties are sticking to you, baby. I can see the split of your lips." She arches her back and moves faster, her knees sliding wider on the seat, bringing her mound within two inches of the fattened bulge beneath my zipper. "I can see how bad you want to grind down on it."

Teresa sobs, the swaying movements of her body faltering. "Please. Yes."

My hands cup her backside, kneading the naked flesh roughly. "No. Not this time." Saying the words is painful, but I'm seeing this experiment through—to the very end—because she *will know* her needs are fulfilled by *me*. And fuck, it's getting me off, too, because she's shaking like a leaf, whimpering in her throat like she can't take much more. "I'm paying you to dance." My hand rains down a blow to her ass and she gasps. "Keep your soaking wet pussy up in the air above my cock where it belongs."

"Please. Please. I'm…" She grabs on to the seat behind me, her hips moving in tight figure eights, making her tits bob, her thighs flex. Jesus, it's getting hard to breathe, hard to restrain myself, hard to do anything but focus on getting her off. "I don't know h-how, but I'm so close. If I could just—"

I reach between her thighs from behind and slap her pussy—*smack*—rolling her unfocused eyes back in her head. "You heard me the first time. If you grind your cunt down where it hasn't been invited, your mouth is going to pay the price."

Her knees try to squeeze closed, but they can't, because my thighs are blocking them. We both stare down at her soaked panties, straight through to the pussy beneath, that sways left to right above my brutal erection. "I-I…what is it? The price."

The way she licks her lips tells me she knows exactly what it is. "You're going to find out if you can't help being a bad girl."

"I can't," she whispers, lowering another inch. "I can't."

A growl builds deep in my chest, a bead of sweat rolling down my spine. I'm not sure I've ever wanted anything as much as I want her to drop that appetizing pussy on my cock and ride herself to an orgasm on it through my pants. Just thinking about it is causing precome to dribble from my tip in anticipation of my balls emptying for Teresa. Like they did last night. And again this morning in the shower. My hand and imagination were a billion miles from the real thing—and she's so real, shaking and whimpering and attempting to dance above me, I know I'm wrecked for anyone else.

Sensing she needs a final push, I reach over and pluck several hundred-dollar bills off the door handle. One by one, I tuck them under the thin side strap of her thong, memorizing the way her head falls back, mouth open, hips writhing. By the time I'm finished, there's so much green around her hips, it looks like she's wearing a short, ripped skirt. There's literally a half-inch separating her from my erection now and I have to clench my teeth together to stop from thrusting up and ending the agony. "Don't you dare." I run my palms up her thighs. "Don't you dare go any lower. I don't care how hard your little clit is throbbing inside those panties. I don't care how good it would feel to have something fat and firm against it."

"Please."

"No."

"*Please*," she cries out, her thighs sliding the final distance wider. And then she's finally seated on my lap, her pupils dilated, mouth dropped open.

Yes. Heat swarms my balls, my cock jerking at the soft but demanding friction. "Oh God. Oh shit," she whispers brokenly, burying her face in the crook of my neck. "I n-need this. Just, just, please…"

Flush against me, every part of us touching, her hips begin pumping hard, dragging her hot flesh up and down my aching cock. She's like the goddess of flexibility, her thighs so wide, she's doing the goddamn splits right on top of me, giving me such insane pressure and—Jesus, *the rubbing*—a ragged moan scrapes up my throat and fills the car.

"I'm going to come." Her eyes meet mine and she looks so exhilarated, shocked and turned on, I forget how to speak. "Feels so good. You're so *hard*."

"Tell me something I don't know," I grit out, grabbing her ass in both hands and pulling her drenched juncture tight to my dick. No way to stop myself, I punch my hips up again and again, listening to the scream build in her throat. "I'm going to need this pussy for house calls, too. It's worth its weight in gold."

Teresa sucks in a breath and goes off, her body trembling violently, her hands twisting in the material covering my shoulders. "Oh. Oh. Will. *Jesus*."

She bears down on me, twisting, hips spasming. Heat leaks through my fly. I feel her teeth sink into my neck, an involuntary search for anchor, and I feel like a God, knowing she found it in me. In my body. "There you go, baby. Thought I'd let you get on a bus? No. *No*. Fuck that. *Mine*."

I'm not sure if she hears me—hears *anything*—but when her head lifts and our eyes lock, there's no discussion about prices or penalties. Or what happens next. She can feel how bad I need release. Hell, she just rode it like a prize horse. And my jaw is about to shatter, sweat bathing my forehead, so I'm pretty damn sure I look like a man possessed. I sound like one, too, as Teresa positions herself beside me on the seat, bent forward, sweet ass in the air. Our hands collide, trying to get my pants unzipped and my cock out. Only takes five seconds, but might as well be centuries.

So, she doesn't make me wait longer than necessary, this incredible girl with the warm, welcoming mouth that slides halfway down my length on her first suck, sending my fist up to punch the ceiling. "Yeah. Fuck yeah, woman. Just like that." I bury my fists in her hair, twisting the silk around my knuckles and wrists. "Suck my motherfucking dick."

Her hands join the action, twisting down to my base, followed by her eager mouth. So I give her my touch, too, scraping my palm down her arched back, stopping to squeeze her ass like I own it, before venturing between her thighs.

"*Fuck*, you wet little thing. You want more?" The vibrations from her affirmative answer echo down my cock, so I don't hesitate to sink my middle finger inside her, twisting it to search for her G-spot. When I encounter that rough patch, her body jolts and she moans, her mouth sinking down lower on me. "You can take more when you're grateful, is that right?" I abuse the spot with the pad of my finger, watching her thighs dance around with a second climax. "Couldn't take it for long, baby? That makes two of us. Get ready for mine."

Pressure has already been mounting like a raging river caught behind a dam inside me, but saying the words out loud seems to give my body permission to set loose the fire Teresa stokes. My stomach muscles seize, blood pounding in my head—and Christ, pleasure spears me like a weapon, robbing me of my ability to do anything but groan like a depraved bastard. I let go of her hair in case she doesn't want to swallow, but I think I'm chanting at her to drink me down, my body heaving its way through the best peak of its life.

I'm not sure how much time passes before Teresa sits up, her hair and clothes in disarray, eyes wide. If she's feeling anything like me, she just got hit by a train and doesn't know where she landed. I don't want her to feel like that—ever—especially with me. So I hold my arms open and after a deep breath, she falls into them, sighing in a content way when I arrange her sideways on my lap.

That's when we notice Southpaw watching us from the hood of the car, with an expression that could only be described as disappointment in our self-control.

"What's it going to take to forget what you saw here?" I ask, before dropping my voice to what I imagine is how a Great Dane would speak. "The ribeye. Rare. And this all goes away."

Her bright, clear laugh makes my chest feel tight. Makes me wish I'd never called New York to order her background check. Because the longer I spend with Teresa, the more I need her to trust me. If I didn't need to trust her in return just as much, I'd call off the intrusive exercise and wait.

Wait for her to tell me her secrets, instead.

But as I watch her get dressed and notice the tension creep back into her shoulders, the solemn expression stealing the smile from her face, I know I can't call off a damn thing.

CHAPTER ELEVEN

Teresa

WELL, *SHIT.*

It doesn't matter how many times I fix the dress, I still feel naked on the way into the restaurant for lunch. My nipples are chafed from sliding up and down the front of Will's shirt, my ass is smarting from being slapped. Don't get me started on my vagina. She's down for the count. Do not disturb.

Lord. In. Heaven. Will might be the only man I've ever met who talks a big game and doesn't *only* back it up, but overshoots the mark. I'm literally walking funny through the entrance and he wasn't even inside me.

I'm going to need a medevac when that happens.

Wait. Whoa, whoa, whoa. That is *not* going to happen. I am not doing thrust squats in his cucumber patch.

I can't.

He's just making it so damn difficult to say no. *You're going to work this little kink out on my lap so we know its flavor, woman. Understand? Then I'm going to hold the door open for you on the way into that restaurant. Going to pull out your chair and dare anyone with a dick to look below your neck. I'm going to be the same man after you take off that dress for me.*

And he does. He holds the door for me, kissing my shoulder as I walk by.

Everyone in the small, homespun bar and grill turns in their seat or barstool when we reach the hostess station, probably because I look like a woman who just screamed through two orgasms in the backseat of a Chevelle. Getting hundred-dollar bills stuffed in her thong while a dog watched at least a partial viewing of the show.

Not bad for a weekday.

Logically, I know letting Will touch me is a mistake. Because it's not just touching. He's...seeing me. Right through the top layer none of the men who passed before could even put a *dent* in. My heart starts to slam into my jugular thinking about the way he held me afterward. Not like a woman who'd stripped and given him head. Like a woman he could cherish.

Do you hear yourself? I barely know this man and he's making me lose sight of what's always been most important. My brother. I need to pull it together and stay objective, but that's easier said than done when I can't distance myself from Will. Not if I want to achieve my goal of getting him to New York. Which will never happen if I go to bed with him.

Why is my conviction on that score fading so fast?

Waiting for the waitress to approach, I cast a casual glance around the restaurant, searching for the man in the white baseball cap. Why? If he was indeed sent by Silas—and I'm still not sure my imagination wasn't working overtime—I didn't see the black sedan at all during the last twenty minutes on the highway. He didn't pull into the parking lot behind us, either. At least not before I became occupied. Unbelievable. I didn't think of our tail even *once* while I was...getting tail. Part of me is almost hoping to spot the man, just so I'll be reminded of the situation's severity. Maybe then I'll stop mooning over a certain hedge fund manager.

Of course, Will makes that impossible. He twines our fingers together and tugs me into his side, that warning look I remember from last night in his eyes, directed at a group of men at the bar. I take the opportunity to study his chiseled profile. How long can his possessiveness toward me last? I never took myself for the kind of woman who liked an alpha male growling around her, but I can't deny it makes me feel powerfully feminine.

This is very bad.

"What are you thinking about?"

I've been so absorbed in my own thoughts, I didn't realize Will was watching me. Very closely. "Food, mostly."

His mouth twitches. "She lies."

There's a sharp, invisible jab in my chest. "Thank you for not, um…"

The amusement fades from his expression. "For not what?"

"I don't know. For not offering to let me keep the money." My face heats, thinking of the crisp slide of bills against my hips, my tummy. "For already knowing I wouldn't."

Understanding dawns and he dips his head, resting his mouth against my ear. Staying there for a beat before speaking. "I won't let those lines get blurred, Teresa. Because if you decide tomorrow you want to play something different, you're going to trust me enough to come get it right here." He moves back, tilting his head at me. "I also put that money back in my wallet because I like my nuts right where they are."

Appreciation makes me featherlight. "Smart man."

"Mysterious woman."

It's hard to keep my smile intact while he's so close, scrutinizing me, interpreting every blink, every breath. What is he seeing? Thinking? I'm about to lose our staring contest, when I'm saved by the hostess.

"Y'all can follow me." We turn to find a teenager with braces waiting with two menus. She almost drops them when she sees

Will, her shoes squeaking on the floor as she scrambles to keep them in her arms. Apparently, I've been so distracted by Will's personality, I forgot how freaking hot he is. "Uh. Can I sit you all in the bar area? We d-don't allow dogs in the grill."

Will gives her a patient smile. "That's fine. Thank you."

"Sure."

The hostess doesn't move for at least a five-count, beaming up at Will the way I used to look at my Spielberg posters. Eventually we start heading in the direction of the bar, though. It's an ancient place, much like the biker bar where we ate dinner last night, but the clientele is way different. The way they lean on one another's shoulders and share features tells me they're either related or they've known each other so long, they've started to look alike.

Southpaw breaks the ice with the group of men Will tried to kill before with his icy death ray stare, a couple of them going down on one knee to greet the pooch. Southpaw asks Will for permission with a glance, receives the nod, then plods over to receive a round of ear-scratching and belly-rubbing.

As we take our seats, Will is fighting a smile, his phone elevated to snap a picture of the scene. "Caption," he drawls. "Rub and tug."

A laugh escapes, but I still shake my head at him. "Do you ever get jealous?"

"Over Southpaw making new friends?" He stows his phone in his front pocket and throws me a devilish wink. "Only if the guy is better looking than me. So it's happened—"

"Never?"

"You said it, not me."

My mouth will not stop trying to smile. "I was speaking in predictive text."

His laugh rumbles across the table, sprouting goosebumps

everywhere I have skin. Which is *all of the places.* "Now if you wanted your belly rubbed by someone else, we'd have a problem," Will says, the smile no longer reaching his eyes. "Tell me something about you. Something I don't know."

My pulse is still spiking after his comment. And whether it's a habit to distance myself from anything too serious with a man...or a caution signal going off, reminding me I'm getting too close to the man I'm conning, I speak without thinking. "You say all these growly caveman things, like you're going to drag me back to your cave. But we're only on a detour together."

A more screwed-up one than you realize.

His expression is unreadable. Guarded. "Then we should take advantage of the time we have."

"I have a brother." The words are out before I can stop them. As if telling him as much about me as possible will balance my guilt over lying. "That's something you didn't know."

Still can't read him. "How old?"

"Few years younger than me. We live together in Los Angeles."

There's a subtle tick in his jaw. "How does he feel about your job?"

"He doesn't know." I recall our phone conversation at the airport. "Not the specifics, anyway. Just that I'm not studying for film school at night, like I said."

A young man stops at the table and drops off a pair of waters, before beelining for Southpaw to join in the petting frenzy. There's an uncomfortable weight on my lungs, probably because I'm talking about my brother, who I'm worried sick about. The orgasms probably only shook me up more, not to mention the orgasm *donor* radiating possessiveness across the table. His patience and quiet encouragement compel me to make him understand on some level that my choices are limited.

"My brother didn't hit a growth spurt until he was a senior in high school." After we'd already moved across the country, thus making him the new kid on top of being five feet tall. "He wasn't alienated or anything—he had friends. Tons of them." My lips tug at one end. "You really can't help but love him. He once got off with a warning after covering the high school principal's car in honey and feathers for a senior prank. Getting mad at him is almost impossible because he treats everyone like they're in on the joke, too. No one is…left out when he's around." I shrug. "But people who weren't close to him always made fun of his height, before he grew. Older neighborhood kids, mostly. They called him Armrest. Sometimes it became too much for him and I'd…"

"Step in and knock heads together?"

"Yeah." We trade a small smile, but I can't maintain mine. "But I stepped in too many times, you know? I never let him fight his own battles. He needed to brawl with Henry Bamford behind the bleachers after school instead of me showing up with a ponytail and no jewelry to take his place."

"The black eye would have faded, but the lesson wouldn't have?"

"Exactly."

I'm the real reason Nicky is in this mess, aren't I?

Will crosses his arms. "You didn't really fight Henry Bamford, did you?"

My mouth forms an O. "You saying girls can't fight?"

"I'm *saying* if a man gave you a black eye, I won't be able to eat."

"Then order big, because Henry went down like a sack of spuds."

A booming laugh from Will brings Southpaw clip-clopping for the table, but Will is still looking at me. He props his elbows on the table and leans closer. "So this brother of yours. He still depends on you?"

I press my lips together to keep the truth from tumbling out. "Old habits are hard to break."

"He's alone in Los Angeles now, no sister to take care of him. Might be late in the game, but maybe that's what he needs."

"Yeah, maybe." My nod is too vigorous, so I stop and pick up the menu, searching for a distraction. And holy hell, do I get one. In big, block letters at the top of the menu are the words BEAT PAULA IN AN ARM-WRESLTING CONTEST AND EAT FOR FREE. "Who's Paula?"

I'm in the process of asking the question when the waitress approaches. She winces, signaling me to lower my voice. "Paula is the owner's sister," she mutters, plucking a pad of paper from her apron and casting a quick look over her shoulder. "It's not meant to be taken seriously."

"Are you sure?" I ask, matching her tone. "It's a pretty eye-catching font."

"That's because Paula designed the menu," she explains, leaning in closer. "If you flip it over, there's also a list of her gator-wrestling championship wins."

Will coughs. "Gator wrestling?"

"Damn right, gator wrestling."

The waitress's slump tells me everything I need to know. That gravel-scraped, whiskey-drenched voice belongs to Paula. And those boot thunks on the floor mean she's headed our way.

Leaning sideways to see around the waitress, I wonder how I missed Paula on the way into the restaurant. She's easily six foot three and wearing a miniature cattle skull bolo tie. A black, wide-brimmed hat sits low on her head, nearly covering her eyes, but as she gets closer, she flicks it up with her index finger, proceeding to dissect me and Will through narrowed eyes.

I glance over at Will and quickly realize I shouldn't have. For two reasons. One, his casual amusement makes me like him even more. And two, it surprises a giggle out of me. The giggle is abruptly cut off, however, when Paula hip bumps our waitress out of the way and slaps both hands down on the table.

"Guess I shouldn't be surprised that a couple of city folk have never heard of God's game." Paula says, following up her statement with a long sniff. "I meant gator wrestling."

I nod. "Right. I got that."

Will nudges me under the table with his foot and I kick him back.

Paula straightens and splits a look between Will and me. "Did I hear someone was interested in a little competition?"

Discreetly as possible, I check the muscle definition in her arms. She could put The Rock in a chokehold. My spaghetti arms don't stand a chance. "Oh no. No." I fan my face with the menu. "I was just reading out loud."

"Size sixty Helvetica," Paula says, jabbing a finger at the menu. "It's a trap."

"I see that now." Why couldn't we have driven through a Wendy's? "Having weighed the chance to eat free and getting my ass whooped, I'm going with paying."

Looking disappointed, Paula points at Will. "What about you, Big Sexy? You're awfully quiet over there."

He does a double take at the nickname. "What do you get if you win, Paula?"

"The only thing worth living for, slick. Bragging rights."

Southpaw lays his head on my thigh and I smooth a thumb between his solemn, curious brown eyes. For a second, I'm taken out of the conversation, because I swear the dog is asking me if everything is all right. "Shhh," I murmur to him. "They're friends."

At that, the dog lies down on the ground, covering both my

feet, and I feel an odd sense of contentment. Right in the middle of being challenged to an arm wrestling match. A prickle on my neck compels me to look across the table and I find Will watching me with a strange expression.

"How about this," he says, still looking at me. "If Teresa can hang for five seconds, everyone in the bar eats and drinks for free."

Southpaw's head comes up. I make a strangled noise, my stomach bottoming out and splattering on the floor. "Excuse me. *What* was that?"

In seconds, everyone in the bar is gathered around the table, the possibility of free drinks and grub hanging in the balance. There's a loud crack to my left and I realize with sickening clarity that it's Paula's knuckles.

"Oh no." I shake my head and pick the menu back up, pretending to read it. But all I can see is size sixty Helvetica. "You're all crazy."

There's a chorus of *awwws*.

Will leans across the table, his expression cajoling. "Five seconds. You can do it." His head tilts. "You're the girl who beat up Henry Bamford."

Am I? Until this very moment, it never occurred to me that I haven't felt like that girl in…kind of a while. *That* Teresa wouldn't have turned in a secret application for film school and written off her chances before the mailman even arrived. She would have marched up to the admissions office and demanded to see who was in charge.

I've been in a holding pattern, haven't I? Working a job that isn't safe and doesn't have a damn thing to do with my hopes or dreams. I've been mothering Nicky, paying rent, falling into bed late at night, and I've forgotten to be excited about things to come. Possibilities. Potential.

There's no way Will should be able to see past my confident surface. No way at all. I showed up in his room topless, for chrissakes. I sassed, I teased, I *just* performed a private striptease for him. But he does. His mouth is smiling, but his eyes are serious and I know he's seeing things about me that I'm only beginning to decipher for myself. There's more, too. As if he understands because he's been here.

Have I really set aside who I am? What I want?

"City people, my ass." I slap the menu down on the table. "It's on."

The cheers are deafening. Will hoots and rises from his chair, moving into a spot behind mine. Paula takes his place across from me. Everyone crowds in on all sides. And suddenly my world has been narrowed down to an arm wrestling arena.

"All right, baby." Will's voice smokes into my ear. "Here's how we get to five seconds. You're going to top-roll."

"*We*? And what is that?"

I sound like a hysterical cartoon character, but Will continues undaunted, his breath on my neck, his thumb massaging me between the shoulder blades. "If we make this a bicep game, she's got you beat, so we're going to make it about hands, fingers and wrists, to ease the disadvantage. You're going to work your palm upwards, along hers, like you're trying to wrap your hand around the top part of hers. Just hold firm and focus on coming over the top of her."

Paula is mean mugging me across the table, gum being mutilated between her teeth. "I thought you ran a hedge fund," I mutter to Will.

"I didn't always," he mutters, laying a kiss on my cheek. "Five seconds. You got this."

"I was wondering why you aren't already married. Mystery solved. You get a lap dance and your date gets her arm torn off."

Another kiss and this time his lips linger on my temple. "You could look at it that way. Or you could look at it mine. Thank fuck I'm not married or I'd have missed the girl who gave me a lap dance, then took on the local gator-wrestling champ. All before lunchtime." His fingers slide up into my hair and tug, firm and gentle all at once. "Thank fuck, right?"

I don't have a chance to respond, because Paula props her right elbow on the table, brandishing her baseball glove hand. There's a tattoo on her wrist that says, "No Weakness, No Pain, No Mercy."

"That's a quote from *The Karate Kid*, right?"

Pleasure floods Paula's expression. She's actually quite pretty beneath the promise of terror. "Yes. It is. Thank you for noticing."

I swallow and take her hand, trying not to dwell on the size difference.

Voices pipe up from all sides, some shouting for Paula to win, others praying out loud for free beer. But I do my best to tune them out and focus on Will's steady presence at my back. Behind me, beneath me or on the other side of a wall, nothing seems to dull his potency.

A man steps up to the table. "Are both parties ready?"

"Yes, sir," Paula pushes between her teeth. "I was born that way."

This woman really thinks I'm going to be an easy victory. Seems to me a pro would have done some warm-up stretches, if she was taking a match seriously, right? Especially Paula. It's these thoughts that get my adrenaline pumping. I tighten my grip on my opponent's hand—a lot—and only get to savor a split second of nerves flitting across her face, before the man yells, "Go!"

It's the longest five seconds of my life.

Forget alligators. This woman could wrestle a fucking stegosaurus.

I'm glad Will is behind me, because I'm pretty sure my face is the kind of mottled red only worn by women giving birth to watermelon-sized babies.

But I win.

Or at least, I last for six seconds, before my arm gives out and goes crashing down to the table, but I don't even feel it. Don't even hear the *thunk* above the cheers and back slapping and high fives. I don't hear it above my *heart.*

"I won. Ish." I leap up from the table and stand there, dumbfounded, satisfaction wrapping around me like a bear hug. "Holy shit."

There's eight tons of adrenaline coursing through my veins and I need an outlet, so I turn and walk straight into a proud-looking Will, pulling his mouth down to mine for a kiss. It's only meant to last long enough to serve as an outlet, but Will's tongue sinks into my mouth, owning it. He lifts me off the ground and kisses me like we're at the bottom of the ocean and he's passing on all the air left in his body so I can survive.

I absorb every addicting second of it. While I still can.

CHAPTER TWELVE

Will

THERE'S A FIRST time for everything. Today was the first time an arm-wrestling contest gave me a hard-on. And the son of a bitch still hasn't gone away.

We stayed a lot longer than expected at Boney's, mostly because Teresa couldn't seem to stop charming the pants off everyone after her impromptu victory, posing for pictures and signing a copy of the menu to be stapled to the wall. Even Paula couldn't keep the grudging smile off her face around a flushed and exhilarated Teresa. There was a change in Teresa that might have been subtle to anyone else. To a man who tries to interpret her every word and gesture, the change was bigger. I thought she was confident before, but I'm willing to bet there's a bottomless well of it inside her, just waiting to come out.

She's young—a little younger than I originally thought—and she's got time to be exactly what she wants to be. I can't go back and resume the life I dreamed of before my father rearranged my priorities. Watching Teresa, though? It makes me wonder if going back is even necessary. These moments with her feel fresh. Part of something new that has nothing to do with before. Or after. Just…right now.

I glance at Teresa where she sits in the passenger seat, giggling at Southpaw's big panting mouth where it hangs over her shoulder. Damn, I'm hungry for her again. If she wasn't giving me sex eyes every thirty seconds back in the restaurant, I might have carried her out of there over my shoulder, just to get her undivided attention for a few minutes. But all afternoon, she had this...*way* about her. A way of making it clear she was with me. Whether she swayed over and twined her arms behind my neck or tugged on the hem of my T-shirt and winked, it felt like...a relationship.

I fucking loved it.

Every time someone walked into Boney's, Southpaw danced around and yipped until the newcomers greeted Teresa. Whether he was introducing Teresa or wanted her to make introductions, I couldn't figure out, but hell if my damn heart didn't climb up into my throat every time.

Distractions. I needed them. From the question mark that still hangs over Teresa's head. From the truth of what's coming with Southpaw. So while the locals commandeered her in the bar, I ducked outside and made a hotel reservation. We're about halfway to Nashville and close enough to Ouachita National Forest to stop for the night. But no way am I checking her into another shithole motel where I have to be concerned about her safety if she leaves to get ice.

Since leaving New York, I've been existing in a different kind of world. Money is available, but it's no longer something to flaunt to keep my financial heavyweight image solid. Most of the time, I have no predetermined persona among strangers, which has left the door open to just be myself. It costs money to stay in a place like this one, though. A good chunk. Teresa knows I'm well off, but she hasn't seen proof of it yet and I'm not exactly anxious to make the transition from before to after. Falling back on my pile of resources takes me a little further away from my *own* before...and the quest to find out if that part of me still exists.

My hands flex and tighten on the steering wheel. Up ahead, the trees are clearing to reveal a sweeping ranch-style hotel, an opulent fountain bubbling in the covered, circular driveway. An army of bellhops stand at attention, prepared to retrieve our luggage and speed us through the check-in process, knowing there'll be a fat tip on the other end.

Based on the way Teresa has been sitting forward in the passenger seat since we checked in at the front security gate, it's not what she was expecting. "Oh no. I can't afford this."

"You're my guest."

There's a slice of panic in the look she cuts me. "Aren't you taking this whole call girl fantasy a little too far now?"

Acid boils in my stomach. Is that what she thinks? "That's not what this is, Teresa. Jesus."

Some of the tension leaks from her shoulders, but a lot of it remains. "What is it then?"

We stop in front of the bell hop podium and I pop the trunk, ignoring the flurry of activity taking place around the car to focus on Teresa. "I want you to be safe. You were already staying at the motel when I showed up. But if I take you somewhere, everyone better damn well call you ma'am. And not that I don't enjoy putting assholes in their place for commenting on your appearance, but I'm still pissed from the last time. Having it happening again so soon wouldn't be pretty. All right, baby? We're going to a place with fountains."

She shakes her head slowly. "I would call you arrogant, but you've probably been called worse."

"It's part of my charm." Maybe it's the way she looks at me like I'm see-through, but once again I'm compelled to reveal more to this woman. "I want us to be on equal terms like we were in that shit-bag motel, but I don't know how to do that. Not without denying you the things you deserve."

"Damn," she murmurs, rolling her soft-looking lips together. "Stop switching lanes, Will. I can't keep up."

Christ, I want to be inside her so bad. Want to test out this live wire connection between us while I'm so deep she can't hide a single thing. She thinks she can't keep up with me? I've never been so fascinated by a woman in my life and ready to do what it takes to earn her secrets. "I think we're about even right now."

I don't want another man opening the door for her, so I climb out and circle the car, passing along instructions to the bell hop to bring our luggage to the check-in counter. Teresa is already exiting the car when I reach her side, earning her a growl of disapproval. She only gives me a pinky wave in response, before turning to move the passenger seat forward to let out Southpaw. He sniffs Teresa's hand and nudges her thigh, then bounds over to me, tunneling between my legs.

"Someone is excited," Teresa says, passing me on her way to the lobby. When we draw even, she slides a glance down to my lap. "I suppose the dog is, too."

"Cruel woman," I return on a low laugh, adjusting my cock, which has been hard for so long today, I forgot to hide it. "Technically I was supposed to call a doctor two hours ago."

"Poor baby."

She continues on her way toward the entrance, swishing her tight little ass around, my dog at her heels like a faithful soldier. The image gives me no choice but to catch up, wrap an arm around her waist and draw her back against my lap. "Just so we're clear, I love being hard for you. Feels like an honor."

"Feels more like an eggplant," she breathes, wiggling her butt. "Did you book one room or two?"

"Both. I booked a suite with two bedrooms."

"Cheeky."

I press tighter against her bottom. "Interesting choice of words." Her husky laughter turns every head in the lobby when I lead her inside. "Right this way, ma'am."

"Unbelievably, I think I prefer you calling me *woman*."

"You'll be hearing that plenty."

She hums in her throat. "You know what happens when you *ass*ume."

"Enough with the butt talk. You're obsessed."

She claps a hand over her mouth, but not before she laugh-snorts, drawing even more attention. Pretty sure my smile is the definition of shit-eating, as I throw an arm around her shoulder and stroll toward the check-in desk.

The way Teresa leans into me is almost enough to make me forget about the missed call on my phone.

Almost.

My APARTMENT IN Manhattan has an unobstructed view of New York Harbor, heated floors, a twenty-four-hour concierge and a rooftop swimming pool. I purchased the place without a viewing and didn't set foot inside until a week after I bought it, because I was working around the clock. I can still remember pressing a hand to the living room window, ships passing through my fingers, and wondering how the hell I got there. None of the furniture or artwork was familiar. It was a stranger's home. Sometimes I worked longer hours so I didn't have to go home, which is one of the reasons I didn't spend enough time with Southpaw.

Other times, I would stand on the roof deck and command myself to appreciate what I'd earned. To stop behaving like some poor little rich boy, when there were so many people out there who would kill for what I had. Sometimes, I could manage to feel satisfied for a few hours, before I started to feel anxious and left. Some days it only took a few minutes. Bottom line, though, I haven't felt right in a long time. Like I wasn't some imposter who didn't belong. My unique brand of high-risk, high-return investing put my fund on the map, right? Made it viable? So why did taking credit feel wrong?

Everything I built was for someone else.

My heart was never in it. Only my head.

Having lived as an imposter so long, I kind of understand Teresa's reaction when we enter the room. Because even by my standards, the suite I booked is fucking impressive. Teresa stops on the threshold and backs up, like she's getting ready to bolt, so I pick her up and carry her inside, choosing to ignore the bell hop's choked laugh as he follows with our luggage cart.

There's a panoramic window overlooking the golf course and the wide body of the lake beyond. To the right is a sliding glass door leading to an opulent outdoor space, complete with a bubbling hot tub and lounge area, flickering lanterns sitting on every available surface. White curtains flutter in the summer breeze blowing in through the open slider. Straight ahead is a sunken living room with a suspended television and enough cattle-patterned throw pillows to drown in. Off to the left is a hallway with a series of doors I assume to be bedrooms. They're right across the hall from one another.

"Can I get you anything else, sir? Ma'am?"

The bellman's interruption makes me realize I'm still holding a limp Teresa in one arm. Setting her down, I slide a bill out of my pocket and hand it to the bellman. "That's all. Thank you."

"Sure. Let me know if you need anything else."

"Great."

A second later, the door bumps shut. When time continues to tick by and Teresa doesn't turn around or say anything, I start to consider that I've made a mistake. I would have kept her safe in a run-down motel, same as I will here. Yeah, more vigilance would have been required, but at least she wouldn't feel like a fish out of water. I know what that's like, dammit.

"I need to make a phone call," she says finally, rubbing her bare arms as she turns around. "Just want to check in with my brother."

"Sure."

She starts toward the hallway but stops short. "Um. Which one..."

"Your pick."

There's no logical explanation for why I follow her—clearly she needs to be alone—only that it's a natural, undeniable response to her withdrawing from me. It's a power surge in my blood, shooting me into step behind her. There's a slight tensing of her neck, but she doesn't turn around, doesn't break stride as she pushes into the right bedroom at the hallway's end.

With one foot inside the bedroom, she's already scoffing. Probably because it's a pink, over-the-top cowgirl theme. Without stopping to acknowledge the room beyond a sweeping glance, she continues to the bathroom, tossing me a fired-up look over her shoulder. If my dick was hard before, it's a heat-seeking missile now.

"You *want* me to come after you."

She keeps walking, her ass swishing left to right beneath her red dress in an absolute testament to God's creative talents. "How'd you come up with that?"

I follow her into the dark bathroom, where she's all ready to face off, chin up, hands fisted at her sides. "When a woman like you wants a man to fuck off, she tells him." When I step into her personal space, she doesn't back away. A shudder goes through her when our bodies brush. That telling reaction tempts me to tangle my hand in the hair at her nape and tilt her head back. To turn her until she's pressed to the marble vanity, her mouth breathing in quick puffs up at mine. "Tell me to fuck off. Or tell me to fuck you. Dealer's choice."

Her lashes flutter down, but not before I catch a hint of conflict in her eyes. "And if I'm not ready for either?"

I've never pressured a woman for sex in my life. I've also never wanted to be inside one so goddamn bad I felt my sanity slipping. The fact that she asked the question at all keeps me in check, though. Sex between us is going to be right. Filthy, with a lot of swearing, but right. In the meantime, I'm not going to forfeit the chance for a preview. Not when I sense she needs something from me and I'm turning into a madman with the need to touch her. "You want me to show you how it would be between us?"

"I don't want the fantasy right now. It's too real after—"

"Seeing the room. This place. I get it." Regret collides with my lust and now? Now I'm not just horny, I've got an undeniable urge to correct my misstep. "Just you and me right now, Teresa. No games."

After a moment of studying my face, she nods.

CHAPTER THIRTEEN

Teresa

*J*UST YOU AND *me right now, Teresa. No games.*

Will has no idea how much I needed to hear those words. They're like a double shot of absinthe to my system, loosening my muscles and inhibitions, making me feel like I've just been made boneless inside a sauna. Now I'm walking out on shaky legs, skin slick and hot…and there's a man waiting to loosen that one. Final. Knot. The one tight as a bow in my loins. Yes, loins. I've never been more aware of that sinful southern region since meeting Will, and I'm *throbbing* there.

When I give my permission, his eyes flash and then I'm being turned, turned just as I hoped I would be, to face the sink. We're just Will and Teresa right now. Not boss and call girl. Not a hedge fund manager and the liar luring him back to New York. We only exist inside this garish, overdone bathroom, and I'm letting myself believe that for the next little while.

Will's fingers are still threaded through the hair at the back of my skull. He holds me there for long seconds, like an intermission to let me know the second half of the play has begun and he's taking control. Slowly, so slowly, he tilts my head to the left, letting his mouth hover over that sensitive flesh, while his hips dip and press to mine, wedging me hard against the sink.

A whimper falls from my mouth, my hands slapping down on

the marble. And that's when he begins to assault my neck. There's no leaning into his lips or pulling away when the raking of his teeth and tongue becomes too much. No, I can't move because my hair is held prisoner in his grip. There's simply no coming up for air, so I gasp and shift between two immovable objects, his mouth relentless, marauding from the curve of my shoulder to my ear over and over, until I'm sobbing.

"Will…"

His voice is pure cigarettes and sex against my ear. "If we were going to fuck, I'd wait until you said my name just like that, like you can't believe how wet I'm making your pussy…" His hand disentangles from my hair to drag down my spine, sending my head pitching forward on a moan. "Then I'd lift your skirt to see if I'm satisfied with the damage."

I arch my back, giving him permission with my eyes in the mirror. He takes it with a growl, gathering my hem in his fists and leaving the material bunched at my waist. Now, when he presses in against my nearly bare backside, there's no mistaking the oversized bulge. It parts my cheeks and makes itself at home, like a king settling into his throne.

"If I have you bent over the bathroom counter, it's because you don't want to wait. Not even for my tongue to give your pussy the same treatment I just gave your neck. So I'd give you exactly what you wanted." I can barely hear him, my voice is rasping in and out so loud, so I try to hold it in, but it bursts out of me almost immediately. Because I need—*need*—to hear what he's going to say next. Will angles his upper half away and I hear the sounds of metal ticking and tinkling together.

His belt.

He reassures me with a kiss to my shoulder that he remembers the boundary I set, but that breezy balm of comfort only lasts a split second, before leather slaps the surface of the sink—

whap—and slides, flat side up, in front of me. There isn't a hint of warning before it pulls taut. So taut, it bites into the lowest section of my belly and hips, which should hurt, right? But no. *Jesus, Mary, Joseph and the Angel Gabriel,* no. It's the pressure I didn't even know I needed. The move jerks my bottom tighter into Will's lap and my gasp is still hanging in the air when he bends me forward, over the sink—the belt positioned between me and the marble.

My expression is one of such naked, desperate lust, I duck my face to hide it, but the sight of Will's fists wrapped around the ends of the belt, like reins, drains any self-consciousness from my body. If he has the balls to truss me up like a horse, I can summon the nerve to enjoy it.

Enjoy it?

My breasts have almost completely fallen out of my dress, I'm so winded from the intensity of the man behind me. With his shadowed face, curled upper lip and corded biceps, he's every movie villain I've ever secretly been attracted to. My panties are uncomfortably wet and I can't do anything about it, except shift around on my toes and suck wind, waiting to see what he'll do next.

"This is the part where we would both remember the condom," Will says in that scorched earth voice. I'm so hypnotized by the dark rhythm of his tone, I'm taken off guard once again when he thrusts his hips hard, yanking back on the belt at the same time.

Oh my God. Oh my God. My breasts finally give up the battle and fall out of my dress, the rush of metallic bitterness in my mouth telling me I've broken the skin of my lower lip by biting down too hard. None of it matters, though, because Will is talking again and I'm dangling on the end of a string he's holding.

"Yeah, we'd remember protection at the last second, wouldn't we, baby? I'd have my cock in one hand, your throat in the other. I'd be pressed right up against that wet hole, ready to finally pump myself into it. To lose myself while you hold on to the counter for dear life." Another *harder* drive of his hips shocks a moan from deep inside me. "There would be a few seconds where we'd look at each other in the mirror, trying to decide if stopping to suit up was worth waiting to fuck. Tell me I'm wrong, Teresa."

I shake my head and it loosens my thoughts, my inhibitions even more. Did I really just say no to that question? Yeah, I did. There's nothing but total honesty and...exposure happening in this bathroom and I'm all in. I couldn't lie or be anything but the barest version of myself right now if I tried.

"We'd think of what would happen if we left the rubber off. That moment where I empty inside you and there's no turning back." His hands twist in the ends of the belt, his hips tilting and rolling, his mouth falling open on a guttural groan. "Would that moment excite you?"

"Yes," I whimper, moving my backside in circles. "I can't help it."

"Good. I'm inside you bare, then. Right. Fucking. Now." His open mouth lands on the curve of my neck, giving it that purposeful treatment from before, which I didn't even realize I was craving like a drug until his teeth abrade my sensitive skin and my clit begins to throb like it's sore and ticklish at the same time. "I'm not going to last as long without that layer between my cock and your tight little pussy, so my fingers are going to help get you there. And that won't be very hard, will it? Nope." He shakes his head, raking me with lust. "Look at your stiff nipples. A strong wind would make you come." His tongue licks up the side of my neck, those teeth catching my earlobe. "Someone is a very horny girl."

"Look who's talking," I manage, my voice shaking along with my thighs. "You're just as bad."

"I'm *worse,* baby. A million times worse." Will drops the belt but keeps me flush to his front with strong, desperate hands, sliding them up to cup and squeeze my breasts, back down to clutch my hips. "I'm so damn deep inside you right now," he rasps into my ear, beginning tight, measured thrusts against my bottom. "I go slow at first, dragging my cock in and out of you, trying to find a way to fuck you without coming. But you make it so hard, don't you? Your sexy porn star tits are bouncing around and you're pouting at me in the mirror, begging to get it rough."

I am. I am. I want nothing more than to be bent over this sink and treated without mercy. I'm not sure where I'm storing that final, remaining ounce of my earlier resolve, but I call on it now, searching for a way to completion without giving in to what my body craves. "Touch me," I sob, writhing my backside on that thick part of him. "Please, Will."

Before the words are out of my mouth, his hand wedges in between me and the sink, no-nonsense fingers tucking into my panties. Two fleshy pads trap my clit and gently squeeze, sucking the air out of my lungs, blinding my eyes. My body jerks like I've been slapped with medical paddles. *Lord oh lord oh lord.* I'm…can I even call this an orgasm? I've had those. They didn't make me feel like I was dying and being resurrected at the same time. Or like every nerve in my body was spinning in mad circles, vibrating and colliding in a frenzied dance.

"…*Will. Will. Will…*"

How many times have I said his name? He's growling louder into my neck with every recitation, his two incredible fingers now beginning to thrum my clit, teasing my blood back to a fever pitch. And all the while, he rocks into the separation of my bottom, fucking me through his jeans and my thong, up against the sink. "I'm starting to get desperate now. Slamming harder and harder into your little body. Getting pissed when I hit the end. You don't like not taking all of me, either, so you try to spread wider. Don't you?"

As if my muscles have decided Will is the master they must obey, my stance inches wider and I arch my back, moaning at the ceiling when his drives turn into grunting, hunger-driven grinds into my bottom. Will is using that forbidden curve to get off, and just when I think nothing about that could be hotter, he dips down and comes back up, that humongous bulge pinning the underside of my wet, feminine flesh to the sink, pumping, pumping against it, those fingers continuing to worry my clit up and down.

"Take a good look in the mirror, Teresa. Look at us. Look what I'm doing to you." When I don't move fast enough, he threads powerful fingers into my hair and tilts my head back, forcing me to acknowledge my pink, dewy skin, my slack mouth, my breasts that shake every time his hips punch up and forward, dragging denim over the twisted, cotton thong covering my drenched, sensitive flesh. "You're giving yourself up to me and I'm taking it—*keeping* it—like a greedy motherfucker. Do you understand?"

Another orgasm is swelling south of my belly, constricting muscles that are still sore from the first time. What he's saying is important and I shouldn't make decisions that involve my brain right now, but Will seems to own that, too, at present. I think I want him to own *everything* when we're together like this, bodies straining, hands grasping for purchase. "*Yes*. Yes, I understand."

"Good." His fingers move faster on my clit, so fast, so fast that I scream when the climax strikes, like bowling pins at the end of an alley, my senses scattering in every direction. I try to slump over the sink and squeeze my thighs together to combat the intensity of what's overtaking me, but Will doesn't allow it. His fingers in my hair keep me facing the mirror so I can watch the bliss crash down on me. "You're the most beautiful woman on the planet," he rasps, staring at me from beneath heavy lids. "Jesus *Christ*."

The pain in those two words snaps me out of my post-orgasm stupor and turns me into a scrambling servant. There's no other way to describe the way I disentangle myself, turn around and drop to my knees, whimpers falling from my mouth as I unfasten his jeans with clumsy fingers. "Y-you can have my mouth."

"Had it today, baby, and I'll damn well have it again." He reaches behind me and grabs a folded towel off the sink, unfurling it and tossing it to the floor. "But I've been watching your tits jiggle around longer than my cock can handle it, so I've got a taste for those. You going to let me fuck them?"

Being that I've never done what he's asking, it actually takes me a moment for my brain to project the logistics. But as soon as the haze clears, I'm lying down on top of the towel, pushing my dress down farther, leaving the bodice around my waist and my breasts on display for his pleasure. In my haste to get on the floor, I neglected to free Will's erection entirely from his jeans, so he does it now, in the most erotic display of masculinity I've ever witnessed.

There aren't enough religious figures or saints in the world to invoke here. The girthy root of his manhood is visible in the unzipped V of his fly...and he smirks, as if knowing how the sight of it affects me. But he leaves that teasing peek of flesh right where it is while reaching back to grip the rear of his shirt collar, dragging it off in one, seriously hot, practiced move.

As he kneels, his pecs and abdomen tighten beneath a sheen of sweat, making my nipples pucker even more. He bares his teeth, nostrils flaring at the sight of my body's reaction. And I don't have to wait any longer to see what's inside his jeans. He reaches in and draws out his swollen arousal, pumping it with his fist while walking toward me on his knees.

"I might take you to fancy hotels, baby. Might walk you through those elegant lobbies and demand you be treated like a queen." He drops forward, bending down to lick a path between my breasts, up and down. Again and again, before lifting his head. "But I will always be the man who fucks you nasty on the floor once we're upstairs, with your thong twisted around your dripping cunt. We clear?"

Oh hell. I'm screwed, aren't I? My back arches on a gasp, hands flying to my breasts to push them together. Tempt him. I'm a mess of heat and need, heels sliding on the tile. Can't stop moving until he's satisfied as I am. "We're clear," I breathe, tossing my head back. "Come closer, please. Have me."

His hand supports his erection until it's just above me, then he lets it go, dropping the substantial weight into the slick cradle between my breasts. An animal groan splits the air between us, the volume of it increasing as I push my breasts in around his engorged flesh. He begins to tunnel through the wet passage we've created, his sack slapping the underside with every drive.

"Fuck," he grits out, pumping faster. "Stop looking at it like that."

My lips are dry, so I lick them, seeing his expression darken. "L-like what?"

"Like you're just dying for me to slip and land in your mouth." His head pitches forward, neck and shoulder muscles straining. "*No.* Can't stop, even for a suck. I'm going to put a claim on every part of you."

Claim. There's a part of my brain that knows such a thing is impossible, but right now, with this gorgeous, compelling man needing relief from me—desperate for it—I can't think of something I've ever wanted more. To be claimed by Will.

Once again, I arch up and squeeze my breasts in around his fat, tunneling inches, watching the head turn purple, hearing his groans grow more and more strangled. "I want you all over me, hot and sticky," I whisper, giving in to the out-of-body experience. "Get it all over my nipples. My neck. *Please*, Will?"

He goes from man on the verge to man in the throes almost immediately. His thrusts become more thorough but less skilled, his breath bursting out of him in a staccato beat. "Horny girl," he barks, neck veins standing out. "Bad, horny girl. You stick your tongue out for a taste, too. Do it now or I'll pry your jaw apart."

Oh God. I've never opened my mouth so fast. Not even for cheesecake. I'm rewarded with salty spurts of wet liquid landing on my tongue, lips, throat, breasts. Will continues to thrust his hips, all while moaning down at me, his eyes alternately blazing and blanking with lust. That large body shudders and quakes and it's amazing, watching him drain, *feeling* it happen. Because of me.

When Will is spent, I think he's either going to fall down on top of me, clean me off, or ask me if I want Chinese food. Instead, he does something unexpected. He scoops me up and rises to his feet, setting me on the bathroom sink.

And he steps between my dangling legs and kisses me. Not like a man who has just finished titty-fucking a woman on the bathroom floor and wants to gloat. Or remind me who dominated the round. No, it's a grateful kiss. His fingers comb through my hair, caress my face, gently tug down my chin so his tongue can invade. I'm a hot mess, my dress askew, makeup probably all over my face...not to mention his come is sliding down my chest. Lest we forget. But somehow he makes me a goddess with that kiss. A certified deity that he lives to serve.

"We good, Teresa?"

Too good. While I was pretending there isn't a single man alive who could get under my skin or make me want to trust again...that's exactly what Will did. I've been denying my feelings, but with that denial bandage ripped clean off, the full scope of them robs me of breath. He's not even asking about us—if *we're* good—he's asking if I'm still angry about the palatial hotel room he surprised me with. Right? So why am I suddenly contemplating his possible reactions to the truth of why I'm *really* here? Am I crazy to consider coming clean about my deal with Silas? It's too soon to trust him, isn't it? It's too soon to trust *anyone.*

Right?

When I don't answer right away, a worry line appears between Will's brows. "Something serious happens in my gut when I look at you, baby. I need us to be good. If we're not, I'll get us there."

My own gut does a somersault. Along with one, all-powerful, severely reckless organ in my chest. "Will..." I can't. I can't risk him turning on me and putting my brother in jeopardy. "We're good. *So* good, actually." I give him a saucy smile. He doesn't return it, the wheels behind his eyes only turning faster. "But I really do need to make that phone call."

He holds my stare for a beat. "Yeah. I need to make a phone call, too." The way he says it sends my heart up into my throat, but I focus on keeping my expression neutral. Before I'm ready to lose his warmth, he drops his hands from my face and turns toward the door. Facing the bedroom, he pauses with a forearm propped on the frame. "You can tell me anything, you know. I've been told a lot of shitty things lately. I can handle it."

What shitty things? Southpaw's diagnosis? Or is he talking about the missing puzzle piece, also known as what exactly happened between him and Silas?

I want to slide off the sink and throw my arms around Will, to kiss him and beg him to confide in me. But the lies hanging over my head render me immobile. I don't deserve his secrets. Even though a voice is shouting *coward* in the back of my head, I stay quiet, holding my breath until he finally leaves the room, taking all the air with him.

And sitting quietly in the dark, I can't help but wonder who he's calling across the hallway. Is the jig going to be up any second now?

Heart pounding, I take out my cell to check the time, then call Nicky.

CHAPTER FOURTEEN

Will

I SIT ON the edge of my bed, staring down at the phone cradled in my hands. Since this morning, my associate in New York has left several missed calls but no voicemails. He knows better. But a significant part of me wishes he had so there would be no one to witness my reaction to whatever he found on Teresa.

At least I'm prepared for the worst, right?

Being blindsided is a million times more fucked up in comparison. It hasn't been long since the *last* time the fabric of my beliefs was ripped down the middle. In the short space of time I've known Teresa, her mere presence has sutured the wounds I'd thought permanently numb. But with one phone call, I could just as easily be creating newer, fresher ones.

Thinking of how she withdrew from me in the bathroom, I push to my feet with a curse, pacing toward the wall. As soon as I make this phone call, everything is going to change, isn't it? There was guilt written all over her, plain as day. And I can't ignore the possibility that she's working for one of my competitors anymore. All I can do is find out the truth, confront her with what I know…and after she attempts to claw my eyeballs out for going behind her back, we can work toward a solution. One that involves me exacting a promise she'll never lie to me again. Preferably while I'm banging her through the cowhide headboard.

Unable to put off the call anymore, I hit the speed dial and hold the phone to my ear. Just like this morning, a faceless voice answers, keys punching in the background, before stopping abruptly. "Yes."

"What did you find?"

I close my eyes and wait.

"Nothing."

My eyes fly open. Disbelief crashes into hope in my stomach. "Nothing?"

"Can't connect her to anyone at a single New York firm, and that includes employees, family members, known associates. I crosschecked several times, right down to their fucking dog walkers. Still working on getting her airline travel records—give me until tomorrow on that—but she purchased a Greyhound bus ticket online last week. Four more over the course of several days, along with some motel charges between California and Texas. She looks legit." He clears his throat, a few keys clicking on the other end. "Teresa Valentini. Age twenty-three. Studio City address. Brother Nicholas. Parents deceased. The only information of note is her employment situation. It's pretty dicey. Underground gambling facility in Sun Valley that has seen an uptick of violence lately, leading to some scrutiny from the police."

"Violence." That word—so vile when associated with Teresa—is the first to cut through my shock. She's been telling me the truth about everything this entire time? Have I become such a cynical prick that believing in this girl was impossible for me? Lightness crawls into my veins, but a weight drops in my stomach, thinking of how I doubted her. I want to kick her bedroom door down, take her in my arms and apologize until I lose my voice. I can't do that, though, without letting her know about the background check. Right now, all I can do is vow to do better by her. And protect her. "Do what you can about shutting down the den in LA. Gather intel, tip off the feds. Buy the building and tear it down, if you must. Whatever it takes." The plan is to keep her with me—not in California—but I'm not taking any chances. "She never sets foot in that goddamn place again."

"Consider it done." A few more key strokes. "There's a steady diet of calls in her cell phone records from a number listed for her brother. Los Angeles area code."

I think of the friend she said she'll be staying with in New York. "No contact with a New York number?"

"Not as of this afternoon, no."

That doesn't mean anything. They could have gone through an internet messaging service—one even I can't get access to. Overall, the information points to her being truthful with me. God, I need to touch her. Now. I can't apologize with words, but my hands and body can do the talking for me.

I recall the way she shut down on me in the bathroom. There's still a lot of mystery surrounding Teresa, but maybe the key is patience. We've only been traveling together since yesterday. Expecting to gain her trust in a matter of days isn't reasonable...even though this thing between us feels like it defies reason.

Trying to shake the intuition that I'm overlooking something, I hang up with my associate and turn to leave the room. But when Southpaw slinks in through the doorway, I stop on a dime. He's moving differently than he was an hour ago. There's a pronounced tilt to his body, like he's compensating for discomfort.

"What's wrong, buddy?"

When he would normally *snarf* or head-butt my legs, Southpaw does neither, walking gingerly toward the bed. He turns to look at me when he reaches the side of the king-sized behemoth. And waits.

Realizing he can't jump the same three feet he could have yesterday is like being socked in the throat. "You need some help up?"

He turns his face away, his tail unmoving.

"All right. That's okay." Gravity is sucking me toward the floor, but I force myself to move forward, picking my best friend up as carefully as possible and laying him in the middle of the bed. With an expression I swear is half embarrassment, half grudging relief, he curls up, closes his eyes and starts to snore.

I can hear the barest hint of Teresa's voice in the other room. She's on the phone with her brother. It's the only thing that keeps me from shouting her name.

Setting my phone down on the bedside table, I stretch out on the mattress and watch the rise and fall of my dog's chest.

Teresa

STAY IN CONTROL.

Stay calm.

"What the fucking *fuck*, Nicky?"

Realizing my pitch is reminiscent of cat having its tail yanked, I march into the bathroom, flip on the fan and close the door. I'm presenting a far different image in the mirror than I did fifteen minutes ago, aren't I? I've gone from sex bomb to atom bomb. My eyes are wide as silver dollars, chest shuddering up and down. The absolute poster child for anxiety.

Or stupidity. Because I have an absurd wish for Will to storm into the bathroom and hold me against his chest.

Which is ridiculous, considering his father is one of two people on the line—and Will isn't even aware I *know* his father, let alone that the stakes of my cooperation have just been upped. Big time.

My brother's voice is choked. "You there, Resa?"

"Yeah. Yeah, I'm here." I shove a hand through my hair, which already looks like a disaster, courtesy of the bathroom floor. "I—we were just going to talk. You and me." I swallow hard, striving for flippant. "I'm not allowed to talk to my own brother in private anymore, Silas?"

There's a heavy stretch of silence. "You got away with disrespect once, but you won't twice." The whip crack in his warning spears my veins with ice water. "Think hard about the way you address me in the company of my employee."

He won't be one for long. My throat aches to scream those words, but knowing Silas is with my brother forces me to swallow them. "I apologize."

"Good." Just like that, he's back to being the grandfather-type who needed eyeglasses to look at Instagram on his phone. "I'm inclined to forgive you, since it appears you have my son moving back in the right direction. I hear Arkansas is lovely this time of year."

How does he know—oh, right. Instagram. With my brother in reaching distance of that monster, my instinct is to assure Silas everything is going according to plan. That I'm well on my way to having Will back in New York. But God—*God*—the disloyalty crams into my throat, making my eyes water. Focus. You're here to save Nicky. That was *always* the plan, you selfish idiot. His life is at stake. "Yes. We're moving in the right direction." Self-disgust closes my eyes for me. "I don't see that changing any time soon."

Silas's laugh is like nails on a chalkboard. "You must be as good as you look, sweetheart."

"Don't talk to her like that," Nicky snaps. "She doesn't deserve this."

I have no time to brace before I hear a sickening slap echo down the line, followed by a pained grunt. Stumbling feet.

"*Nicky.*" Panic erupts in my chest, but I clamp down on it hard. "Shut your mouth. Do you understand me? Not another word. *Not one.*" Seconds tick by and all I hear is harsh breathing. "Apologize to him."

"Sorry," says my brother, his tone suggesting he's barely moving his lips. "I'm fine, Resa. I just can't believe I dragged you into this shit—"

Another thud of bone and flesh. Another. My brother grunts—a harsh, wet sound that tells me he's bleeding. No. This can't be happening. Helplessness wracks me in the form of shudders. "Leave him alone," I whisper, imagining my brother lying on the floor being punched, maybe kicked. Impossible images. He's the boy I used to hang up in a tree wearing wings and a halo. I'm supposed to protect him. "Don't you want to hear how things are going here?" I blurt. "Talk to *me.*"

"*Ahh.*" Silas is breathing heavily. Winded from hitting my brother. "You're going to entertain us with details?" I cringe at the leading question. There's no way I can let him touch these real feelings inside me that continue to build like an out-of-control bonfire for Will. I search for something to say that will distract him from Nicky, but after a moment, he keeps going, sounding perturbed over my lack of response. "I'm more impatient than I realized, you see, Teresa."

I slump sideways against the bathroom door and slide toward the ground. "What do you mean?"

"Your brother has been lifting an easy load, but as you can

tell, that's changing. And there's a little problem that needs taking care of on Friday night, Teresa. He's going to handle it for me. Prove his worth." There's a smile in his voice. "I really don't like problems. You know what I mean by a *problem?*"

God, I wish I didn't. But I know the way he emphasizes the word *problem*, he's talking about a living, breathing human being. One who needs to be taken care of...by my brother. No. This is my worst nightmare. "Y-yeah. I know what you mean."

"Smart girl. I might be persuaded to relieve him of the responsibility if Will is back behind his desk where he belongs by then."

My stomach drops. "You told me I had a week."

"And now I'm cutting it in half," he returns. "When a man is holding all the cards, that's his prerogative."

I'm missing something, right? "There was no giant rush when we spoke in Staten Island. Now getting Will back to New York is an emergency?" I shake my head, my heart silently apologizing to the man across the hall. "What happened?"

"One last thing before I go, sweetheart," Silas drawls, talking over me. "Did you happen to catch the visitor I sent you today?"

My stomach plummets at the confirmation that Silas is having me—no, *us*—followed. I wasn't just imagining things. The man on the highway this afternoon was the same man I saw outside the tavern in Dallas.

I haven't managed to formulate a response when Silas speaks again, in a tone that brooks zero nonsense. "You have two days. I'll be watching."

Sensing he's about to hang up, I speak in a blur. "Nicky? Is my brother okay? Please, just let me talk to him."

"Resa..." A cracking cough. "I'm fine."

The line goes silent.

My hand drops to my lap, the phone skittering across the

floor. Instead of bursting into hysterical tears, though, I feel eerily numb. I'm sitting on a bathroom floor in Arkansas, I just realized the vanity lights are in the shape a cattle horns, and my brother is physically hurt. Out of my reach and at the mercy of a sociopath. I have two days to ensure he doesn't become a murderer.

How am I supposed to walk out of this bathroom and act normal? How can I set aside what I just heard over the phone and not have Will see right through me to the terrified sister beneath? It has been years since I tried and quit yoga—everyone in Los Angeles tries at least once—but I call on those breathing exercises now. In through my nose, out through my mouth. I imagine a marble rolling down from the top of my head, gliding down the curve of my throat, over my arms, hips, legs. There. I'm here and I'm fine. In two days, once I've completed the god-awful task in front of me, I will shatter and break for a little while. No way around that. But I will not break now. I won't let my parents down and I won't let Nicky drown in the life we escaped.

Standing on shaky legs, I reenter the bedroom, intending to change my clothes and go check out the balcony. Maybe the fresh air will help center me more than an imaginary marble and get my head right. But I find myself stopping halfway between the bathroom and the bed, my attention drawn to the door leading to the hallway. Will said he needed to make a phone call, but I don't hear his voice. I don't hear Southpaw's usual shuffles and grunts, either.

I have this paralyzing thought that Will overheard me and left to call the police from the front desk. But no. If Will found out about my duplicity, there would be an argument. A loud one. He might leave afterward—that certainty makes me miserable—but there would be yelling first. Hate sex, too. Definitely hate sex.

With that conclusion in mind, I step into the hallway and jerk to a stop. Will's back is to me and he's lying in the bed with

Southpaw. They aren't touching, but they're cuddling from a distance. And if my gut wasn't telling me to worry, I would laugh at the silly picture painted by these two hulking creatures spooning.

"Will?" I whisper.

His shoulders stiffen, but he doesn't turn around.

My worry increases. Taking a deep breath, I move into the dim room. Twilight has turned to night and no lights have been turned on. As soon as I reach the bed, though, I can still see that Southpaw seems...off. Curled in on himself instead of sprawled out, as is his usual default.

There's a painful twist inside my ribcage as my gaze slides to Will.

He doesn't look back.

"Can I do anything to help?"

His voice is made of smoke. "No."

I should leave the room. Already I've formed a dangerous attachment with this man. After the phone call with Silas, my budding hopes of coming clean are out the window. There's way too much at stake and I'm not in New York to prevent the unthinkable from happening if Silas finds out I've revealed myself to his son. Comforting Will and getting in even deeper will only intensify the hurt racing in our direction, won't it?

Yes. Yes, but I couldn't be dragged from this room by a sumo wrestler. I'm a part of this. I've been painted into this picture and I can't let Will lie here hurting alone. We'll both be doing enough of that in the very near future.

"Hey," I murmur, kneeling on the bed behind Will. When he still doesn't look at me, I begin massaging the stiff muscles of his back. It doesn't help. He only grows more tense, especially his jaw, which flexes in the muted light. But I keep going, dragging my thumbs up his spine, digging them into his neck. Circling.

And gradually, slowly, his breath starts to come easier, his big body turning until he's lying on his back and my hands are smoothing over his chest, his face, my fingers tracing his cheeks and eyebrows. "Hey," I whisper. "You want to talk about it?"

"No," he says gruffly, capturing my wrists and tugging me down beside him so I'm wedged between Will and a sleeping Southpaw. "I want to talk about anything else, baby. Help me out with that?"

There's always sex in Will's eyes when he looks at me, but it's overshadowed now by the plea there. He needs me right now. He's letting me see how much, and it sends my heart into a marathon. "*Anything* else?"

He nods.

"What did you mean?" I slide closer and inhale the scent clinging to his collar. "When you said you've been told a lot of shitty things lately?"

His exhale comes out in a rush. "You couldn't ask me my favorite movie or something easy."

I lay my head on his shoulder and it's the single most divine position I've ever been in. Bar none. "Tell me that instead, if you want."

"No." He brushes my hair away from my face, looking fascinated by how it moves. "No, it's just the kind of story that will make you look at me with sympathy. I don't want that."

"How do you want me to look at you?"

"Like I can spin the world whatever direction you want." His thumb drags along my lower lip. "Like you're frustrated and want me to fuck it better."

So protective. God, if Will knew we'd been followed here from Texas by one of his father's associates, he would shit a brick. Or would he throw me right to the wolf himself? This is a man who takes my safety seriously. Checking into this place proved that. Not telling him of an immediate threat? I'm not sure he could forgive it so easily. "I-I'll have to practice my fuck-it-better look in the mirror."

"Nah, you're wearing it right now. Try to keep it from slipping while I tell you this story, all right?"

"All right."

He nods, his hand beginning to coast up and down the hill and valley of my side, leaving goosebumps behind. "It was just me and my mother growing up, and she was constantly telling me stories about my father. He worked for the government. Some..." He shakes his head. "Some secretive, military operations bigwig who traveled the globe, taking down bad guys. Living with us wouldn't have been safe, so he only came once a year. On my birthday."

I'm frozen to the mattress. Why did I ask him this question? Didn't I know where it would lead? Now he's trusting me enough to reveal secrets I have no right to know. But I can't make him stop. I can't. Because I'm desperate to learn everything I can about him. It's a compulsion and...God, I think my heart has started calling the shots.

"It sounds ridiculous now, but when you've been told something—over and over again—from birth, it becomes this unshakeable fact. You know?"

I nod, unable to speak around the knot in my throat.

"When I was younger, the visits were fun. He'd take me to Hersheypark or to the movies. But when I got older, they mainly consisted of lectures. About school, my grades, my future. And even though I hated school and wanted to use my fists for a living, I fucking listened to him. Because he was this bright, shining military hero who sent money to my mother, wishing he could be with us, but knowing our protection was more important. He was a presence in our house without even being there. A god."

He pauses to swallow, his hand turning into a fist on my hip. I'm fighting a battle to keep from stiffening, but I see what's coming now and I'm outraged on his behalf, whether I have the right or not. "The day I found out Southpaw was sick, I got an anonymous file in the mail." His eyes shift away from mine. "There are men on my payroll who deal in information and I'm sure it came from one of them. Looking out for my interests so I'll remain in a position to continue looking out for theirs."

For a long time, he doesn't say anything. The silence stretches so long, I have no choice but to prompt him through parched lips. "What did it say?"

A muscle jumps in his cheek. "I didn't always want to wear a tie to work, Teresa. I was a fighter and I loved it. It suited me. My father...he's the reason I quit the sport I loved and started studying so hard. He's the reason I've been living this life that makes me feel like a stranger in my own skin—and it turns out he's nothing more than a criminal. Not a small-time one, either. He's done horrific things. All this time, I thought of him as this noble superhero and he's been lying to me, along with my mother. I built myself into the man I am for him. And he's not even real, Teresa." Shrewd eyes shift back to mine. "You want me to fuck it better. That's how you're supposed to be looking at me."

"S-sorry," I rush to say, willing the pressing heat behind my eyelids to disappear. Doing my best impression of a pouty Revlon commercial, I tug him closer by the collar. "Is that better?"

"Hell yeah." He drags his lips side to side along mine. "That's the stuff."

"Will?"

"Yeah, woman?"

I rub my hand up the center of his chest. "He didn't touch

the man on the inside. He didn't even come close."

We breathe into each other's mouths, eyes open and locked. The intimacy of the moment, the way he looks at me like he's half in awe, half grateful, is something that will probably haunt me forever. Now that I know what Silas did to Will, this betrayal of mine is so much deeper than I thought. But not tonight. Tonight I'm the woman who's falling for him and his dog, heart, body and soul.

As I turn over and snuggle into the curve of his body, our fingers laced together, I say a prayer that he'll think back and remember us falling asleep together beside his sleeping dog.

And know deep down it was real.

CHAPTER FIFTEEN

Will

THE TERESA I fell asleep holding last night is not the same Teresa I woke up with. A few minutes ago, we pulled into Ouachita and I watched from my lean against the car as she attached her GoPro to Southpaw's collar, instructing him in murmurs to act natural. As soon as she finished her handiwork, he went hurtling down a path toward the trees, last night's bout of exhaustion apparently a thing of the past. For now. Teresa walks beside me on the path, her eyes looking shaded and tired, telling me she didn't catch as many Z's as I did. Christ, I haven't logged this many hours of sleep in a decade—all since Teresa showed up.

Neither she nor Southpaw were in bed when I woke, shocked to find daylight filtering in through the white hotel room curtains. But I could hear the happy jingle of Southpaw's collar out in the living room, his exuberant *snuffs* telling me I could afford to lie in bed a few extra minutes. And I needed them, because the relief that I had another day with him was followed by the bracing reality of how I feel about Teresa. She knew exactly what I needed last night, even when I didn't and all I could think of was dragging her back to bed so I could worship her pussy.

When I walked into the living room, intending to do just

that, I found her already showered and dressed, twisting a cup of coffee side to side on the breakfast bar, looking distant. Anxious. Not in a *fuck it better, Will* kind of way, either, otherwise we would still be wrecking the bed. I don't have experience with women beyond casual sex, but there's nothing casual about me and Teresa. She's got something on her mind and I need to know about it so I can fix it. Then we'll get to the wrecking.

After the phone call with my associate yesterday, one of my theories is she's on the run after some shady shit went down at her job. Something worse than just the illegal activity she initially told me about. If that's the case, it's already being handled. I can't tell her that, though, or she'll know I dug into her personal life. And we're not solid enough yet to put a potential crack in the foundation we're building.

One I intend to *keep* building, no matter what.

Teresa is mine. My bones know it. My head. Even the heart I thought was too damaged and scabbed over to be touched knows she belongs with me.

The hard part is being patient while *she* figures it out.

"You're quiet," I say. "You're missing your pink cowgirl room, aren't you?"

Her surprised laugh hits me right in the stomach. "You caught me." She rolls her lips together on a long pause. "No, it's just...I've had a change of plans, Will."

My feet stop moving on the path, a boulder coming to rest inside my stomach. Tamping down on my instincts is hard as a motherfucker. I want to get right up in her personal space and tell her yes, they have changed. To include me. But I don't think I'd get another word out of her if I followed those impulses. And I need to know what I'm up against.

Teresa stops on the path, too, looking everywhere but me while continuing her explanation. "I-I guess I've been debating when and how to tell you. Or if this thing between us…if it's substantial enough that I even *need* to tell you I'm—"

"It is."

A puff of air leaves her. "Okay. I'm flying to New York tomorrow morning." She adjusts her sunglasses. "The friend I'm staying with is leaving on a trip soon. We have to do the apartment key hand off, plus I want to see her before she goes."

"When did you speak to your friend?"

Her right eyebrow arches. "She messaged me last night while we were sleeping. I got it this morning."

"Her trip kind of came out of nowhere, didn't it?"

"Um. Welcome to the age of spontaneous millenials. Make yourself at home."

We're squared off on the path, almost-lovers to adversaries in a matter of seconds. I've never wanted to fuck her more than I do right now, the other park-goers be damned. I'd plant her open knees on the path and give her my cock from behind, while I patiently explain in her ear that I'm becoming more than a little obsessed with her. And her getting on a plane without me isn't an option if I want to keep my sanity intact. "Fine." As I move past her, I plant a hard kiss on her lips. "I'll handle plane reservations."

She jogs after me. "Reservations *plural?*"

"Yes."

"Will," she mutters, grabbing hold of my arm. "Would you stop for a second?"

I quit moving even though I want to jump out of my skin. "Let me ask you a question, Teresa. Do you *want* to leave?"

"Leave you and Southpaw?" she whispers. I give a single nod and attempt to prepare myself for her answer. When she shakes her head, it's like I've just been given a stay of execution. "No. I really don't."

"Okay. That's good." I clear my throat of rust. "Do you *have* to leave?"

"*Yes.*"

I can't pinpoint what is it about her too-fast answer that makes me suspicious, but there's something off about the hint of pleading in her tone. The way she's trembling even though the sun beats down on us. "Is this friend of yours really a man?" The question is out before my brain gives the formal command. No, when it comes to Teresa and other men, my brain vacates the building. "I hope for his sake that's not the case."

"It's not." Fire kindles in her eyes—and I was wrong before. It's possible to want to fuck her even more than I already did. "I'm giving your macho attitude a lot of leeway."

"I appreciate that."

"Good. Don't push it."

We're both breathing heavy, but we're forced to put our stand-off on hold while a family of four passes. No, their arrival doesn't make me any less horny, and as soon as they're out of earshot, I take a step closer to Teresa, putting our faces a few inches apart. "You don't want to leave us, but you have no choice. I do have a choice. So I'm making it. Because I'm not letting you get away from me."

The flames in her eyes are doused, her mouth softening. "But this trip is important to you." She looks off toward the tree line, her words halting. "It's important to him. Y-you should think about it a little harder."

"Jesus." Frustration snaking into my throat, I reach up to shake her shoulders but let my hands drop before I can follow through. "Maybe this trip wasn't just about giving Southpaw the final days he deserves. Maybe it was about meeting you. No. You know what? It was." I pace away and come back, energy snapping in my joints. "I used to wake up at five in the morning. And now, it's like I'm making up for every single minute of sleep I've missed my entire life. Maybe I was missing sleep because I knew you were out there, baby, and I hadn't met you yet."

"Will. *Stop*," she breathes, covering her face with both hands. "Oh God, this is moving too fast. I didn't expect you to be you. Didn't expect any of this."

"Yeah? Me either." I pry her wrists away from her face, alarmed to see panic in her expression, before she can hide it. "Am I really moving too fast or is there something holding you back? I will demolish it to keep you with me, Teresa. Just talk to me."

"Yes, it's moving too fast," she blurts, jumping on the explanation I wish I hadn't offered her. The step she takes backwards might as well be the length of a mile, her eyes staring at nothing over my shoulder, same as they were this morning. "I only left home a *week* ago. I don't want to be tied down before I even get where I'm going. *God*."

The strong sense that she's not being truthful doesn't completely ease the blow. What I hear is that she doesn't feel the same—and considering what I'd be willing to sacrifice for her now and in the future, considering I'm aching just looking at this woman, those words are unacceptable. "You've got *me* tied down. How about that? I'm tied the fuck down."

"Will..." she whispers.

"For the record, baby, I think you're full of shit. It's going to kill me to ask you this, but when was the last time you slept beside someone?"

No hesitation. "A long time ago."

"Yeah. Good." I twist a fist in the hem of my shirt. "You spent the night warming every inch of your skin on mine, purring for back rubs and tucking your hands and feet in places so I could heat them up. It's been a long time for me, too, but I know it's not supposed to feel that goddamn natural and right. Your mouth needs a little longer to admit we've got *each other* tied down? Fine. But I'm going to end up back in New York sooner or later, and if you think I'm not going to knock fucking walls down to get to you, you've got another think coming, woman." I pause to let her sputter. "Give me until morning to convince you to let me fly you there *tomorrow*. That's what I'm asking."

"How did this happen?" she says, seemingly to herself. I miss the second half of what she says, but it sounds like, "He's trying to convince *me*..."

"Tomorrow morning, Teresa." I move into her space and capture her dropped open mouth with a hard kiss. "I'm going to get us a map at the visitor center. Stay on the path and I'll catch up."

Leaving her standing there looking half stricken, half impressed is one of the hardest things I've ever done. But I harden myself against the need to turn back and kiss her until she's convinced *right now*.

Instead, I keep walking...and start to make plans.

CHAPTER SIXTEEN

Teresa

I STUMBLE BLINDLY down the path in the direction of Southpaw. It's kind of like we're playing Marco Polo on dry land, because every time I manage to croak his name, his bark seems to be coming from a different spot in the forest. Finding him is giving me something to focus on, though, and I desperately need to be distracted or I will crawl into a shrub and petrify into part of the landscape.

Did I really just talk Will out of following me to New York?

Yes. It appears I did. My life as a con woman can be summed up in two words: brief and unsuccessful. *The Hapless Con*, Thursdays on Fox. Maybe someday, if the impossible happens and I make it through film school, I'll shoot the pilot. I'll tap Nina Dobrev to play me, the well-meaning but utterly doomed heroine who wears overpriced shoes and discount push-up bras.

No matter who I chose for the hero, he would never live up to the original Will, though. I'd secretly refer to him as The Un-Will.

Tears fill my eyes and I blink them away. "Southpaw!"

Bark. Bark, bark, bark.

"Wait. You're behind me now?"

I turn on a heel and head down a different path, overgrown brush sliding against my bare legs. In the pilot episode, we would meet The Hapless Con as she competes on *Survivor*, searching for a good place to tan while everyone else forms alliances. Hapless Con can't even save her brother, even when the key to doing so is handed over on a silver platter, can she?

God, there wasn't even a fleeting sense of victory when Will said he'd handle the plane tickets. No, not tickets. *Reservations*. Probably on a private plane. Not even *that* gave me the tiniest spark of satisfaction. Nothing but guilt and dread. And more guilt heaped on top. When it came down to it, something inside me wouldn't let me deceive him any further.

It was your heart, idiot. That thing that feels broken right now.

Realizing my hand is pressed to the center of my chest, I swipe at my eyes with it and let it drop. Come tomorrow morning, I'll have no choice but to take Will's offer if I want to help Nicky. Every part of me rebelled against taking that final step to get Will back to New York, though. Am I going to be even less inclined to take that leap tomorrow morning after another night with him?

Resisting the urge to run, just run away from the trap I've laid and never look back, I turn in a frustrated circle. "Southpaw!"

The bark is closer this time. I hear it the same time I hear water rushing. A few more steps bring me to a rise in the path and I cross over, my breath catching at the beauty spread out before me. It's a river. Or more accurately, a rapid. White wash goes whooshing past, down small waterfalls and bumps where rocks stick up in the water. Southpaw dances on the shoreline with a stick in his mouth, like something out of a pioneer movie. I'm the loyal, hard-working wife coming to collect fresh water to do the laundry.

"Sure, that sounds just like you," I mutter, climbing down the rocky embankment toward the small beach where the dog waits, head tilted. It reminds me a lot of how Will looked at me back on the path, as if to say, *what are you scared of? I'm right here.* "Hapless Con Woman in the Wilderness," I blurt in a rush, trying to distract myself. "At first glance, she's the Plain Jane wife of a Hapless Mountain Man—always plan for a spinoff—but under her handmade cloak, she's hiding the body and mind of a former con and assassin—"

Southpaw barks, toeing the edge of the water.

"I'm coming. I'm—"

He leaps into the water.

"Whoa!" My laugh sounds sad, a total contrast to the carefree behemoth reveling in his freedom. "You're lucky that camera is waterproof."

All I can see of Southpaw is his head sticking out of the rapid at first, but then water starts to splash in front of him. Is he trying to paddle? Yeah…but. Hold on. It's not working. He's struggling to get back to shore, but can't. He's moving farther away from me, little by little.

"Shit. Oh shit."

I turn in a circle, looking for a branch long enough to hold out so he can grab on with his mouth, but nothing. "There's no fucking branches on the ground in a forest? Seriously?" I jog to the end of the water and kick off my Gucci sandals, noticing Southpaw is a good five feet farther away than the last time I checked. And I don't know a lot about rapids, but I'm pretty sure they move in the direction of a drop. Because physics. "Oh no, no, no." I gather a scream and let it loose, loud as I can muster. "*Help!*"

No way I can wait around on the off-chance someone heard me. Southpaw isn't even paddling anymore, fatigue probably setting in, so he's traveling along with the current. Crap. This is *not* happening to me. I'm just The Hapless Con.

But I've never run as fast in my life as I do now, sprinting barefoot down the shoreline to get ahead of Southpaw and jumping into the rapid. "Oh, God. That's cold. Holy shit." He starts paddling again as soon as I hit the water, barking at me like this is my fault. And I paddle, too, finding my inner swimmer and introducing her to the situation from hell. It takes me a few seconds to reach Southpaw, which is when the next clusterfuck presents itself.

He's a huge dog and I'm a petite woman.

Suddenly I've got one hundred and eighty pounds of wet dog trying to climb me and it hits me that I have a limited amount of time to get us to the shore. I can't tread water long with the added weight—and we're obviously headed to a drop.

"Okay." There's calmness in my voice I don't feel in any way, shape or form. "Okay, buddy. It's fine. Just hang on."

I start to kick, but we're pushed sideways into one of the miniature waterfalls—did I once think they were beautiful?—and it rains down on my face. It shocks my lungs into emptying, and my body instinctively searches for oxygen but gets water instead. Panic slices into me hard. I'm choking when we finally shoot out on the other side, my shoulder ricocheting off a rock and spinning us.

Someone is talking. I realize it's me, rambling in between sucked-in breaths. I'm being tossed in a green and white kaleidoscope, water climbing up my neck. Southpaw is whimpering above me. He's sitting on my chest and I can't—I can't get in enough air. Dizziness hits me at the same time we go flying down another small waterfall, but I cling tight to Southpaw and he does the same. How much longer can I do this? I can barely breathe, let alone swim to the shore.

"*TERESA.*"

I hear Will shouting from somewhere in the distance, but I ignore him. He can't help us. We're moving too fast now. The water is up to my chin. I take the biggest breath I can manage, reach for my deepest reserve of willpower and kick my legs hard, one arm wrapped around Southpaw, the other paddling.

The effort starts to drain me almost immediately, but I close my eyes and kick through the screaming strain in my muscles, prayers for a miracle sitting on my lips. When I feel the hand clamp down on my neck, I must be reaching the edge of delirium, because my first thought is *sea monster.*

"*Goddammit,* Teresa. Baby, *what the fuck?*"

Southpaw barks in my ear, mimicking Will's distress. I can't see Will, because he's behind me, his fist wrapped in the neck of my T-shirt, but I feel myself and Southpaw being tugged sideways, against the current. Thank God. Thank God. I have a second of alarm when Southpaw jumps out of my arms, but the sudden lightness allows me to turn around and see him splash through the shallow edge of the rapid and jump onto shore. I join him a moment later, pulled by Will—and sucking in rasping breaths, I'm hauled into his arms.

"I'm going to kill you, woman. I thought you were gone." I can't tell which one of us is shaking, but the particulars don't matter because Will is raining kisses down on my face and head, cursing in between each plant of his hard lips. "You screamed like you were being fucking attacked and I couldn't *find* you. *Jesus.* Is anything hurt?" His hands run down my arms, stomach and legs, making me groan over the warmth. "I swear to God, if you're hurt…"

Southpaw starts licking my face, reminding me why I jumped into the rapid in the first place. And I don't know what happens inside me, everything that has taken place in the last week—and especially the last five minutes—catches up at once, twisting me in knots, tightening, tightening, until they snap and I burst into tears. "He jumped in and I couldn't find a stick to hold out. In

the middle of a *forest*. The water was carrying him away—"
Remembering the way the water kept climbing higher toward my
head renews my shakes. "I'm not a good swimmer. I'm not good
at *any of this*. I thought I would be, but…"

Will pulls me more firmly onto his lap, clutching me to his
chest, as if trying to physically stop me from trembling. "You're
not good at any of what, baby?"

Lying. Using people. In trying to save Nicky, I've become the
very thing my parents took us away from. I've become someone
who hurts people. I need to protect Nicky, but I don't think I can
do that while hurting Will. Sitting here on this damp riverbank,
I'm a part of a family. A small one. One I didn't earn, but a
family, nonetheless.

I won't let him get on that plane without knowing the truth. I
make that vow to myself right now in the woods with Will
crushing me to his chest. Even if it makes him hate me forever, I
won't accept his help. Not unless he offers it with the full
knowledge of the deal I made with Silas.

Making that decision fills me with the kind of peace I've
never experienced. Being honest with this man will always be the
right decision, whether or not that honesty makes me lose him
forever. And if that's my fate, I'm going to take advantage of this
day. I'm going to live in it without reservation.

"I need you, Will," I whisper against his mouth. "Now."

CHAPTER SEVENTEEN

Will

FUCK. I'M NOT okay. I'm eight million miles from okay.

When I came over the incline and saw Teresa being carried by the current, I left my heart on the goddamn ground. It has only just reentered my chest and begun to beat again. Was I worried about Southpaw? Yes. But his entire upper half was above the water line, while Teresa was rapidly sinking and—

Jesus Christ. I can't think about it.

She's crawling onto my lap, wrapping her legs around my waist, and she looks so beautiful, so fragile and brave and determined and everything in between, I drop the niggling certainty that she's keeping something from me...and I let the hunger that has been building for days take over. It takes over without mercy, too, turning my cock to wrought fucking iron in my wet jeans, just in time for Teresa to settle her cunt over it and work, work, *work* her hips like temptation in the flesh.

She goes in for my mouth, but I fist her hair in my grip, stopping her. Not sure why, since my balls are so high and tight, I can feel them in my throat. Maybe it's a last-ditch effort to get inside her head before lust makes me its servant and I can't think anymore. Maybe I'm still shaky from seeing her flying down the rapid, knowing I only had a limited time to reach her before the beach ran out. Whatever the reason, I want to hear some of her husky voice. I'm craving it. "I put us up in the presidential suite at our hotel…" I twist my fist in her hair and she bucks in my lap, mouth falling open on a whimper. "Could've taken you the first time in a bed, a couch…a whirlpool. But no. You want my dick in the forest."

"Not want. Need." Her wet T-shirt is showing me everything. Those peaked nipples. Hell, the exact tint of dusky pink is obvious because this little temptation isn't even wearing a bra. Not a damn thing in this world can stop me from leaning down and sucking on her through the sodden cotton, gently tugging on the bud with my teeth. "Will, *please.*"

I give her other tit the same thorough attention. "We could get in trouble."

"You love trouble." Teresa pulls the T-shirt over her head and drops it with a *glop,* knocking my hands free of her hair in the process. "Asking me to dance for you in the backseat of your car. The way you look at men, daring them to check me out. You *want* trouble, Will. Come and get it."

Christ. Does Teresa see me, or what? A lot of our association has felt like a game of chess, but the game board is made of solid stone. The way she's looking at me, half naked and mind-blowingly gorgeous in the fractured forest light…it makes me feel new. Who the hell cares which life path I'm supposed to be on, so long as it led me to this day, this moment, with this woman.

"You said it yourself last night," she purrs in my ear, rubbing her tits against my chest. "You might take me to fancy hotels, but you fuck me nasty on the floor. That's you, isn't it? Best of both worlds?"

Blood roars in my ears as I stand, Teresa's legs wrapped around my hips, her naked breasts bouncing around with every step I take. To where? I don't give a damn. She's getting it fast and rough against the first solid surface I find. Southpaw has taken a hint and gone off into the trees, away from the water. Thank God I don't have to worry about him, because my head is full to bursting with Teresa.

Her fresh water and female scent is a drop kick to my senses, curling in my nose and throat like an airborne love potion, stroking my cock with an invisible hand. Getting inside a woman has never been about more than release, but it's like I'm already worried I won't get close enough to her. Won't absorb as much of her as I need to live. Jesus, when her mouth meets mine and our tongues flick together, I really wonder if needing her to live isn't so crazy. My pulse is slamming up against the sides of my veins, like it wants to join with hers.

The kiss ends and her neck goes loose, head falling back. "*Will.*"

In my periphery, I see an upright boulder with a broad, flat front and change direction to get us there. "Go on, baby." I flatten her between me and the rock, baring my teeth against her mouth. "Whine my name again. Whine to me about the achy little pussy inside your shorts."

"Oh God." Her tits lift and shudder between us. "Make it better, Will."

There's a thread of vulnerability in those words, compelling me to press our foreheads together, search her eyes. "Tell me you're really okay, Teresa."

"Yes," she whispers. "But I was scared."

Fuck. Based on the way my heart free falls into my stomach, it does not like hearing that. "Is that why you want this?" I frame her face in my hands, keeping it tipped up when she tries to look away. "Because you were scared?"

"Only a little. Like I need somewhere to put the fear. But mostly it's you." Disbelief dances across her face. "It's…this. Us."

Hearing her use the word *us* knocks over a bucket of warm

wax inside my chest. "You're not afraid of me tying you down. You couldn't even look at me when you said it."

"Arrogant man." A ghost of a smile passes her mouth before vanishing. "It's not fair. Nothing is fair."

I press my lower body tighter to the notch of her thighs and she gasps, digging her heels into my ass. "Like what, baby?"

"I-I don't know. Just circumstances. Timing. Responsibili-ties." In the distance, there's a happy bark, but it sends even more distress cutting through her needy expression. "You...having to lose Southpaw. I couldn't let it happen earlier than it's supposed to, Will. I just couldn't. But you'll still lose him and it's not fair—"

"Shh." I quiet her with a kiss, while my heart breaks out in a riot. For the rest of my life, if anyone doubts out loud in my presence that a man can fall for a woman overnight, I'll be the first to tell them they're dead wrong. Because I've damn well fallen for this woman who just saved my dog's life and goes from sex bombshell to honest and afraid in mere seconds. She's a mystery, she's truth, she's black, white and gray. She's *mine.* "Here's the thing, Teresa," I murmur against her lips. "We're *not* dying, you and me. We get to live. This isn't an end for us." *It's just the start,* I add silently, not wanting to overwhelm her. "You want to feel alive right now, baby?"

"*Yes.*"

Teresa

My ADRENALINE IS still firing from my impromptu swim meet, but it's quickly being overtaken by lust. Hot, sticky, undeniable lust. Will asked me if I want to feel alive, but I already do. I've felt more alive around him in the past couple days than I have in years. Maybe my entire life. And with his hips pumping between my open, eager thighs, I refuse to think of this—of *Will*—being taken from me. Just for now, for today, we're two people who collided, and upon standing, maybe found a better version of themselves when the dust settled.

It hasn't settled yet, though. No, *settled* is definitely the wrong word for being dry humped against a boulder in a national forest. Topless. Soon to be pantless, too, because the way Will is kissing me means one thing: it's going down. No turning back. I don't want to, either. My shorts are still saturated from the river, but they grow wetter the old-fashioned way every time Will leans back and looks down to watch his erection grind between my legs.

"By everything holy," I say, my voice shaking. "Please take off our pants. M-mine and yours. Both."

He snags my mouth in a blatant kiss, teasing my tongue with his until I don't know whether to slap him or beg for more. "Woman, how am I supposed to do that when your thighs are wrapped around me like a boa constrictor?"

I nip at his bottom lip. "Figure it out."

There's only a split second to savor his heated amusement, before my legs are pushed down Will's powerful hips, my feet meeting the ground with a crunch of foliage. Not an inch of space is put between us, though, as Will continues to abuse my mouth with growling, provocative kisses, his big fingers busy on my zipper. When he lowers it with a metallic zing, I expect him to shove my panties off and get down to business. But he lowers them slowly, his fingertips trailing lightly down my hips. A slow, slow, never-ending *drag* of flesh on flesh raising goosebumps on my skin, head to toe. I'm panting by the time the material slips down to my ankles, my vagina singing falsetto.

I make quicker, clumsier work of his fly and lower the front of his briefs, groaning like a damn lady when his thickness bobs free, slapping off his stomach and loitering there. Just like the night when I knelt for him on the motel balcony, I have a strong urge to fall to my knees and serve. To please. So I don't fight it. But as soon as my knees dip, his grip closes around my throat and I'm positioned back against the boulder, pinned by the single hand.

"None of that pretty mouth for me this time." His free hand separates my thighs, his knuckles rubbing against my sensitive skin. "I'm saving all my misery for this." His middle finger surges up into my entrance hard, his hand tightening on my throat at the same time—and in the space of two seconds, I'm trembling, my loins constricting around his one long finger. "Remember that, baby. Remember that your man's pleasure is tied up in pain. Every little bounce of your cunt is going to feel like heaven and hell. Like medicine and murder." He adds a second finger, pressing deep until I scream through clenched teeth. "I love the way we've been getting each other off, but the hunger for fucking you only builds every time. So if it seems like I'm angry with you, try and remember I'm just trying to get through pain to pleasure."

"Okay." I wobble around on my toes, sucking in a breath every time the heel of his hand grazes my clit. "O-okay, I'll remember."

"Good news is, it's going to be all pleasure for you." Will steps close and yanks up my left knee to waist level. He doesn't take his eyes off mine as he dips down, positions his blunt-headed erection between my thighs...then drives home, lifting me off the ground. "*Yeah!*" he roars. "*Fuck.*"

My scream is trapped in my throat, eyes watering from the intrusion. But he's right. Oh God, he's so right. Despite his size, there's nothing but blinding, impossible pleasure, probably because I'm a human lubricating device and Will could turn a nun into a sinner. "Move, please." I open my thighs wide, my backside propped on the boulder, writhing, writhing. "Move. Please."

"I got you, baby." His hot breath pelts my neck, hips dropping and punching upwards again, making me see stars. "Christ, Teresa. You're like threading a fucking needle."

"Thread it harder," I whimper.

His groan is ragged. "You planning on making me feel guilty later, telling me your pussy is sore?" He starts to thrust in tight, even pumps. "It'll work like a charm, you know. My girl pouts and can't get comfortable in her seat because I fucked her too hard? I'll sit you on my lap, apologize, rub your clit through your panties until you're smiling again." He gives me a savage drive that rattles my wisdom teeth. "Yeah, I'll massage the ache until you forget my dick is the bad guy and you want him to fill you up again."

The words *fill you up* make my eyes fly open. "Oh. We didn't...condom."

"Shit." He tilts his open mouth against mine, our gazes locked. "Shit."

I can't manage a swallow. "Huh."

"I'll pull out."

With a wince, he starts to ease his hips back, but denial clamors through my blood, my legs locking around him involuntarily. "No."

He slams back into me with a vengeance, roaring into my shoulder. "Remember what I said about the pain, Teresa," he grates at my mouth. "It's going to get worse. I have to wrap it up now, or stopping to leave you is going to kill me. It's so hot and tight..." Another series of desperate thrusts. "Jesus, I thought I knew how good you'd be, but I had no idea."

"I do have an idea," I whisper brokenly, working my hips, my bare backside scraping on the boulder, but barely a hint of pain registers next to the epic, increasing pressure between my thighs, all centered around Will's smooth, swollen flesh. "Feels so *good*."

"Goddammit." He slants our lips together, kissing me long and wet until I'm lost in a fog of impending climax, no idea where to focus. His mouth or his pumping erection that seems to grow larger with each drive. "Can you get pregnant, baby?"

"No. I'm taken care of." Thank God he's asking. That must mean this isn't about to end, even for a second. I've been on the pill since I can remember and it seemed like a waste during my long stretch without sex, but I'm so grateful I stayed on it now I could cry. "Don't stop. Don't stop."

"Can't. I can't."

I don't realize until this moment that he's been holding back. Compared to how he claims my body now—raw, deep, hard and *fast, fast, fast*—before was only a muted preview. One muscular arm bands behind my backside, the other braced at my back, so my bare skin is no longer rubbing the huge rock. The intimacy of being pressed to Will so tightly, his arms wrapped around me to possess, protect...it makes it hard to breathe. His eyes bore into mine like he's trying to read my mind, all while he pounds into me like a man with little control.

"Feel me, Teresa. You can't walk away from this and neither can I." He angles his hips and rolls into me, dragging his hard flesh over my clit. Like our bodies were molded with the specific intent to please each other. "There's no end date on this. Every time you try to put one on us, it's going to end with you moaning and telling me I don't need a rubber."

The buildup to my climax is too intense to stand. I'm looking right at Will, but I'm seeing gold plumes at the edges of my vision, my thighs beginning to shake violently. "Don't move. I'm coming. I'm...please."

His growl and the stuttered pace of his hips tell me he's close, too. "No end date. Say it." He crushes me closer, our wet mouths raking up and down together. "*Say it.*"

Even though my common sense is firing warning shots, I would say anything in the world he needed to hear right now. I'm an animal desperate to be pleased and to please her mate. "No end date," I wheeze.

"Good girl." He dips his head, bathes the side of my neck with his hot tongue. "Now tell me you can't walk away from this cock, either. Tell me it services your dick-tease body just the way you need it."

My climax begins to pump through me in dark, radiant waves, choking off my air supply, so I can only gasp the words. "Can't walk away." I throw my head back and moan, grinding the back of my skull against the boulder. "Need it. Need it."

"Get used to having soaked panties," he rasps against my ear, giving me crude upward drives, bouncing me and holding there, exploiting the elevated peak I'm living in. "I'm going to keep them that way. When I'm not fucking you, I'll make damn sure you're thinking about when and how it's going to happen."

I'm limp by the time he finishes speaking, head lolling, barely capable of keeping my thighs wrapped around his waist. It's sheer pride keeping them in position at this point. Pride and that still-fierce need to give him the same bliss he's given me. My hands lift and cup my breasts, my teeth sinking into my lower lip, and I watch in satisfaction as his nostrils flare, a curse scraping out between his teeth. "You like the way I feel, Will?"

"*I fucking love it.*"

"Filthy man," I whisper, not sure of the woman I am in this moment, but so comfortable and confident with her, I think she's been waiting in the wings. Waiting for Will to free her. "You big, filthy man. You need to come so bad, don't you?"

"Yes." A tremor moves through him, his pumps turning violent. "*Jesus.* Yes."

With his breath growing more and more labored at my forehead, I clamp down around him with my inner walls—and his answering groan is the hottest thing I've ever heard. It's a masculine battle cry that fades into surrender, cracking at the end as he comes. "Goddammit. Teresa. *Shit.*" His mouth opens wide over mine, his eyes squeezing closed. And I've never been more satisfied in my life than I am for the next few seconds, his heat flooding me, my intimate muscles flexing around his flesh—*tighten, release, tighten, release*—milking him dry. A stream of dirty speech comes out of Will, slurred and incoherent. Words I would slap any other man across the face for saying out loud, but this man who accepts my fantasies without flinching makes them...right. Praise spoken in the heat of passion, singular to us, whether it's truth or fiction meant to heighten the moment. "*Fuck.* That's a greedy pussy you've got, woman. Stealing the come right out of me." Will bares his teeth as more liquid warmth releases. "Little liar. Want my baby, don't you? *God.* This body tells me the truth. Take it."

"Yes," I moan, licking salty sweat off his face. "Give it to me."

One final thrust and Will collapses against me, his face finding a home in the curve of my neck. My legs lose their battle and drop, Will's embrace keeping me upright, pressed between heavy male muscle and stone. We stay like that for long minutes, catching our breath, until we hear the jingle of Southpaw's collar approaching. We glance over to find Southpaw watching us, head tilted, a moss-covered stick in his mouth.

A laugh climbs my throat, Will's low timbre joining me a second later.

"All right, buddy." Will presses a slow kiss to each of my cheeks, humor dancing in his eyes. "My stick has been looked after, now we'll worry about yours."

"I *knew* that was coming." I shove Will off me with a laugh, but he comes right back, whipping his shirt off over his head and carefully pressing it between my thighs, his earlier humor fading away. It's such an unexpected move that I suck in a breath, unable to move as he cups me through the fabric, dragging it up and back, then moving lower to collect the stickiness on the insides of my thighs.

While he completes the task, his eyes never leave mine, the intensity in their depths holding me in thrall. "Mine now."

I nod like I've been hypnotized. Or Will-notized.

"Can you stand to put those wet clothes back on for a few minutes?" He kisses me slowly, thoroughly. "I'm going to jog back to the visitor center to get you something dry to wear." His lips twitch. "Pretty sure I saw a tie-dye dress in there that says Nature Girl across the front."

"It won't match my shoes, but I think I'll live."

His thumbs brush my cheeks, a shadow crossing his face. "Too soon after I pulled you out of the river to go making jokes about living and dying, woman."

Stepping back with a low sound of reluctance, he tucks the T-shirt in his back pocket, zips up and leaves me to dress.

And I know that no matter what happens, whether he wants me or not when the dust settles, I am his. The question is whether or not he'll still want to be mine.

CHAPTER EIGHTEEN

Will

I LIFT MY hand to knock on the doorframe of Teresa's room, but I pause in the action, literally unable to do anything but stare at her and breathe. God, she's fucking beautiful. The lamp glow highlights her sun-reddened cheeks, her hair has dried messy from her dip in the river. She's sitting cross legged on the end of her bed—which she hasn't and won't be sleeping in—still wearing the tie-dye dress I bought her today. After we played with Southpaw in the park until late afternoon, we came back to the hotel and now I'm focused on feeding her. But she seems more focused on the laptop she's holding.

She looks up when I clear my throat. "Hi."

"Hey." I walk into the room, noting the way she watches me with an air of anticipation. As if she's wondering if I'll push her backwards on the bed and take more of what she gave me in the woods. Make no mistake, after she wrecked me for every other woman today, I want back inside her as soon as possible. Want her bucking and twisting and scratching. I'm more than a little obsessed with this woman, actually. But I have one more night to make my mark, and that requires more than fucking. "I came to ask what you want for dinner."

I set the room service menu down in front of her and she picks it up, setting it on her laptop keyboard. "Mmm." She looks up at me through a squinted eye. "Want to get a bunch of appetizers and share them?"

"Read my mind—"

"And then...maybe I can show you some of my work over dinner?" She slaps her hands over her face. "Oh my God, that sounded like a bad pick-up line."

Laughing, I sit down beside Teresa on the bed and pry her hands off her face. "It would have. If we weren't well past that point."

"Are we?" Her face is scarlet. "I've got that nervous first date feeling all of a sudden."

The mere implication that she's been on dates tightens my skin all over my body. "You don't seem the type to get nervous about dates," I manage.

"I would with you, I think," she says slowly, easing my strain. "If we'd met and gone through that whole process of exchanging numbers and feeling each other out...I think I'd be nervous on our first date."

She's hedging because she doesn't want to show me what's on the laptop and I'm perfectly content to let her get there in her own time. "Do you really think we could ever go through a patented dating process?"

A beat passes. "No."

"No." Leaning in, I drop a kiss on her shoulder. "I couldn't date you, Teresa. Dating implies I don't have you locked down. Until we were solid, the gaps between us seeing each other would drive me crazy."

"Yeah?" She turns her head, bringing our faces an inch apart. "So you would just take me hostage until I agreed to be your..."

"Girlfriend. Yeah." I'm not sure I've ever said that word out loud. It sounds pretty damn good when I'm looking at Teresa. "You wouldn't realize I was holding you hostage. I'd simply keep inventing reasons for you to stay."

She tosses her hair back, feigning only mild interest, but I can tell she's interested as hell. Might have something to do with the pulse going wild at the base of her neck. "What kind of reasons?"

A series of images flips through my mind. Bringing Teresa a glass of champagne while she soaks in my bathtub. Fucking her on hands and knees in front of my fireplace. Stuffing dozens of drawers with ridiculous French underwear for her to wear. This desire to treat someone like a queen is new. It's specific to her. "If I talk about spoiling you, baby, I'm going to get turned on. And if I get turned on, we're not going to talk about what's on that laptop."

As if on cue, the computer tilts and almost falls off her lap, but I catch it, forcing myself not to look at the screen. Teresa chews on her lower lip, splitting glances at me and what she's clicking on, until I finally sense her turning the device in my direction. "Okay. Okay, so I work with this girl at the parlor. Mara. She's kind of an unofficial manager. Doesn't say much, but her word is law, you know? She's a single mother with two kids and she takes three buses to get to work." Her expression warms. "I admire her a lot. She's tough, but this...*good* just kind of pours out of her when you least expect it. Once, a customer was giving me a hard time because I cut him off. He owed the house too much already. But he wouldn't let up. Kept demanding I change his money into chips and he was getting belligerent. Mara grabbed a bag of Lays out of her purse, ripped them open with her teeth and dumped them on his head. 'There's your chips, asshole,' she said."

We share a quiet laugh. "If she made you feel more safe in that place, I'm grateful for her."

"Yeah. She did. More than once." On the screen, the arrow hovers over a movie, Teresa's finger shaking where it gets ready to click. "I asked if I could follow her around for a day. She took my best shift as payment, but…I—it was worth it."

She clicks, and images roll. Mara getting her children dressed. Making breakfast. Sitting on the edge of her bed staring into space. Transferring buses. Arguing with a man outside a supermarket. Cursing over a rip in her stockings. Counting poker chips. Rolling her eyes behind a customer's back. Picking up her children from the babysitter and fawning over artwork they present her.

The film is only about five minutes. Just bites out of a woman's life. But that's part of what makes it so poignant. It's like I *know* Mara—everything about her—because Teresa found this way to introduce her in a careful, realistic and sensitive way. "Did you edit this, too?"

Teresa snaps the laptop shut and nods, seeming to chance me a look. "Yes."

I could lead with how perfect and wonderful the short film was, but I want to hear her talk about it first. More than that, I'm interested in her answers. "How did you know which angles to shoot from? Do you try more than one?"

"Sometimes." She sits up a little straighter. "On the bus, I—"

"She sat in the back. But you shot from the very front."

"Yeah, I…wanted whoever's watching to see how easily someone who's struggling, but so important to their family can just blend in. And seem *not* important to the casual observer. That's why I included all the other passengers in the shot."

"And you almost hid behind the doorframe when she was on the edge of her bed. It was kind of like we weren't supposed to be there."

"Yeah," she breathes. "Exactly."

"I could feel through the camera what you were thinking." I shake my head. "Teresa, I'm not an expert, but I doubt there's a lot of people who can accomplish that. You're fucking good, baby. Really good." She ducks her head, but I bring her chin back up. "I can remember every second of it. *You* did that."

There's hope in her eyes when she looks up at me, and I never want to see her looking any other way. "This is the film I sent in with my application."

"Then you're as good as accepted," I respond, with total conviction. "You did mention they have a campus in New York, right?"

We both smile, slowly gravitating toward one another. "I might have."

I growl, stealing a quick kiss from her mouth. "Go shower. I'm going to order."

"Second thoughts on the tie-dye ensemble?"

Garnering my will, I climb off the bed and pick up the hotel phone. "Second thoughts about you being dressed at all." Before I can dial, Teresa bounds off the bed and throws herself into my arms. I don't even have to think. I just drop the phone and hold her against me, wondering if she can hear my heart hammering.

"Thanks," she whispers. "Thank you."

My raw throat won't let me do anything but nod as she floats away, closing herself in the bathroom.

WE EAT DINNER outside, Teresa sitting across from me, framed by the stars and swallowed up in a giant, white hotel towel. When we finish, I leave to take my own shower, and when I return, Teresa has moved inside. She hasn't seen me yet where I stand in the hallway entrance, drying my hair with a towel. There's one around my waist, too, but my thickening cock is about to dislodge it. I don't just want Teresa again. I *need* her with a vengeance. One quickie in the woods with this woman and my definition of sex has changed, never to be reverted.

We're at such ease with each other since this afternoon, I'm having a hard time believing she could say no to us flying back to New York together. But I'm not taking any chances. I've bought myself some time. She's not going anywhere tonight and I'm not going to push for answers right now when the mood between us is relaxed. Trusting.

Yeah, she's sprawled out in a shit-load of pillows on the living room floor, wearing nothing but the white hotel robe, her hair still a touch damp from a shower. She's got a glass of wine in one hand, scratching Southpaw's belly with the other while he rumbles with delight.

This is what contentment feels like. I'm not giving it up.

Haven't I learned throughout my life that actions speak louder than words? I'm going to spend the rest of tonight showing her what we'd be like together. Show her what I do with the trust she gives me.

Like that little fantasy of hers she confided.

Anticipation sends blood rushing south to my dick...and as if she can hear my flesh stretching and growing swollen, Teresa looks at me over her shoulder. Just as quickly, her gaze falls to my towel and the full salute I'm giving her beneath.

"Has dessert arrived?" She sips her wine. "I'm usually more of a chocolate girl."

Woman, you are locked down. I watch the way her robe gapes, teasing me with a sexy view of her right tit and lust begins to expand my lungs, my blood. I'd like to knock the wine out of her hand, flip her onto her stomach and take the razor's edge off my need, but I've got a plan for tonight. One I hope will satisfy her and convince her she can trust me. She *can.* So I only allow a smile to play around my mouth as I join her in the living room, sitting on the edge of the couch. The position puts her eye level with my lap, and it doesn't escape my notice how she squirms a little, wetting her lips.

So I lean back and grip myself through the terry cloth. "I could take this down to the bar and have a drink. Wait for you to arrive." Cataloguing her reaction, I slide my palm over the curve of my cock. "You could be the girl I ordered."

"Could I?" she whispers.

"Only if you want to be." Adjusting myself to one side, I lean forward and reach out to cup Teresa's chin. "Teresa, you already know I'd rather everyone in the room—in *any* room—treat you with respect. I'd rather walk in with my hand on your back and hold out a chair for you. But acting like we're something else in front of strangers we'll never see again…in order to get you off good and hard? Woman, I'll do what it takes and enjoy the fuck out of it."

A few beats pass and she drains her wine, which would make me laugh if my cock wasn't throbbing like a bastard against my stomach.

"What if I want to stop?"

"Then you tell me to stop. I will." My thumb traces her cheekbones, my heart booming when she leans into the touch. "And I'll bring you upstairs for chocolate cake."

She blows out a breath. "With ice cream?"

"A gallon of that shit." Her mouth opens and I let my thumb tuck inside. "We don't have to do this, Teresa. I could lay you down on that carpet and sink my tongue in so deep between those thighs, you'll scream your throat raw."

"God, Will." Her eyes glitter. "The way I let you speak to me."

"Let me?" I ease off the couch and drop to my knees, putting me a good foot above her. "If I stopped speaking to you how I do, you'd hate it."

"Maybe. Let's not find out," she murmurs, head tipping back to look up at me. "I always thought this would stay in my private thoughts. Playing it out in real life never occurred to me. Not until you."

"I'm telling you, baby. Chocolate cake and—"

"Your tongue. Believe me, I remember."

"I was going to say ice cream, you pervert."

A laugh breaks free of her lips and hits me right in the stomach. "No, I'm not backing out. I...oh my God." She slaps a hand over her eyes. "I think I'm excited."

I lean down and laze my tongue into her mouth, rubbing it against hers until she moans, her fingers climbing my bare abdomen, like she's unconscious of the action. "How far do you want to take it, Teresa?"

Thoughts zoom behind her eyes. "I trust you to know how far to take it." A crease forms between her brows. "I...trust you."

My pulse goes fucking wild. Not throwing her down on the carpet is growing harder by the second, so I stand up, helping Teresa to her feet. "I'll get dressed. After I leave, give me fifteen minutes before you follow." I tip up her chin, waiting until she's focused on me, our breaths matching. "You come straight to me. As far as you're concerned, there are no other men in the room. That's my only rule."

She goes up on her toes, her eyes steady on mine. "I think...you being the only man in any room where I'm standing is a given, Will. It's just you."

I'm left with my heart lodged in my throat as she goes to change.

CHAPTER NINETEEN

Teresa

I STARE BACK at my reflection in the full-length mirror, which, of course, has giant steer horns mounted on top. Might as well face it. In six-inch heels and a little red dress that ends just below my butt, I look like I'm hoping this story ends with Richard Gere scaling my fire escape. Or Will, rather.

Definitely Will.

The man won't stop surprising me. Or turning me on. And I'm so turned on right now, I could hump another sink. When Will said he'd rather I be viewed with respect, I know he meant it. So this effort he's making tonight is totally about me. Oh, he's going to have a good time. I'll make sure of it. But that kind of selflessness in a man is something I haven't seen before...and it's pulling me in deeper.

I've fallen hard.

There's a vicious twist in my middle, but I force my chin up and ignore it. I'm not going to think negative thoughts tonight. Tomorrow will be soon enough. I've been a dutiful daughter and protective sister for a long time. Maybe I can let tonight just be about Will and me? Without letting anything else intrude? Whatever happens when the lid comes off the box, I'll have this night to remember.

Fighting back another wave of dread, I lean toward the mirror and apply the nude lipstick in my hand, flipping the tube over to add a glossy sheen. I can't believe I'm getting ready to go downstairs and role play. To trust a man to be my partner in this scene created by my own imagination. I've always been a little embarrassed by this secret of mine. Not anymore.

Since I met Will, I've won an arm-wrestling contest, saved a dog from drowning, and I'm about to fully embrace my wayward libido.

When a flash of nerves hits me, I remember Will's face after watching my film. I think I'll replay that moment every day until forever. Maybe I *am* good. Maybe film school isn't such a pipe dream after all. Saying those things to myself and remembering the awe in Will's tone while he peppered me with questions give me the push I need. I got this.

Taking one final look at myself in the mirror, I tug on my light, black, belted jacket and step back to survey the goods. I'm not a shy woman by any stretch, but then again, this isn't my usual crowd downstairs. At the club, I'm surrounded by older men, but they've either fallen on hard times due to their gambling addiction. Or they're low-grade criminals on the take. This hotel is bursting at the seams with money and influence—and I'm going to strut in wearing stripper heels, looking like I have nothing but my birthday suit beneath this jacket.

When I said I trusted Will in this, though…I meant it.

My palms start to sweat on the way to the elevators, so I blow on them, shake them out. I bypass the main bank and travel to the farthest ones on our floor, which I noticed earlier will take me down to the hotel's side exit. Thankfully, I don't pass anyone on the way out of the hotel. I circle around to the front and enter, ignoring inquisitive looks from the front desk and taking the first right hallway to the hotel bar. It's noisy. Crowded. Before I step one heeled foot inside, I can tell that some sporting event is showing on the television, thanks to the cheers and groans.

A lot of the patrons have their backs turned to the entrance, most of them facing a large projection screen on the far side of the room. Some of them do turn, though, eyeing me top to bottom beneath heavy eyelids—and their lack of any discernable expression almost makes me lose my nerve. There is one man off to the side wearing a white baseball cap and I stop breathing, but he turns with a laugh and it's not him. Too old to be the man who was following us. Still...our tail could be here. Couldn't he? Could be watching from the shadows and reporting back to Silas. I haven't spotted him since the day he drove past us on the highway. I've been hoping he either didn't make it past hotel security without a reservation and the cost for a room was too astronomical, but it's impossible to be sure. And that damn baseball cap is all I remember. His features are a blur, so if he wasn't wearing the hat, I'm not even sure I'd recognize him.

When I see Will, everything fades into the background. My nerves, my fear. All of it. There's only him.

He's sitting at the dark end of the bar, away from the crowd, turned sideways in his seat, a highball of whiskey resting on the bar beside him. He sits unmoving, while somehow crackling with animal energy, his eyes burning like twin brands. The sound around me fades. The heels on my feet stop feeling ridiculous and make my calves tingle instead. Or maybe it's the way Will's eyes slide up from my ankles to rest on my thighs, the hem of my jacket.

There's no one in the room but us, so moving toward him in the void of noise is the most natural thing in the world. Like being pulled slowly, sensually by a humming magnet. Except the magnet is hotter than sin and talks about giving me head like it's an Olympic event.

I stop when I reach Will, who is already calling to the bartender for a glass of white wine. Thankful for the extra seconds to collect myself, I turn to face the bar and set down my purse. "Mr. Caruso?"

"That's right." While the bartender drops off my wine and glides away, Will takes a long drink of whiskey, letting his gaze travel over my bottom. "Very nice."

Heat climbs the insides of my thighs and sinks low in my belly, colliding right in the middle. "Thank you."

He sits forward, his hand opening wide to palm my hips, squeezing, testing. "Would you like to take off your jacket and show me the rest?"

Dampness forms between my legs. This is it. It's happening. I'm the merchandise, just like I've thought about in the dark so many times while touching myself. I'm already so hot, I could climb on his lap now and ride him into the sunset, but the thrill of the game is only beginning, isn't it? Good Lord. By the time it's over, it could kill me. "Sure, of course," I breathe, unbuckling the belt and tugging it off my shoulders—

Will's hands find my hips, turning me toward him in a blur. I'm caught off guard and the loss of balance sends me into the V of his thighs. "The preview is just for me." A muscle flexes in his jaw. "No one else."

"Right." That reminder of Will lurking beneath the surface, possessive and steadfast, gives me a boost of confidence. Enough to let my jacket fall to the floor, leaving me in the tiny red dress. "Am I to your taste, Mr. Caruso?"

"You inspire tastes I didn't even know I had." Out of the corner of my eye, I see his hand ball into a tight fist on the bar. A hungry sound leaves his mouth, but he tries to hide it by clearing his throat. Nonetheless, his voice sounds like ripping Velcro when he speaks. "I bet those pretty tits get you into a lot of trouble." His eyes tick to mine. "Do you like being in trouble?"

My bottom tingles where he slapped me yesterday, the memory sending a bead of sweat sliding down my back. "Yes. If that's what you want," I rush to add.

"You'll like what I like, won't you?" He runs his tongue along the inside of his bottom lip. "That's the advantage of ordering only the best."

Oh God. I'm trying not to breathe like I just ran a marathon, but I'm slipping into the role of call girl, letting it become me, and it's intoxicating. Just for tonight, my only job is to satisfy this man and I'm placing all my focus in that single basket; every other worry or insecurity rolls off me like lush, morning dew. "Yes, Mr. Caruso."

He stands and picks up his whiskey for a lazy sip. But for all his casual male grace, when he moves to my opposite side—partially blocking my view of the other patrons—I can see the sheen of sweat on his upper lip. "Turn in a circle. I want to see your ass in that dress before you spend the rest of the night naked."

My panties are soaked, clinging to my skin as I turn slowly, pivoting on the toe of my high heel. As I turn, I can see one of two loners at tables in the back section of the bar, watching the show we're putting on, and it should make me want to shrug my jacket back on, right? Should make me want to vamoose out the side door. No, though. I'm not shying away from this experience I've apparently needed so badly without realizing. This chance to be bought. To be an object of such concentrated lust. And there's no doubt that Will is lusting as his hand slides over my left bottom cheek and squeezes, grunting in satisfaction, the way he might while buying a sports car—and it makes my knees shake. Knowing he's in on the act and would start a brawl over someone *actually* disrespecting me only heightens my enjoyment.

"Let's get this upstairs before someone tries to outbid me," he growls, inspecting my other cheek with a rough, testing palm. "I wouldn't let that happen, but nothing is going to hold me up from getting inside you."

I complete my turn and come face to face with Will once more, but I'm only given a second to appreciate his hooded eyes and concrete jaw, before my jacket is wrapped around me and I'm being escorted from the bar. I've been so absorbed by Will that I wasn't aware exactly how much interest we've drawn, but there's no ignoring it now. Several men are turned in our direction, some of them whispering to each other, all of them looking me over. Like bidding to take me home isn't that far outside the realm of reality. Once again, though, my trust for Will just turns it all to background noise. Part of the dream we're weaving.

Once in the hallway, Will punches the call button for the elevator, his focus straight ahead, his thumb brushing the small of my back. As soon as the doors roll open, however, and I'm dragged inside to the empty car, his façade cracks.

Hard.

CHAPTER TWENTY

Will

THE LAST TEN minutes used up so much of my self-control, I'm running on very little as the elevator doors smack shut behind Teresa and me. *Very* little. She knows I'm close to the edge, too—my jealousy coiled inside me like a snake—and it excites her, those hard nipples teasing me forward as she backs up toward the wall, like prey.

One step. Two.

And then I'm on her, one hand curved around her throat, guiding her the remaining distance until I have her pinned loosely against the wall, my other hand shoving up beneath the hem of her indecently short dress. Red. She shows up in fucking red, those stupid shoes putting her ass lap-level for every man in the room. I can't breathe around the grip of possessiveness shackling my neck…but the jealousy loosens its grip when I take a handful of her pussy and find it hot, drenched beyond belief. She gasps, her eyes going blind, as if the single touch has her on the precipice of an orgasm. It's the reminder I need that she was mine the whole time we were inside the bar. My Teresa. Who needed her man to rise to the occasion and feed her fantasy.

"This wet pussy is for me. Because of me. Only."

"You know it is," she rasps. "Oh God…I can't…did we press the button for our floor?" She licks parched, swollen lips. "I'm actually hurting."

Since I did apparently press the button in the midst of my green haze, the elevator car slows to a stop on the top floor. Even with the doors opening, though, I can't stop myself from massaging her through the soaked panties one more time. Again. *Again.* Christ, she has no idea how hot she got me in that damn bar. This night is for her, but a dutiful Teresa is the full moon to the hungry werewolf that is my dominance. "Not for long."

"Please," she moans, raking her fingernails up and down my stomach, tugging on my belt buckle. "Please."

I reach over and hit the *hold* button, before leaning in to speak right up against Teresa's mouth. "You've been hired to put that gorgeous body to work and get *me* off. Or did you forget?"

A shudder passes through her, those exposed thighs squeezing together between mine. My cock lifts and swells more in my pants, knowing how bad she needs to sit on it. "I didn't forget," she whispers. "Take me inside and—"

"And we'll talk about what I'd like?" I scoop my hand into her panties, pressing my middle finger to her slippery entrance. "How much is full use of this going to cost me per hour?"

More moisture finds my fingers, her hands scrambling up to my shoulders, and I'm fully prepared to play her john every day for the rest of her life, as long as it makes her this desperate, this turned on. It'll be my privilege. She's trying to wrap her thighs around me now and I step back, giving her enough room to do it, unable to control my groans every time she makes contact with my throbbing dick. As soon as she's got her legs clamped around my waist, her open mouth hot on my neck, I turn and take the elevator off hold. We exit a moment later, taking the few steps to our hotel room. We're inside with one swipe of the key and I head straight for the sunken living room area, the pillows still strewn about on the plush carpet from earlier.

Instead of laying her down on her back and thrusting deep between her thighs, I put her on the lounge chair, already pushing her knees open as I drop into a kneel. "Are you going to charge me extra to lick it?" Holding her legs open wide, I curse over the damp, black silk stretched across her pussy. "You should. It looks as delicious as the rest of you. I'd let you fleece me just to get the taste in my mouth."

She arches her back, her fingers twisting the hem of her dress. "In that case, y-yes, it's extra."

This combination of needing to fuck this woman and feeling my heart squeeze for her, so deep in my chest, is like nothing else in the world. My hand travels up her body to press over her own pounding organ, while my mouth comes to rest on the silk path of her panties. "Thousand bucks a lick." I nip at the material, dragging it to one side. "That sound about right?"

Her fingers fly to my hair, tangling there. "Yes. Yes."

"You have to keep count, baby. Can you do that?"

"Mmmhmm."

I hook a finger in her panties, twist and rip them off her body, tossing them over my shoulder, giving me such a sweet view of pink I might go back to church on Sundays just to praise God for making it. "If you come, the fee you're racking up drops down to zero."

"What?" Her stomach hollows and lifts on a whimper. "Why?"

"Because you're going to ride me next—and I want you with eager hips." With my index and middle fingers, I separate her lips and swipe my tongue up the center of her pussy. Her sugar and female flavor turns the crank of lust in my gut, so I'm forced to grind my cock against the edge of the couch. "Start counting."

"One..." I kiss the insides of her thighs, then—keeping our eyes locked—I start to lap at her clit. Fast. "T-two, three...oh my

God. Twenty?"

Still flicking my tongue against her bud, I let my fingers travel lower, pumping the middle one inside her entrance. Immediately, her flesh clamps around my digit and she close-mouthed screams my name. "Damn, that's tight," I manage through the need, twisting my finger. "Go ahead and double that fee."

"Stop talking." One of her hands pushes my head away, while the other one pulls it closer. "I'm not going to last."

I lift a hand and slap it down on her pussy, right over the top of her clit. "You will if you want to get paid."

Her strangled scream hangs in the air. "*Please.*"

"Take just a little bit more." I deliver another sharp smack, dropping down right away to lick at her swollen clit. "How do I want your hips?"

"Eager."

"That's right."

"I can't...I can't..."

"Don't come, now." I suction my mouth over her clit and jiggle my finger inside her at the same time. Her hips buck off the furniture and she screams. But just as she begins to contract around my finger, I slide it out of her and take away my mouth, resisting the urge to finish her when she sobs.

She sits up, looking like a sex goddess in a bad mood, her nipples in sharp peaks, her mouth in a pout and *fuck*. I might be prolonging this game, but I'm a raging beast on the inside that is seconds from calling it quits and taking what I need. It's her flushed face and labored breaths that keep me in the moment, but I can't stop myself from yanking her forward by the knees until she drops off the chair. The move pulls her down to me, and she lands with her thighs open, straddling my lap. "Feel how ready I am to see what a good little earner you are?"

Her eyelids flutter, but not before I catch her excitement,

both of her hands dropping to my belt to begin unfastening it. "*Yes.*"

I recline in the mess of thick carpeting and pillows, stacking my hands beneath my head. My casual position is only a show, though, because she's the most incredible thing I've ever seen, red cheeks and teeth-bitten lips, her hair in a mess from wiggling around while I gave her head. And instead of sitting there like a client enjoying the show, I want to kiss her mouth until she comes from that alone.

It seems like I've only been given a few seconds to marvel over her, before she gets my pants unzipped and I'm locked in her right hand. "Ah, fuck, woman," I grit out, my hips shifting on the ground. "Give me what I need."

These sexy whimpering sounds are falling from her mouth as she guides me between her thighs and tucks my head inside of her. "Oh my God." Her hips drop in one fell swoop and my balls wrench tight, her name leaving my mouth in what sounds like a prayer and a curse at the same time. "*Oh my God.*"

Understatement. She's slippery and hot around my dick, her lips in an O above me, because I'm pushing at all her walls. And the woman earns my undying gratitude by not taking the time to get used to my cock, but starts to ride as soon as she's seated, rolling forward and up before sinking back down with a smart-ass little hip tweak that makes my vision flicker.

"That's right. Show me all your tricks. Show me what I can't get anywhere else." My stomach knits up on impulse so I don't go off right away, like I almost did this afternoon. Christ, she's sliding up and down my cock exactly like I'm paying her, and now I'm halfway lost in the fantasy, too, of being serviced by a woman. Because that's exactly what she's doing, working me with slick bounces of her pussy and blowing my mind. I want to devour her, touch and see every inch of her, the impulse so strong that I jackknife into a sitting position and rip the zipper down her back. "Take off this motherfucking dress. I'm paying for naked."

I whip the dress off, leaving her completely nude, and being exposed seems to push her desperation to the next level. Fingernails digging into my shoulders, she rides me harder, her mouth raking up and down mine. We're flush, her bare flesh pressed to mine, her pussy grinding down on me and it's *so fucking good*, I drop my head back and moan. It doesn't even sound like it's coming from me, it's so unrestrained, so starved—and something about it brings Teresa's movements to a pause. "I…can you…"

"What, baby? What?"

"I love that sound you made." She pushes her face into the crook of my neck, her hips starting to pump out of control, her fingernails now breaking the skin on my shoulders. "That m-moan."

It occurs to me in a flood of heat that being an object of lust goes hand in hand with satisfying that lust. Shit, I'll do anything to show her how well she's doing exactly that and more. "Never had it this good," I rasp, honesty gathering between us like sauna steam. "Look how you spread your sexy legs so I can get so fucking deep. Snapping your hips and getting wetter with every stroke, too, huh, baby? You're the hottest thing I've ever seen."

She's shaking now, laying bites and licks on the curve of my neck, and I do it again, I moan loud and long because I can't help it. My dick is being treated like a king, being hugged up and down by clenching and releasing flesh, while my hot, whimpering girl rubs her tits on my chest. And the sounds I can't help making turn her even more wild. Her legs clamp even tighter, her hips moving like kinky machinery. "Again," she pants, pushing me down into the pillows—and I let her, watching her through a fog of need so thick, I can barely cut through it. "Again."

This time, when I groan loud enough to shake the windows,

it's out of pure pleasure/pain, the effort of holding back the release she seems determined to wring out of me. Desperate to last, I drop back into the pillows and squeeze my eyes shut, hoping if I can't see her, it might give me the added strength. My body has a mind of its own, though, and no sooner do I hit the pillows, my hips start pumping, driving my cock up into her tight pussy, slapping noises filling the room, along with her gasps. "Dammit. *Dammit*," I push through clenched teeth, watching as she teeters toward the edge, her body vibrating with the force of my upthrusts. *Get her there.* "Consider this your last appointment. I'm purchasing you for my own personal use." I find her clit with my thumb, pressing down and massaging roughly. "I'd bankrupt myself to reserve this for whenever I need it."

Her head falls back, exposing the gorgeous curve of her dewy throat. "Maybe I don't want to be on reserve."

The back of my neck tightens at those words, but I know from the flush of excitement on her cheeks that this is part of the fantasy. And hell, did she ever pick the right man to play it out. "That's too bad, baby. You work for me now. My cock is your new employer." My thumb blurs on her clit and her muscles seize on top of me. "You're going to weep all over him with gratitude."

Her fingers twist in the front of my shirt and she screams. I'm barely aware of buttons popping off the front of the garment, because the vision she creates demands my attention. Christ. She's a force. A life force. Fuck it, she's life itself, her stomach trembling like a leaf, her cunt tightening around me with feminine violence. Her hips heave and twist, trying to make the most of her climax, and wet sex sounds pound in my ears. "Will. Will. Oh my God. *Will.*"

Teresa's use of my name almost makes me drop the scene we've woven, but I hang on tight, determined to see it through to the end. "God, woman," I say, gruffly. My hands find her tits, my thumbs rubbing over her nipples in genuine reverence. "I'd let you bleed me dry for the privilege of making you come."

She yanks the sides of my shirt open, running smooth palms over me. Up and down. Side to side, through my chest hair. All the while, she worries her lower lip between her teeth, well-fucked but still visibly turned on. *Hallelujah.* "I don't usually get so hot while I'm..." Pink brightens her cheeks. "Working. Maybe I have to consider that offer."

My dick is throbbing like a son of a bitch inside of her, and it hardens further with irrational jealousy, just hearing her talk about *working.* Which implies other men besides me. Reality or fiction, my blood starts to drum in my temples, my fingers digging into her hips. Without a rational command from my brain, I move fast, sitting up and flipping Teresa onto her hands and knees. "Need some convincing that I'm it for you, is that right?"

The game blurs now—hard—along with my control. In my mind's eye, I see her in the park this morning, hesitating over us returning to New York together. And a hurricane starts spinning in my chest, toppling my plan to be patient, to conquer her body first, mind second. Those intentions flutter to the ground like a house of cards, then whip into the frenzied storm happening inside me.

She's still wearing her shoes, and I grip the long, skinny heels now, using them to pry her thighs apart with a growl. It leaves me a nice view of her sweet ass and the drenched strip of pink flesh beneath. I take my cock in my hand and drag the sensitive head up and down that hot, little path, nipping at the center of her spine with my teeth. "Every place I'm touching is mine." I drag my tongue up her back and don't stop until reach her ear, breathing against that soft shell. "Every square inch."

"Please..."

There's a catch in her voice, like maybe the act is becoming hard for her to maintain as well. I want to question her, but she tips her head sideways for my mouth, backing her tight backside into my lap…and lust wraps around the base of my spine, buzzes in my skull like a swarm of locusts. "Please, what?" I position my dick at her entrance, take hold of her hips and plow forward. "This what you want?"

"*Yes.*"

I'm laboring to breathe through my nose—in, out, in, out— ignoring the pressure threatening to burst free of my balls. Knowing once I begin to thrust, I'm not going to stop, I grab two pillows with my right hand and wedge them beneath Teresa's hips, making sure they won't slip. "I'm going to go rough now. I have to. Feel how impatient you've made me?" I rear back and give a hard, testing drive, grunting my satisfaction when I hit the snug, firm resistance of her pussy, the pillow barrier holding fast. "*God*, yeah. Be a good girl and stay still while I do some convincing."

Her whimper is a mixture of yes and nine different names for her Creator.

I drop myself down on top of Teresa, curving my body over the ass-up angle of hers, and need roars through me like a living thing, jerking my hips forward and back. *Jesus*, the feel of her will haunt me every hour I'm not buried there. My knees slide wider, taking hers along with them, so every part of us is low to the ground, besides her ass and my hips. She's crying out every time I slap deep, my balls rebounding off her slick underside, and I love the sound. Her voice is making me miss her face, her eyes, but I picture them in my head and go for broke, living for her broken sobs and moans.

"Here's how this is really going to go, baby. Whether I'm paying for you or you're letting me in because you feel something for me." I fist her hair, tilting her head so I can speak up against her ear. "I'm going to fucking worship you. Every day. You want to play a prick tease who performs for what's in my wallet? Hell, I got you. You want me to slap a diamond on your neck and fly you around the world? That might be more for me, but I got you there, too. *I* got what you need. And if I *don't* have it, I'll go find it." Just voicing the possibility of having her beside me every day shoots me closer to my end, possessiveness turning my vision bright and hazy. Below my waist, everything starts to tighten, tighten, tighten, bolts twisting that I wasn't even aware were part of my body. Her. It's just *her*. "You're giving me your body right now, Teresa. Dig a little deeper and give me the rest. I *got* you."

"Will..."

I know I'm playing dirty, but she's still on the fence, and if I don't get some kind of sign that we're together for the duration, I'm going to go insane. So I reach around her hip and rub her swollen clit, my cock swelling to the point of blinding pain when she strains beneath me, her voice cracking on a scream. "I need you, Teresa. Let yourself need me back."

We turn our heads at the same time, meeting in a furious kiss over her shoulder, while I continue to take her from the back like a goddamn savage. Somewhere in the middle of the kiss, she hands herself over. It's a gentle sound and a nod. "I do," she murmurs haltingly. "I need you."

Triumph and relief explode in my chest like twin bombs, turning everything around me clear as crystal, filling my lungs with oxygen. "You have me. *You have me.*" I don't realize how hard I'm taking her until her knees kick out from beneath her completely. She's draped over the stack of pillows I created, her fingernails clawing the carpet, her voice hoarse as she screams my name. "Now let's see what we can do about getting rid of this ache between my legs. You started it, now you need to finish it."

My pace is full speed now, my fingers busy on her clit. She writhes beneath me, but my full weight presses down, giving her nowhere to go. "Is this what I can expect my life to be like now? You parading around in tight dresses, making men want to outbid you from under me?"

A rush of wetness follows my words, followed by a winded, but excited, "Y-yes. I can't help it."

"Oh, you *will* help it." I give one brutal thrust. Another. My climax breaks free, barreling up the hard stalk of my dick, scalding hot and more intense than I've ever experienced. That mind-melting pleasure and the intuition that Teresa needs something a little dirtier to find her second release brings words growling out of me. Are they part of the game? Yeah. But shit, when they make her come like a wildcat, they become a signal of other games to come. And Jesus, that's fine by me. "Daddy is going to buy you anything you want. No need to go anywhere else."

"*Will.*" She spasms around me with a cry, more moisture turning her slippery for my throbbing cock. "Oh *God.*"

I slam into her one final time, bellowing through the orgasm of my fucking life. It tears through me in a painful tirade, setting fire to my awareness. Making everything burn, ache, release, ache, burn. Until there's nothing but a void of sound, my body slack, aftershocks passing through me in tremors as I work to regain my ability to breathe. "Teresa." With an effort, I lean my weight on an elbow and drop kisses into her neck. "Baby, you okay?"

"Mmm." She lifts her head, but it drops just as fast, face first into the plush carpet, the edge of her mouth lifting in a lazy smile. "Mmmhmm."

My heart climbs the column of my throat. Stays put. "I need to turn you over."

"Why?"

I try to put into words what's sparking the growing urgency in my gut. "That was…goddamn, Teresa. Good isn't even a start. I'll be the guy who paid for your time any day of the week. But when it's over…" Her head lifts, curious eyes training on me. "When it's over, I need to kiss you, talk to you like you're Teresa. The girl who everyone treats like a fucking queen or I'll break their jaw."

Slowly, she turns over on her back. *Wow.* I'm not known for being nostalgic, but apparently that's going to change. For the rest of my life, I'll remember how beautiful Teresa looks, rosy and naked, limbs loose, as she nestles into the pillows and tilts her head at me. "You need to be kissed and talked to like Will, too, don't you?"

"Yeah," I say, clearing my throat hard. "Didn't know I did until you said it."

Teresa takes hold of my ripped shirt and tugs me down on top of her, welcoming my hips between her thighs, which she wraps around me. Heaven. That's where I've landed. Especially when she slides her fingernails into my hair, raking them lightly along my scalp. "When we were in the bar, you kept angling yourself so no one would see me, even when you were saying all those perfect things. You made me feel so safe."

Warmth floods my chest, loosening everything in its path. "Yeah?"

She nods. "You were there the whole time. I could feel Will behind everything you said, everything you did." Her breath releases in a cool stream against my mouth. "And I loved it. A lot."

My cock wakes up, sliding through the sexy mess between our legs. "I told you, Teresa. I got you." I drop an open-mouthed kiss on her neck, lapping up her incredible taste with my tongue. "Now let me say all the things I didn't say."

"Go ahead," she murmurs, playing with my hair. "I'm listening."

I trace her collarbone with my lips. "You're so damn beautiful, baby. On the outside, yeah. But you've got it on the inside, too. The kind of beautiful that makes you jump into a river to save my dog. Or film people so you can appreciate the things in life no one sees." Her eyes shine as they train on me, her fingers going still in my hair. "You make me crazy, too. Crazy in a way that makes me want to rearrange the earth so it's laid out exactly the way you want it."

She shakes her head, opens her mouth and closes it. "Kiss me, Will."

I do. And I don't stop for a long time, wanting to put off tomorrow.

Teresa pours her entire heart into kissing me—I do the same, I couldn't help it if I tried—but I still feel like we're standing on the edge of a precipice...and I have no idea why.

CHAPTER TWENTY-ONE

Teresa

I DON'T WANT to face reality yet. It's too scary. A fire-breathing dragon that can burn me to a crisp with one well-aimed flame. At the moment, I'm encased on bajillion thread count cotton, my head resting on a manmade cloud. Warmth is a never-ending commodity on all sides, but I've chosen the smoothest, most masculine source, snuggling into Will's back like I'm trying to burrow beneath his spine. My arm has snaked over his hip during the course of the night, our fingers loosely joined.

Oh, please. Please fuck off, dragon.

Just for a little longer.

Hitting my mental version of the snooze alarm, I crack an eyelid and absorb my surroundings. Dim, cool room. The outline and slope of a muscular back, facing the backlit rectangle of encroaching sunshine. His bulk rises and falls in time with easy, rolling snores. They're not coming from Will, though. They're coming from the bathroom floor where Southpaw chooses to make his bed.

I could stay like this—just like this—forever.

I've already made my bed, though. And it's one of nails, not warmth.

After Will carried me to bed last night, he disappeared for twenty minutes, but not before I saw the purpose, the resolution squaring his big shoulders. That flight to New York is as good as booked. When he returned to bed, he seemed to tell me so with his body, rolling into the space between my thighs with a firm thrust, tilting my chin up with his hand so I was forced to look him in the eye while he took me. Took me hard. No words were exchanged this time. There were no games. Just Will letting me know I'm his, without question.

My chest twists and I suck in a breath, scooting closer to his solid presence. His breathing changes pace and I close my eyes, savoring the experience of wakefulness reanimating him. His muscles expand, his back arching against me in a lion-like stretch. His bare ass shifts at my belly, making my palms itch to grab two handfuls. I let my fingernails scratch at his belly instead, and he grunts, low and hungry, his abdomen knitting together.

God. *God*, he's a beast. I knew it when I saw him in that photograph what feels like a million years ago. I'm a pile of smiles and satisfied limbs and still—still—my clit begins to tingle knowing its lord and savior is awake. My heart does more than tingle, though. It sprints into high gear, trying to burst out of my chest to get closer to Will. Last night he gave me a lifetime of fantasy fodder...but it was so much more than that. Is it ironic that being treated like a call girl has made me feel empowered? Yeah, probably. But just like the fantasy I kept stored in the deepest recesses of my libido, I've hidden away so many other things I want.

I want to go to film school. To take it seriously. I want to stop selling myself short and working shit jobs, because I'm afraid to fail.

I want Will.

No. No, I think I might need him.

My hand is enclosed tightly in Will's, and he guides it lower, scrubbing my palm over his coarse happy trail, sending my already speeding heart up into my throat. Need. He needs again. And that need is mine, even if it might just be for a short time longer. Anxiety tries to cloud around me, but I shake it away, focusing on the heat. The lust stirring inside me.

From their position of honor smashed to Will's back, my nipples pucker and begin to ache. He rubs my hand against his thick shaft, once, twice, before bringing me to his mouth, licking a path up the center of my palm.

"Help me out, woman," he rasps, wrapping my hand around his erection, helping me give it that first stroke. "Gonna blow real fast thinking about you lying there, taking it last night. Wet, screaming little thing."

On a hoarse moan, my thighs squeeze together. In two seconds flat, I go from pretty horny to a bridesmaid who caught the bouquet, then took three shots of tequila and fell down a Tumblr rabbit hole. I'm lying naked in the dark with this sex god's arousal in my hand, stickiness forming between my legs and I have no inhibitions. None. He threw them down the garbage disposal last night by refusing to let me be ashamed of what I like. What I need. I know what Will needs, too, and I'm going to give it to him now.

While my hand eases down to his base, then chokes up to his tip in slow, firm strokes, I slide up to whisper in his ear. "You take such good care of me, Will."

His stomach was already bottoming out and shuddering, but with my words, it hits rock bottom and he groans, his big body twisting in the sheets. "Do I, baby?"

"Yes," I murmur, tracing my tongue along the curve of his ear. Just like my long-hidden fantasy, there was truth threaded through the act, but there was no harm in the occasional blurred edges of those truths. Do I need to be taken care of? No. I pride myself on the opposite. But we'll both get pleasure out of setting that reality aside. After the selflessness he showed me last night, I happily throw my pride out the window—same as he did for me—and the freedom is inebriating. "No one has ever made me feel this safe. Or given me a bed this soft to sleep in."

His back heaves with two punctuated grunts, his flesh swelling in my hand. "That's right. There'll only be safe places from now on for you." His grip covers mine, squeezing once, then dropping to handle his balls. I'm almost outraged that my other hand isn't available to do that for him, but I'm appeased when his body vibrates with pleasure against mine. "Going to treat you like a goddamn queen. My lap is your throne. Sit on it, make a wish and get whatever the fuck you want."

"Really?" I breathe, awe lacing that single word without me having to think, my intuition simply informing me what Will needs. And that need is so damn hot, because his wanting to play my provider isn't about him showing off or throwing money around, it's about him having a deeply woven desire to give. To satisfy.

And I've read him right, because with a snarl, he begins thrusting into my fist, hips pumping like a repressed animal. "That's right, baby." His groan is choked. "Can't stop thinking about ways to spoil you rotten."

"Tell me."

The drives of his hips slow but remain intense, every inch of him sliding through my fingers to take advantage. Luxuriating, almost. "I'm flying you to New York today on a private plane." Against my wrist, I can feel his forearm contracting with a rough squeeze of his balls. "Going to introduce you as my girlfriend, going to sit back and watch you sip champagne."

An even sharper ache begins between my thighs, a hot throbbing that makes me plaster myself against Will even closer, my tongue and teeth going to work on his neck. "And once I'm half drunk on champagne…then what?"

"*You know what.*" A shudder passes through him, and a spurt of liquid leaks out over my knuckles. "When there's only five minutes left in the flight, I'm going to take you in back and fuck you so hard against the bathroom door, your legs will still be rubber when I buckle you into our car."

I'm grinding myself against his ass now, dragging the lips of my sex over the hard slope of the closest cheek. I'm a mindless Will addict with two goals. Make him come in my hand, and find an angle where I can get a single rub of friction for my poor clit. Just one and I'll lose my mind. "And…and…"

"And what, Teresa?"

His use of my name is what loosens the words stuck in my throat. "When you're taking me in the bathroom, am I…thanking you for treating me so good?"

I feel it in my stomach. My chest and head. The exact moment our two newborn fantasies combine into one. His need to be a provider and my desire to be possessed. A possession. It's like having an oxygen mask slapped over my mouth, air inflating my lungs. Will is right there with me, pausing in his relentless thrusts, only to begin anew, pistoning into my tight grip like a man hell-bent on destroying himself. "You want to open your legs and pay fealty to your king, baby?" His words are gritted out. "I'll accept like the town fucking beggar."

Will's body seizes against mine, a choked curse bouncing off the walls of the dark room. Hot moisture coats my still-pumping hand, his back heaving against my front like violent ocean swells. I'm almost there. I'm almost there, but my angle isn't right and I blindly push at Will's hips, begging him to understand what I'm asking for, even though I barely know. I've never done what I'm thinking and don't even know if it's possible, but I need, I need, I need…

Still panting, he turns onto his stomach I climb on top of him, burying my open mouth in his back as I drag my soaked and aching pussy up and down the right curve of his hard butt. In my periphery, I see his hands twist in the sheets, a roar breaking from his throat. "Goddamn. You get that hot jerking me off?"

"Yes," I sob, pressure climbing my throat, my private inner walls beginning to contract wildly. My writhing movements have parted my flesh, giving my clit the glorious friction it needs, and my orgasm shatters me. A scream ripples up through my chest and I fall forward, stabbing my nails into Will's flexed biceps, my heart slamming around inside my head. Beating, beating. All of me is beating and clenching until it's not. I'm not. And I'm just a blind lump of human parts glued to Will's strong, incredible back. "Morning," I manage around a yawn.

He shakes beneath me with a warm chuckle. "Damn, Teresa. Just *damn*."

I try to lift my head and fail. "What?"

"You make me feel in charge and used at the same time."

My gut trembles. "Is that good or bad?"

He turns slowly, nestling me back into the pillows, those cut arms like pillars on either side of me. And for the first time this morning, we're making eye contact. I drown in it willingly, losing my breath all over again. "Good doesn't cut it, Teresa. I'd kill for what we've got here. I'm out of my damn head for you."

"Thanks for clearing that up," I say in a shaky whisper. The real world is beginning to creep in around the edges now that Will is talking about the future, the long term—*us*. I desperately want to block it out, but when I grasp for a distraction, all I find is the driving urge to confess how I feel before it's too late. "I couldn't have predicted you, Will. Which seems impossible, doesn't it?" There's a hot press of tears behind my eyes, but I will them away. "How could I miss you coming when you make the earth shake beneath my feet?"

"Teresa," he says on a rush of breath, like I've caught him off guard, but he's still going to collect his unexpected fortune greedily. "Just let it shake. I am."

"Okay." I nod, threading my fingers through his hair and wishing I'd had more foresight. Wishing I hadn't let my lie fester this long. "I-I'll try."

"I need you to know, baby. This thing inside me...wanting you spoiled and respected and *safe*...I've never wanted or needed that for anyone else. *You* did this to me. You're the only one who could. Understand?" He leaves a gentle tongue kiss on my lips. "We can get nasty in bed and play like you're a grateful girl. Or like I'm paying for privileges. But you remember that my fucking ground is shaking because of you, too."

Oh God. Oh God.

This feels like love. Or if not love, something that is rapidly germinating into it. My chest is a wide-open cavity, but I'm also wrapped in security, courtesy of the man above me. I have no experience with love, so I don't know how to identify it, but...shit, what else feels this way?

So this is it. I have to come clean. If I have a chance in hell of keeping him, I can't let him climb out of this bed and leave this cocoon where I have some chance of reaching him. "Will."

His eyebrows draw together at my tone change. "Yeah?"

Southpaw bounds onto the bed, his head tunneling into the scarce space between our bodies. His tongue catches me in the nose and cheek, making me gasp and try to squirm away, eventually giving in to a giggle. Will's own laugh booms through the dark room as he pushes up, wrapping the dog in a bear hug. "How's that for a wake-up call, huh?" Will noogies the dog, who reacts with absolute tongue-lolling delight. "Time for his medicine, actually, then I need to get him outside. It's late." He winks at me. "For some reason, I've been getting the best sleep of my life lately. You know anything about that?"

"Maybe," I manage around the lump in my throat, seeing my opportunity to tell the truth slipping away as Will throws on a pair of jeans. "Um. I—"

I'm interrupted by a bark, and my nerve fades, fades away like it was never there. Will watches me a moment, before they head out the door and I'm left sitting up in bed, covers clutched to my chest, feeling as though there's a whirlpool swirling on all sides of me, preparing to suck me down.

CHAPTER TWENTY-TWO

Will

SOUTHPAW'S MEDICINE IS missing. Like a greedy motherfucker, I wanted to get back to Teresa, so we jogged around the hotel grounds two quick times, before Southpaw took care of business. Now, I'm riffling through my suitcase and every jacket I own, looking for the little orange pill bottle so I can crush it up and put it in his breakfast. He's sitting on his hind legs, looking up at me with a classic head tilt on the kitchen floor and my throat is starting to tighten with panic. He's never missed a dose before and I don't know what happens if he does.

"Teresa." Her name is out of my mouth before I realize it. "Baby."

"Yeah?"

I look up to find her walking into the kitchen, looking concerned, hair wet from her shower. She's in a T-shirt and panties, like I interrupted her in the middle of getting ready. Not even my worry can keep me from formulating a plan to fuck her up against the counter as soon as I get Southpaw his meds, but I'm struck more by how much less alone I feel as soon as she gets close. Like I'm on a team. I've always been solo, whether while boxing or running a company from my cold, quiet office. Not right now, though. Christ, I want to drag her up against me and breathe her scent until I'm back on solid ground.

"Can't find his medicine," I say instead. "Any ideas?"

Obvious worry sends her hand fluttering to her throat, and guilt pinches me in the sternum, but I still can't regret calling for her. Not when she makes my load feel so much damn lighter. "I saw you put it in your pocket yesterday. In the morning."

"Right." Mentally, I retrace my steps. "Before we went to the park."

"Oh God." Her eyes widen. "You don't think it fell out in the water, do you?"

"Shit. It's possible." I scrub a hand over my face. "If it did, it's long gone."

She gets on her knees and scratches Southpaw behind the ear. He edges closer, propping his jaw on her shoulder. "Well, maybe we shouldn't waste too much time looking for it. There has to be a vet nearby that can fill the prescription."

"Okay. Yeah. We'll have to push back the flight, but this can't wait."

"No. Don't chance it."

I'm man enough to admit my hands aren't completely steady as I find my phone on the counter and pull up a search engine. Teresa drops into a cross-legged position and stays there while I dial the closest vet and make an emergency appointment, filling them in on the details of our New York vet to save time when we get there. When I hang up, Teresa smiles at me and I'm back in control. "I thought I'd figured out how to take care of him. Looks like there are a couple holes in that theory." I shake my head, wishing she was closer. Unable to keep myself from telling her everything. "Maybe this road trip wasn't a good thing for him. Maybe it's making things worse."

"No, Will. You're doing great. He's loving every second." I start to correct her—that *we're* doing great now, the three of us—but she stands, looking...troubled. Worse. Like she did back in the bedroom. My body seems to brace itself, head to toe. "Sometimes you throw a solution a dartboard when you're trying to do the right thing for someone you love. I've done that for my brother, thinking I was acting out of love. I thought love meant the randomness didn't matter." Her hands meet at her waist, twisting in her shirt. "Turns out, it matters a lot."

"Talk to me, Teresa."

"I'm trying."

When her voice cracks, something inside me does, too. I don't know exactly what's coming, but I know it's bad. Bad enough that her teeth are chattering and she's swaying on her feet. "Come here," I rasp, compelled to wrap my arms around her, no matter what she's about to tell me. "Come here." I step forward, holding out my hand. "You look like you're freezing."

My cell phone goes off and she jumps, backing away. "Will…"

I glance down and find the name of my associate in New York flashing on the screen. With a hollow chest, I slide my finger across the screen and hold it to my ear. "What is it?"

"Mr. Caruso. Can you talk?"

He's asking if I'm alone. Meaning the information he has is sensitive. Enough that he's pretty positive I don't want anyone around when he relates it. My heart wakes up with a vengeance, firing around my ribcage in every direction. "Yeah."

"I've obtained the travel records for Miss Valentini." It's made clear by Teresa's sudden wheeze that she can hear every word being spoken. My instinct to comfort her is resounding inside me, but I'm cemented to the ground, waiting for the axe to drop. What the fuck is this? "She was in New York as recently as last week. I still couldn't connect her with any of your competitors, but…on a hunch, I ran a cross check against another, older report I compiled for you." My stomach plummets, because I know from his tone which report he's speaking about. Disbelief plows into me like a semi truck. "The one—"

"Jesus. Don't say it."

"I'm sorry, sir." He pauses. "I called in a favor with my contact at the NYPD. Teresa Valentini's father is a past associate of *your* father. Quite well known, in fact, for leaving their ranks roughly a decade ago. He's since passed away, but I have a hard time believing Miss Valentini arriving in New York, then appearing in Texas with you, is a coincidence."

So did I. In the beginning, I was suspicious as hell, questioning every move she made, every word out of her mouth. Until I stopped. Until I couldn't hear my own common sense over the volume of my stupid heard pounding for her.

I hang up, refusing to listen to any more damning information. Jesus Christ, I'm an idiot. A crashing sound starts in my ears, the white noise accompanied by a stab of broken glass in my chest...but when I look down, there's nothing there. Only my numb hands that don't look familiar. Betrayal tightens them until my knuckles are white and it's so familiar. So fucking familiar. Wanting to make someone happy and only getting played in return.

"Will. Listen to me."

Her tearful voice tries to intrude on my rage, but I refuse to hear the suffering in it. No, I only want to increase that suffering until it amounts to even a *fraction* of mine. Nothing. This woman felt nothing for me and all the while I was falling in love with her. "What did my father offer you, Miss Valentini?" She flinches at my use of such a formal address. "Why would you make a deal with the devil?"

When she walked into the kitchen, she was so comfortable in her panties and T-shirt, but now she tries to shield herself with useless hands and I shouldn't ache watching it. I shouldn't want to wrap her in a blanket. *Goddammit.* "I-I was going to tell you *everything* this morning—"

"Well, here's your big chance."

She squeezes her eyes closed, seemingly against the chill in my voice. "My job was to bring you back to New York. Back to the business, before it fell apart without you. That was all. There was no money involved. Will, please *listen.* He has my br—"

My chest is being crushed between two spiked walls and they close in tighter with each new confession. All her phony hesitation over us returning to New York together was a sham. None of what happened between us was real. None of it. "Back to the business. Before it fell apart." Confusion pierces the edges of my misery. "Why would he give a shit about my company?"

"He…" She swipes at her damp cheeks, confusion beginning to dawn in her eyes. "In some backwards way, he wants you to succeed. Doesn't want you to throw it all away. That's what he told me." A shudder catches her. "That's the only way I could justify this to myself."

"That's bullshit, Teresa. There has to be another reason. Didn't you stop to think that this man who makes a living off the backs of honest people—this man who lied to me for thirty-two years—could be lying to you, too?"

"Yes. I did. I did."

"Well, why didn't you tell me?"

"Because you'd hate me. Because he sent someone to follow us." She sniffs. "He was back in Dallas and I saw him again on the highway. If I told you the truth and you freaked out or left me behind, he could have reported it—"

"There was someone *watching* us?" She nods slowly and a buzzing starts in my head, the sharp tip of violence spearing me. "Of all things, you should have told me we were being followed, Teresa. You knew what your safety meant to me, but you'd already taken away the privilege of ensuring it."

Her shoulders sag. "No. Please don't think of it like that."

I barrel straight through her plea. I don't want to hear it. She could have been hurt and I would have been in the goddamn dark. "Is he here now? In *this* fucking place?"

"No," she rushes to say. "No, I think he's gone. It was probably just to scare me into…"

"Into screwing me over faster." The lifeblood in my veins freezes over and I'm just fucking numb. "Into screwing me, period. Christ. That's how you planned to get me back to New York, isn't it?"

Nothing moves. This time and place is frozen, along with my blood. Except for Teresa, who shrinks in on herself, cupping her elbows. "I wasn't going to sleep with you. I was just going to…go far enough that you followed me east. But you're you. And I couldn't…I-I couldn't…I didn't know you'd *get* to me this way. Every time you touched me it was real. *We* were real."

"I don't believe you."

She sinks down to her knees slowly, knuckles crammed to her mouth and I lurch forward to catch her. Old habits I need to kill hard. She doesn't want this thing between us—it was just a job to her. I'm a job. She conned me—and she is still trying to dupe me with this wounded act. Still lying about how she feels. I'm not going to make myself more of a fool by letting her know *my* feelings haven't faded by one fucking degree. That they never will.

That truth only serves to strengthen my anger. None of it was real for her, but it was for me. She knew that. She knew how I felt and used it against me to do my father's dirty work.

"I'm *sorry* about everything," she whispers. "Can we please find out what Silas really wants together? Can we…fix this together?"

"No." The need to lash out rises up and swims in my head, turning my stomach. "You knew how I felt about him. You had to know that when I found out—because I was *always* going to find out—that I'd shut your game down fast enough to make your head spin."

She reacts like she's been slapped, but sobers fast, putting her hands out in an imploring way, inching forward on her knees. *God,* I hate her down there. I hate it and love it at the same time. "He has my brother." Her sob is anguished. "You...I haven't told you everything about my family, but if you knew what my parents did to get away from Silas, you would understand why I was scared enough to-to risk hurting you."

Light tries to pierce the fog around me—maybe even hope— but it's too late. I'm enshrouded in thick blackness. Back in that nauseated state I was in before leaving New York. How did this happen so soon? How did I *let* it happen? "If I haven't convinced you by now that I would have moved mountains to help you, Teresa, this was nothing but a waste of time."

"Don't say that. I'm sorry. I'm so sorry."

"A little late for that, baby." Despite my harsh words, optimism dances across her face at me calling her baby. Seeing her optimism sparks my own and I need to douse it. Need to. Before it grows and I forgive her. Before I open myself up for being burned a third time. No more. I'm done. And I need her to be done, too, so the avenue back to her is closed for good. Ignoring the buzz of warning in the back of my head, I pick my wallet up off the counter and take out all the money inside, tossing it on the ground in front of her. "Guess it wasn't such a fantasy after all."

I turn away from her shock and pain before it can force me down to my knees to apologize. I almost do, though. I come so fucking close because she's dug herself a home inside me and her

215

suffering is unacceptable.

"Will, please. Please don't call him. If he knows I told you, he could hurt my brother. Promise me."

The fact that she's asking for promises now—after everything—makes it possible to force my armor into place and command myself to register nothing. Nothing as I snap on Southpaw's leash and walk out the door, focusing on one task at a time. Keep moving. Get the medicine. Keep breathing. It's all I can do when I've had the heart ripped out of my chest.

CHAPTER TWENTY-THREE

Teresa

A KNIFE TWISTS in my gut as I stare down at the money on the floor.

I can't move.

At least until a sob wells up, the force of it tipping me backwards onto my ass.

What have I done? *What have I done?*

Shit. Oh God. Deep down, I didn't expect him to react this way. Which I realize is ridiculous. Utterly stupid. But I honestly believed when I told him Silas had my brother, he would snap out of it and understand I had no choice. I did have a choice, though, didn't I? Will was right. He has given me every reason to confide in him, despite his father's increased threats and my trust issues with men. Will proved himself. His reward was my betrayal.

Every single part of me hurts. My face is blazing hot and covered in tears, but lifting my hand to wipe them away seems like more of an effort than I'm worth.

No. Screw that. That's not right.

I'm worth more than the pile of money mocking me on the ground. If I've learned anything during my time with Will, it's that. Or my self-worth was always there, but I needed a little push to recognize it. I need to concentrate on that newfound confidence now. I can collapse later. I can mourn the man I've lost with my bad decisions and fears, but not right now. Not when my brother is still in danger and my only hope of saving him just stomped on my heart and walked out the door.

I try to stand up, but my muscles shake and I drop down again onto my butt. Tears streak down my cheeks, carrying loss and nerves over the task ahead…but looking at the money piled on the floor, I'm…humiliated. Yeah. Wasn't that the point? He wanted to hurt me and he has. He has. He turned what we did together into something ugly to get me back. Whether it was done with malice or purely out of damaged male pride, it hit the mark. Hard.

Taking a deep breath, I replay that image of him tossing down the money and I hold on to it. Tight. I disregard the conflict in his eyes and remember only the curled lip, the cold way he turned his back. The fire it lights inside me is what I need to get off the floor. Slowly. In degrees. My legs don't want to work, but I force them to support me as I walk to the bedroom. Momentum and adrenaline kick in within seconds and I'm packing like a mad woman, shoving things into my suitcase, ripping my cell phone charger out of the wall and donning the first available pair of pants. In the process, I step on one of Southpaw's chew toys and very nearly falter, but I keep going. And going.

Until I'm out the door.

Will

ENDING UP IN the vet's office so soon is not the plan. Southpaw has more time. We were going to live every day like it was his last, until it actually was. His last. We aren't supposed to be in a quiet, beige room, waiting for another man in a white coat to tell me he's got a limited amount of time. I don't need to hear the words again. Don't need them to rip me wide open when I'm already walking around like I'm half dead.

Southpaw is sitting on the floor between my legs, his head resting in my lap. He senses I'm fucked up and it shouldn't be that way. I should be able to get my head together and get through this appointment for him—after all, I'm the one who lost his medicine...while pulling him and Teresa out of the rapid.

An arrow of doubt attempts to break through my defenses, but I harden myself further, letting it bounce off. Teresa was lying to me the entire time we were together. Nothing is going to change that. Not even the selfless act of jumping into the river.

Right before she almost drowned saving my dog, she'd turned down my offer to fly her back to New York. Why? Had she actually felt guilty?

No. She was just that good. I'd walked away from that conversation twice as determined to make her let me in, which was probably her intention. Little did I know I was nothing more than a means to an end from the moment we met.

A memory of her face as I emptied my wallet on the floor makes my skin feel like it's covered in ice. I shove the heel of my hand into my right eye, trying to get rid of that final, devastated image of her, but it won't budge. *Goddammit.*

Sometimes you throw a solution a dartboard when you're trying to do the right thing for someone you love. I've done that for my brother, thinking I was acting out of love. I thought love meant the randomness didn't matter. Turns out, it matters a lot.

More of that earlier doubt starts to pop up, but I swipe it away, like pawns off a chessboard. Teresa's sore spot might be her brother, but I'm not going to accept that bullshit excuse. She came into my life under false pretenses and maneuvered me to her liking. It might have seemed real—more real than anything in my life—but it wasn't.

I can't forget that.

To my left, the door opens and in walks the vet. I can barely manage an acknowledgment, the goddamn memory of Teresa on her knees is biting into my brain with razor-sharp teeth. "His meds," I force out. There's a sense of urgency closing around my throat with every passing second, but I have no idea why. I have no reason to be anywhere. Still… "I just need the meds so we can go."

"I need to speak with you, Mr. Caruso. About those meds." The vet looks somewhat incredulous as he studies the file in his hands. "Southpaw doesn't need them."

The gut intuition that Teresa has no doubt already bailed hits me—*hard*—but the vet's words knock me even further off balance. "What do you mean he doesn't need them?"

"Before we could prescribe medication, we needed to contact your vet in New York to get Southpaw's records. It was highly unusual of your vet to diagnose Southpaw without having the test results back from the lab, but I have to agree with him, Southpaw's condition seemed clear. I'm not so sure I wouldn't have drawn the same conclusions."

Time slows to a halt. "What are you saying? Is he…"

"Originally, the lump on Southpaw's front right paw was diagnosed as a malignant melanoma. Because of the placement, Southpaw likely spent some time agitating the area by scratching at it or using his teeth to bite the affected area, leading to pretty visible infection. I'm guessing that's what led to the misdiagnosis. The medicine he's been taking relieved him of the infection, thankfully, so he's left with nothing more than a benign melano-ma." I can hear his smile stretching wide, the air is so quiet around me. "Southpaw needs surgery. There'll be some recovery time. Lots of rest and a dip in his appetite. But the good news is he's not..." He lowers his voice to a whisper. "Dying. Your vet in New York has been leaving messages at your office for the last couple weeks. He was relieved to know you'd finally be getting the news."

Knots upon knots untie inside me with such a swiftness, the unexpected relief would have knocked me on my ass if I wasn't already sitting. The reprieve of darkness is so fast I'm immediately suspicious. "But he's been sluggish, on and off. I—"

"That's not unusual. The area is likely tender or sore, especially with all the running around he's been doing. A few weeks after surgery, he'll be good as new."

"Holy shit," I choke out, pulling my dog up onto my lap. He comes happily, wagging and panting, letting out a bark when I wrap my arms around his neck. Every time I've held him over the last month, I've wondered if it was the last time. Not having to speculate on that anymore is like being pumped full of helium. "Holy shit, buddy."

I've fallen through a trap door and I'm floating, no gravity to pull me down. My dog isn't dying. He's going to be fine. *My dog isn't dying.* But I hit bottom hard when I look around, needing to tell Teresa the news...and she's not there. She's gone.

I'VE JUST BEEN handed a miracle. That's the only reason I'm holding on to the possibility that Teresa will be inside the hotel room when we burst inside. She and I? We're not finished having this argument—not by a damn sight. I have more to say. She was supposed to scream back at me this morning, not fall onto her knees like a stringless puppet, dammit. That's the *only* reason I drove here at one hundred miles an hour.

To go another round.

But I know the moment I open the door that she's gone. The money is still scattered on the floor. The plane reservation I printed out earlier remains untouched on the entry table. There's no life inside, just a shell of a place that she had the nerve to make feel like home. When that last iota of optimism dries up, panic stomps all over the barrier I've erected.

If her brother is in New York, that's where she's headed.

Will, please. Please don't call him. If he knows I told you, he could hurt my brother. Promise me.

My stomach rises up in rebellion. She failed to do the job my father gave her. She's returning to New York without me. Empty handed. That puts her in danger—and I sent her right into it. Alone.

"*Teresa!*"

I shout her name, as if it'll conjure her up. I tried calling her cell on the way here even though I suspected it was useless. Now, I storm through the rooms, stopping in hers when I find the drawers open, her things long gone. The floor seems to rise up around me, sweat forming on my forehead.

No. No, no, no. I just need the morning back. Give me the morning back.

Southpaw jumps up on Teresa's bed and sniffs it, glancing over at me. As if to say, *what did you do, asshole?* On the bedside table, there are a couple balled-up tissues. To dry her tears? A sound climbs my throat at the evidence, but I'm distracted when I see a shiny black object peeking out from beneath them. I pounce like a beggar who spies a twenty on the sidewalk, snatching it up.

Her GoPro. She left it.

I start to shove the device into my pocket, but something stops me. Instead, I turn it on and hit play, holding my breath when I see…white, bubbling water on the screen. And Southpaw. It's the rapid. In the confusion of that day, I forgot Teresa had strapped the camera to his collar to capture what he does on his own in the woods.

"Okay," says Teresa's voice, through the camera. "Okay, buddy. It's fine. Just hang on."

Instead, she caught them fighting to stay above water in the river.

"Oh, this is bad. This is really, really bad." Teresa's voice fills the room, full of terror and—incredibly—humor at the same time. Her words are almost inaudible because of the water rushing in the background, so I turn up the volume and press it to my ear. "You have to stay, like, as long as you can. For him, okay? Because I can't. He's not going to want me. Come on. *Come on.* Where's the fucking shore?" The humor is beginning to slide from her voice and it's like I'm reliving the horrific moment I saw her being carried away by the current. "I could love him. Maybe I already do. I could love you, too, even though your giant ass is the reason I'm going to die."

I'm being flayed wide open where I stand. Hemorrhaging blood all over the carpet. She could love me? Maybe she already does?

Everything comes crashing in at once. Snippets of the last few days. Southpaw protecting Teresa in the hallway of that fleabag motel. Her vulnerability the first time I kissed her, like she wasn't expecting to feel that fucking free fall. The same one I felt. The exhilaration on her face when she won that arm-wrestling contest. And threw herself into my arms…

Not fake. Was *any* of the good stuff fake?

I swallow a fist-sized lump, but another one forms in its place. One thing definitely isn't phony. The danger she's in. The danger she would have avoided if we'd gone back to New York together.

We didn't, though. She went. She's gone and I'm still fucking *here*. While the full magnitude of what she could be walking into cuts me in half, an echo of her past fear plays in the room, like a premonition.

"Will," she whimpers through the camera. "This is bad."

"Dammit, Teresa." I drop the camera and punch a hole through the wall. "*Goddammit.*"

Today's nightmarish roller coaster isn't over, though. When I get to the airport, I'm informed my flight has been pushed back because of bad weather in New York. No amount of bribing or threatening can help me. I'm left with no choice but to climb the walls praying Teresa's flight is also grounded, somewhere in the airport. But after searching the place top to bottom—and considering the two-hour jump she got on me—that hope fades way too fast.

In the place of that hope, rage springs up like a demon from hell.

So help me God, if she has a single scratch by the time I reach her, nobody will be safe. Nobody.

CHAPTER TWENTY-FOUR

Teresa

E DITING WOULD BE key at this stage of my film. As I walk through the same side door of Tommaso's to meet with Silas Case, there would be flashbacks to the girl who faced the devil with her false bravado firmly intact. Not a single hitch in her stride or glint of fear in her eyes while looking down the end of a gun barrel and accepting orders that would change her forever. On the inside, that girl with the head full of steam was shaking in her high heels.

What a switch, huh? A matter of days later, I'm full of enough determination and go-ahead-and-fuck-with-me-ness to fill a stadium. I'm here to get my brother back and I'll lie, cheat and steal to do it. On the outside, though. God, on the outside my once impressive façade has crumbled. A glance in my Uber's rearview mirror on the way from JFK to Staten Island reflected back red-rimmed eyes, the corners of my lips weighted down by invisible grief. My pure, dogged refusal to fail in my mission has not reached the fractured pieces of my heart—and that, that is what's showing on my face. I don't have the extra energy to control that.

Will has called me several times. I'm not returning those calls, though. It's over. I'm not looking back. There's only tonight and whatever I have to do to get Nicky out safe and alive. I'll worry about tomorrow when it gets here. Am I worried that this mutilation plaguing my insides might make me less objective when it comes to my own safety?

Yeah. Yeah, I'm a little scared about that, but I'm out of choices.

When I round the corner into the dining room of the restaurant, it's empty except for Silas, just like last time. He's smiling at me, an arm draped over the booth of his usual seat. Craggy eyebrows lift at my grim appearance. After taking a paper towel bath, forgoing makeup and changing into my only remaining clean pair of clothes—a jean skirt and a long-sleeved baseball T-shirt—his reaction doesn't surprise me. I'm a hot mess.

"You look like you could use a drink," Silas says.

I stop in front of his table. "Where is Nicky?"

He twists a rocks glass full of dark liquid on the table. "Not up for small talk, are we?" His pleasant expression fades, his features hardening, making him appear almost reptilian. "Have you returned my son to New York?"

It's deadly obvious he already knows the answer. Did White Baseball Cap track me down again and report back, without me knowing he was watching? This morning, I was so careful to leave the hotel through the side exits, ducking down in the backseat of my Uber as we pulled through security and onto the road, but it's possible our tail watched Will storm off with Southpaw. Alone.

Or did Will simply call Silas and give me up?

Panic flutters in my throat, but I swallow it down. No. He might hate me, but he wouldn't do something that could get me killed. I have to believe that. "No." I clear the cobwebs from my throat. "I guess I'm not as charming as you thought."

"But I thought things were going so well." A thick silence passes. "You wore your special red dress last night and everything."

Bile burns my esophagus, but I don't let him see my utter disgust over the fact that such an intimate moment with Will was tarnished. Even if I didn't know at the time. What does it matter now anyway? All the moments are tarnished now, aren't they? Will thought me falling for him was nothing more than an act. "He wasn't interested past a few days," I say, shrugging off the sting.

"*Nights*, you mean." Smirking, Silas leans back in his seat. One yellowing finger lifts and punches the air in my direction. "He got to you."

No energy. None to lie. Besides, the man has eyes, and I currently resemble the living dead. "Yeah. He did."

"If you told him I sent you, you're dead. You realize that."

The sudden threat is a hammer to my solar plexus. "If I told him who sent me, you would have heard about it by now. I'm not stupid enough to risk it. He hates you."

There isn't so much as a flicker of grief in his expression at the word *hates*—and that's when I know Will was right. There's more to Silas wanting Will back in New York than a father's concern. "He'd risk your life?"

"Like I said, I was just a few nights to him." After my lies and the way he left me devastated on my knees, those words are as good as true. But I harden myself against the hurt. I just need to get through this. Just get through tonight. "I'm done talking about him. Tell me another way to get my brother back."

He tilts his head. "Who said there is another way?"

Don't freak out. "On the phone, you said I had until Friday or Nicky would be sent out on a job." I lick my lips and plunge ahead. "Let me take his place."

His smile is back, but it's got an edge of incredulity that wasn't there before. "If you didn't look like warmed-over shit, I wouldn't believe my son had really kicked you to the curb. You got brass ones, sweetheart. I'll give you that."

"Swell." Despite my attempts to numb myself, his shot finds its mark. Not that I let it show. "Tell me what I need to do. And then swear to me once it's done, you'll let me and my brother leave and never hear from you again."

"Here's the thing." His laugh turns my stomach. "I don't need you to do shit for me. I don't need your brother, either. You had a job and you failed. Why should I send a proven fuck-up out to represent me?"

I can't keep panic from sinking in its claws any longer. "What about...what you said on the phone?"

"Incentive," he tosses out, scratching the corner of his eye. "You were incentive to get Will back to New York. Your brother's job was incentive to get you moving faster. You're a smart girl. I shouldn't have to explain this to you."

"So there is no job?"

"There is." He checks his watch, then returns his attention to me. Several beats pass in silence, before he shrugs. "I guess we'll tie up this loose end one way or another." With that ominous statement hanging in the air, he rattles off an address. "That's the address where your brother is set to be picked up by two of my guys. I'll tell them to swing by fifteen minutes earlier than planned and take you instead."

Air inflates my lungs. "I can take his place? One job and we're out?"

"If you make it through the night." He appears thoughtful. "It occurs to me that if you're lying or maybe even oblivious to how my son feels about you, I could be bringing a fucking war down on my head by putting you in danger."

Snorting, I turn on a heel. "Please. He already forgot my name."

As soon as I hit the curb outside, a sound curls in my throat.

Please, Will, don't ever, ever forget my name.

WHATEVER I EXPECTED when I took Nicky's place, this is ten times worse.

Since yesterday, I've eaten nothing but roasted airplane peanuts and they jump around in my stomach now, leaving me full of holes. I arrived at the address given to me by Silas and was promptly picked up by two dudes in a sparkling new SUV. They weren't surprised to see me, but no pleasantries were exchanged, either. I was coming along to be a witness. An act to make me complicit, so when Nicky and I leave New York, we'll keep our mouths shut, lest we bring charges down on our own heads. The famous one last job trick—there's a reason for it. Insurance.

Whack. The sound of bone crunching sends me cringing into the wall.

Nausea wells up inside me, the airplane peanuts threatening to climb my throat. We're in a storage room in the back of a pawn shop. The two men who drove me here have tied the owner to a chair and…I stopped listening after they demanded money and started hitting him, demanding what they're owed. Or what Silas is owed, rather. The shop owner moans through a bloody mouth and I start to tremble.

"Come here, princess."

I've wrapped myself in a security blanket of fog and I don't realize they're speaking to me. But when I'm dragged forward by my elbow, I have no choice but to rejoin my surroundings. The moaning owner is now directly in front of me, pain glazing eyes that implore me to help. I'm paralyzed just imagining the pain he's in. No one deserves this. No one.

"He knew what would happen. He's not innocent." Something cold is pressed into my hands. A gun. Oh God, it's a gun.

"Silas said to make sure you did the honors."

No. No. It wasn't enough to have me play a complicit witness. He needs this? My humanity? Just like the strip of flesh he took from my father, he's doing the same to me. How could I have expected any less? I sway on my feet at a sudden memory of my father, looking haunted in the moonlight when he didn't know I was watching. If he knew what was being asked of me, what would he say? He'd beg me not to turn out like him. He would do everything to prevent it.

A hand urges my arm up, so I'm pointing the gun. I'm pointing it at an actual human being. It's him or my brother, isn't it? But that can't be the only option. A vision of Will swims into focus, intense and huge and beautiful…and despite what I've been telling myself, telling Silas, heat begins to trickle in through the cold I've encased myself in all day, out of necessity.

I used to wake up at five in the morning. And now, it's like I'm making up for every single minute of sleep I've missed my entire life. Maybe I was missing sleep because I knew you were out there, baby, and I hadn't met you yet.

With those words—words spoken with conviction that no longer exists—tumbling in my head…the echo of that love refuses to let me pull the trigger. I never could have, anyway, and lived with myself. Even if it meant breaking Nicky free of this life, this isn't a cost I can live with. Nor could my brother. "I won't do it," I whisper, dropping the gun to my side where it dangles in bloodless fingers. "I can't."

"Silas asked us to encourage you."

I look back over my shoulder at the men, and seeing their eyes for the first time, I'm alarmed by the lack of life in them. "What does that mean?"

A backhand catches me across the face and I stumble sideways, knocking into a metal rack of merchandise. My ass hits the floor a second later, but I'm too dizzy to stand. The throbbing that screams to life along my eye and cheekbone makes me gasp. That wasn't just a fist—I tasted metal. I take another hard punch to the side of my head and the room shrinks in around me. His fist rises again—

The back door flies open and I whip my head around to find Nicky standing in the frame, his hair in eighty directions.

"Shit, Teresa. *No.*"

I only have a couple fleeting seconds to take notice of how he's changed—grown up, turned wearier—since the last time I saw him, before he lifts a gun and points it at the man who slapped me.

"Nicky, don't—"

But that same man already has his weapon trained on me.

Slowly, Nicky lowers his gun and is immediately cracked across the jaw by the second man, dropping him to his knees, before receiving the second blow. My scream is the last thing I hear before everything goes dark.

CHAPTER TWENTY-FIVE

Will

S OMETIMES IT TAKES the worst fucking day of your life to put
things in perspective.

All the money in the world can't get me to New York on
time. I'm not more powerful than the weather and thus, the
woman I can no longer deny being gut-sick in love with has a
five-hour jump on me. Knowing Teresa, she wouldn't have
wasted any time getting from the airport to Staten Island, so
there's no chance she's waiting for tomorrow to get herself killed.
It's all happening now. Or it already happened and my life has
been reduced to ashes.

I'm in the backseat of a black police SUV, weaving through
traffic on the goddamn Verrazano Bridge. Two officers are taping
wires to my chest and repeating the same words over and over,
but I'm barely aware of their presence. My mind has retreated
into an almost trance-like state, forcing me to think painfully
clear thoughts to distract me from the reality I could be facing ten
minutes from now. Money. It couldn't help me when I needed it
most. It means nothing to me. But that's not some major
revelation. I've been driving in the opposite direction of New
York and my bank accounts for weeks now, trying to figure out
which man I'm meant to be. The man my father built, or the
man I was originally.

What I've learned today—on my hellishly long flight from Arkansas—is that my father could *not* have built the man who loves like this. Loves his dog—who is on the way home in the backseat of another vehicle. And loves a woman like the earth is ending. I am the man I set out to be. The path I took to get here changed, but I didn't.

He didn't touch the man on the inside. He didn't even come close.

More words spoken by Teresa in the dark. Even when I was livid with her for deceiving me, I should have known the parts that mattered hadn't been an act. There's no way I could have been changed for the better by something or some*one* false. No way I could have been this *affected*. Why didn't I listen to my instincts? If I lose her, if I let her walk away and get herself killed, it doesn't matter what kind of man I am. He'll be ripped clean out of me, leaving nothing but an empty husk behind.

I've been confident that my father would one day be held accountable for the lives he's ruined, including my mother's. I didn't expect to be racing the clock, waiting for some sign that he's got Teresa. Or that he's…hurt her. But my call to bring in the cops led to them asking me to cooperate. They think there's less of a chance of Teresa and Nicky—or any officers—being hurt in a crossfire if I go in and negotiate her release.

If it means Teresa walking out of this unharmed, I'll go to hell and back.

Another NYPD unit is staking out a restaurant called Tommaso's and Silas's house, but he hasn't left the restaurant for an hour—and he's alone. They assured me Teresa is nowhere to be seen. So where the hell is she? They're working on finding her brother, Nicky, but apparently he's so far off the damn grid, even the expert I've got working for me can't even find the beginning of a paper trail.

The tires of the SUV squeal as we floor it through a yellow light. The worst of the storm has passed, but water still sprinkles the windshield of the car, the droplets illuminated by passing headlights. I'm distracted by the memory of Teresa arm wrestling in Texas, when one of the officer's phone rings.

I sit forward as he answers. "Yes?" A pause. "The girl, too?"

Frigid cold grips me. We're going eighty down a residential block I don't recognize and I can barely keep myself from throwing myself out the nearest door. *"Where is she?"*

The officer takes a sharp turn and tosses the phone down. "Teresa Valentini and her brother, Nicholas Valentini, were brought in through the back entrance. She appears to be injured, but managed to walk on her own accord—"

Relief is like a whip cracking over my head, even though it's tempered with white-hot rage. Someone hurt her. Someone is going to pay. I don't hear the rest of what he says. I can't. I just focus on getting there. Getting to where I need to be. And when we're parked a few blocks away, I'm out of the still-running vehicle like a demon hell-bent on revenge, taking only the barest of seconds to compose myself before trying the restaurant door and finding it locked.

If any more proof was needed that Teresa was right and the man I've always tried to subdue inside me is alive and well, it comes when I step back and kick the door in. A man spins around in the doorway and reaches inside his coat, but I've taken him by surprise and he doesn't get there in time. I've got a few inches on him, so I swing in a downward arc and his face contorts in pain. I'd be lying if I said it wasn't satisfying. What kind of a monster stands guard while a woman needs medical attention so close by? He might even be the one who inflicted her pain. That possibility has me reaching down and gripping his collar, dragging him up for the punch that puts his lights out.

Adrenaline is pumping like motor oil in my veins, making everything else move in slow motion. It speeds up and narrows down to one thing when I turn at the end of the hallway, the dining room coming into view. Teresa. She's slumped on the floor with her hands tied behind her back. There's blood matting her hair and running a river down the side of her face, stemming from a hideous blow at her temple. Her eyes are so glassy and she's clearly disoriented, barely able to react to me walking in. I don't realize I'm shouting until my hearing returns with a sharp vengeance. The sound cuts off when I see the gun pointed at her head, all remaining oxygen leaving me in a rush.

"If you pull that trigger," I tell my father. "I will murder you with my bare hands."

The man I believed to be a hero for so long continues pointing the gun at an injured woman. *My* injured woman. Black blinks in front of my eyes, the motor oil in my veins turns to cement. Some part of me must have still thought he wasn't all bad. He is, though. He's a motherfucker without a conscience. And that means he'd pull that trigger.

Looking at Teresa, Silas tips his head toward me. "And here you thought he'd already forgotten your name."

"*Teresa.*" Her name sounds like it's being strangled out of me. I want to shout at her that me forgetting a single second with her is an impossibility, but I won't do that when it can be used against us. Still… "Look at me."

She doesn't. Even if—*when*—we get out of this alive, she could already be lost to me. I doubted her. I shamed her. Let her walk into this inferno alone. Why the hell would she forgive me? "Nicky," Teresa says finally, shivering. "Don't let him hurt Nicky."

For the first time, I notice the huddled figure across the room. A young man with the same coloring as Teresa. It's a testament to how distracted Teresa makes me, because he's seething so hard, I can't believe I didn't see him before. His hands are also tied, his wrath is aimed at my father's back. And I don't know what it is about this kid, but I'm instantly on his side. I'd built up some resentment without realizing it, thanks to his existence putting his sister in danger, but through his anger, I see it's about fear for his sister. So we're on the same damn page.

"I won't let him hurt either of you," I say, forcing my blood to go from a rapid boil to a simmer. "He wanted me in New York. Here I am."

"Too late," says Silas. "She chose what was behind door number two. A certain pawn shop owner is going to turn up sooner or later in the landfill and she's a loose end, along with her brother. Aren't you, sweetheart?"

The venomous look she sends my father makes me fall even more in love with her. Fierce, beautiful woman. "What about me?" Subtly as possible, I take a step in her direction. "You going to kill me, too?"

"You won't say shit about this, son." He turns his face up, half of his sickening smile illuminated in the dim light above. "You're going to get back to work now and protect both of our interests. Your little vacation has your investors spooked and there's talk of them pulling out. I can't have that."

My neck goes tight. "Why do you give a shit?"

"You made your mother an investor. She made me her partner. Turns out it pays to go straight. I'm making a nice income off your company, and you fucking off to God knows where isn't going to jeopardize that." By the time he finishes, my blood is rapping in my temples. "There's dirty money running through the lifeblood of your company, son. All traceable back to me. You get me arrested and expose me, you're going down, too."

Am I shocked? Yes and no. I knew this man was capable of

anything. Knew my mother had a weak spot when it came to my father. But on some level, I must have still believed he wanted my success for the right reasons. Not just so he could use me for his own ends. None of this matters now, though. Only getting Teresa and her brother out of here alive.

"I never gave a damn about the company. I never wanted any of it." Remembering the wire taped to my chest, I focus on keeping him talking. "Until now. When I found out what you really are, I looked at the company and saw something you built." I shake my head. "That's bullshit, though. It's mine. Nothing is going to take it away from me. But if you pull that trigger, make no mistake, I will burn it alive."

I feel, rather than see, Teresa's glance shoot toward me, but I'm afraid if I look at her injuries again, I'm going to lose my temper. "This is all hinging on a woman, huh?" He sounds almost curious. "I lied to you. She lied to you. What makes her sins excusable?"

"Your reasons were selfish. Hers weren't. And I don't need to explain another goddamn thing to you. Put the fucking gun down."

"*Will.*"

Teresa's scream pierces the air a second before pain cracks down on the back of my head. Red coats my vision, a ringing starting in my ears. Ignoring the expanding throb pushing behind my eyes, I spin around and catch a fist to the ribs. Not the man I took down upon walking in—no, this is the second man I would have remembered to be aware of if Teresa wasn't hanging in the balance. I'm so pissed about the attack taking my attention off what's happening behind me, I barely take the time to square up before I tackle the motherfucker and deliver my first blow. A second, third. He reaches for a gun in his waistband and my father's *no* sounds like it's coming from another planet. No matter, though, because I secure the weapon first and waste no time pointing it where it counts.

At Silas. Who is now pointing his gun at my attacker, not Teresa.

There is some humanity inside him. Or maybe it's still about money, just like it has always been. Whatever the reason, though, it's decades too late.

"Drop your gun. It's over."

He tries to swing the gun back toward Teresa and I don't hesitate. I fire. And maybe there's some love leftover for my father, because the bullet only catches him in the side. I'm moving before he even jerks back, throwing myself in between him and Teresa, knocking the gun free of his hand in the process. We both dive for it, just as loud shouting fills the room. Cops. Weapons drawn. My father stops attempting to grab the gun and simply goes still on the floor, his eyes closing, fingers threading together at the back of his head.

I spare him a final look, then turn away as an officer presses a knee into his back and cuffs him. I'm desperate to get the goddamn ropes off Teresa's wrists and have her in my arms. Even as I untie her, she still won't look at me, and God, it makes my heart drop to my knees, but I've been paying close attention to this woman. I know her. She takes pride in being independent, especially when it comes to protecting her brother, and she's considering what happened tonight a failure on her part. She doesn't want to be rescued when she's always been the cavalry. Not to mention, she shut me out the second I walked away. I might as well be a ghost here untying the knots around her wrists. I get that.

When the final length of rope is unwound, she mutters a thank you. Then she's off like a shot toward her brother to make sure he's okay where he sits on the floor, giving a statement to a kneeling policewoman. Letting Teresa walk away from me after almost losing her is like having my organs pried out, but I command myself to be patient.

Almost.

"Someone get her a fucking medic. *Now.*"

Teresa

I'VE GIVEN MY statement nine times about what happened at the pawn shop and later, at the restaurant. I'm not sure I'll ever get the memory of that man tied to the chair out of my head. I'm grateful I wasn't conscious to witness what happened to him, but tomorrow I'm going to find out his name. I'm going to do what I can to make things right for whoever he left behind. The blood has been cleaned off my face, a bandage applied to the right side of my head. I would normally hate people fussing around me, but Nicky is sitting next to me, safe and free, so I can pretty much deal with anything.

Except for Will.

I can't deal with the way Will is watching me from across the room.

Damn him for coming after me. For proving me wrong and not only saving me and Nicky, but eradicating the evil that sent my family on the run to California. Who knows how many people have been terrorized by his father? Forced to pay protection money, forced to abandon their sense of right and wrong out of fear. Now they've been freed. I'm not naïve enough to think someone new won't pop up in Silas's place, but his deeply rooted influence on this neighborhood is over.

The way Will is watching me says this battle between us isn't over, however. I know he wants to speak with me—among other things—and his restraint is making me edgy. What does he want? Since boarding the plane to New York this morning, I've been numb to the broken heart he left me with, kneeling on the hotel room floor. But that self-administered novocaine is beginning to wear off and I can't decide if I should let myself feel the fresh pain, to remind myself of how vulnerable these feelings for Will make me. Or if I should re-inject myself with a double dose of painkiller.

"Are we done here?" I ask the detective.

"I am," Nicky drawls, jerking his chin at Will. "You're not."

"Shut up."

My brother squints an eye at me. "Have a heart, Resa. He saved our asses."

"I know." A knot forms in my throat, remembering how I felt sitting on that floor, knowing I couldn't do anything to save myself or Nicky. The utter disbelief and horror of being seconds from losing everything. The traitorous joy and relief that gripped me when Will arrived when I'd given up all hope. "I'm grateful. I'm just…"

Confused. The things I discovered about myself in Will's bed conflict with how I feel right now. I like the illusion of being grateful, being his possession, but after having him throw those new discoveries in my face and walking out, I don't appreciate feeling grateful toward him. At all. Not in the cold light of day. So while I could never thank him enough for coming to our rescue, my stung pride is reverberating like a plucked tuning fork.

"It won't hurt to hear him out," Nicky says, breaking into my thoughts. "He had a bad night, too, you know. If you're into him, might want to consider that."

"I have," I whisper. Silas is going to be fine, health-wise, but Will pulled the trigger and chose me over the potential opposite.

I want to embrace the gratitude that continues to pile on, but then I remember him throwing the money on the ground and my heart rebels. Will seems to realize it, too. Seems to be reading my thoughts from his tense position among the flurry of police activity. "What are we going to do?" I ask Nicky to distract myself. "Go back to LA?"

His gaze traces my profile. "Is that what you want to do?"

"I don't know." There's a welling in my throat pushing the honesty free and for once, the moment feels right. Unavoidable. "Maybe it's time to be on your own, Nicky. I love you. I'll always have your back. But I need to have my own, too."

I turn in time to catch his nod. "It's okay to let someone else watch it once in a while, you know." His smile makes his eyes— so much like my father's—twinkle. "Maybe not as much as I do, but...once in a while. Okay?"

We share a laugh and I lean into him. My eyes clash with Will's. "We'll see."

Will

MY PATIENCE RUNS out right around the time someone else gets to put their arm around Teresa. I don't care if it's her brother. I almost lost her tonight—technically, I *still* don't have her back— and not comforting her when she was almost killed is like a screwdriver twisting in my ribs. *Enough of this.* When the detective dismisses her and she stands, sending me a look from beneath her eyelashes, I stride toward her. And I don't stop until I've picked her up and started toward an empty storage room, away from the multitude of detectives.

Her brother's laugh cracks through the room around the same

time Teresa starts to struggle against me. "Put me down."

"In a minute."

"Now."

I kick the storage room door closed behind me. "Fine."

As soon as she's on her feet, I back her into the wall, leaving only the barest space between us. Hands at my sides, I let her shove me, but I don't budge. "There's nothing to talk about," she says, her voice all over the place. "I was just acting the whole time. None of it was real." Her shrug is jerky, her gaze glued to my neck. "Sorry."

Despite the fact that I know the truth, her strategy catches me in the dead center of my stomach. "*Bullshit*, Teresa. I know better."

Her eyes are full of unshed tears as they lift to mine. "How?"

Jesus. There's so much vulnerability packed into that single word, I can't wade through it all. I did a fucking number on her this morning and I'll never forgive myself. After seeing tonight with my own eyes what she was up against, however, I *do* forgive her lies. She needs to believe that. She needs to know I trust her. Above all else, though, she needs to know I believe this thing between us is real. That it has been real since day one, whether she had an ulterior motive or not. "How do I know better? Because you and that act crumbled underneath me the first time we kissed. Remember that? You looked up at me and I saw right inside your gorgeous head. You might have pulled your little topless seduction performance off without a hitch, but you went down in the second round. Me? I went down in the first. For you, Teresa. When my fucking heart feels like it's being ripped out over here, it's not because of some performance." I reach back and pull the GoPro out of my pocket. "I knew what we had was real before I heard this, but hell if I didn't listen to it a hundred times on the way here."

Her frown clears when I hit play, the sounds of her sobbing river confession filling the tiny storage room. *I could love him. Maybe I already do.* As soon as past Teresa says those words, the gathered moisture spills out of eyes and down her cheeks. "You call that proof?"

I pull her into my arms, wrapping them as tight as they'll go. "I'm sorry, baby," I rasp into her hair. "I'm sorry. Tell me what my father said was bullshit. Forget your name, Teresa? I know it as well as my own."

She stills a moment. "I…think I know."

"You don't *think* anything," I growl.

"Okay, fine. I *know*."

Just for a second, I allow the flame of relief to flicker in my gut. She knows I'm her man right down to my soul. The war isn't over yet, though. "I was fucked up and angry. You're so damn important to me and I didn't treat you that way. I didn't act like the man who earned your trust." My hands tunnel through her hair, bringing it to my nose for rough inhales. "You want to shove me again? Do it all night. I'm not moving."

"*Stop it.*"

"Stop what?"

"Taking all the blame. I'm the one who lied."

"Yeah. And I forgave you as soon as I pulled my head out of my ass." I drop her hair in favor of cupping her face. "You were protecting your brother. You've been doing that alone for a long time. Breaking that habit in a matter of days—"

"I should have." Her eyelids drop and she breathes. In, out. "You never would have let someone hurt Nicky. Same as me. I should have known it was safe to break my habits for you. You showed me that tonight. Before tonight."

"Why does that make you mad?"

Her eyes flash up at mine, swimming with uncertainty. "It

243

doesn't feel right to be grateful to you right now. Or owe you. Even though I really, really do."

Understanding dawns and I suck down the insight like oxygen. The money. I can fucking see it sitting there on the floor where I left it. The trust between us got twisted. I'm never going to let it happen again. Thankfully, it'll only take the truth to fix this. "You came here to take your brother's place. And Jesus, baby, I heard what you almost had to do tonight." Some residual anxiety crops up thinking about her in that position, but I banish it and focus on Teresa. Never again. "If your brother had gone instead tonight, he might have made the wrong decision. You taking his place is what saved him. Not me. All I did was follow you."

"You did more than that," she whispers, her hands softening where they remain wrapped in my shirt. "A lot more."

"I never would have gotten the opportunity if you hadn't been brought back here." I heave a shaky breath. "Fuck, Teresa. I might not have been able to find you."

Without warning, she goes up on her toes and presses our mouths together. Not a kiss. Just a locking of lips, a trading of breath that slays me where I'm standing. "You did." She runs her tongue along my bottom lip, turning my dick to stone inside my jeans. "You did find me."

"I refuse to lose you ever again." In a move I didn't plan, I go down on my knees, running my hands over her hips and kissing her stomach. "You knelt down this morning and begged me to listen. I'm doing the same now." I lift her shirt and rim her belly button with my tongue. "You going to have mercy on me and give the answer I didn't? The answer I was too stupid to give?"

"Yes," she breathes, pushing her lower body toward my mouth. "I'm listening."

I trail my tongue along the waistband of her jean skirt. "I'm the grateful one. I always will be. As long as I can call you mine." Tucking my tongue deep into her belly button, I reach down and unzip my pants, the sound making her moan. "You don't owe me the chance to live my life for you, but I'm asking you to give it to me. As a gift."

I glide my hands up the backs of her thighs, ending in a tight knead of her ass. "Will," she says in a husky voice. "Come up here. Please."

"You want me, woman?"

"*Yes.*"

On my way to my full height, I bring her with me, levering her off the ground and fucking into her tight body, capturing her cries with a cupped hand. "You were hurt. You were *hurt* and I couldn't touch you," I growl into her hair. "Fair warning, I'm going to spoil you rotten to make up for that shit, Teresa."

"I love you," she whispers, taking me off guard and squeezing my chest until I can't breathe. "Not because of the spoiling. Just because of you."

"I love you, too." I lay kisses all over her face, her lips, her head. "That's what I should have said this morning. I should have picked you up off the goddamn floor and said it until you got sick of it."

"Never."

I rear back with my hips and drive her up the wall, earning a close-mouthed scream. "Let's test that theory." I'm slamming into her like a madman and I can't stop. Her legs are wrapped around my hips like ivy, her eyes blind, fingers clutching my shoulders as I work us through the nightmare day we spent apart. A day that could have ended without us together, like this, and just the possibility makes me jerk her legs higher, thrust harder, waiting in agony for her to come before I shove my cock as deep as I can and release in hot, mind-blowing waves, our mouths moving in a frantic kiss…until we're left groaning each other's names as the aftershocks pass.

Several moments later, when our immediate fever has cooled, I smile against her temple and she lifts her head, returning it with a drowsy one of her own. "What?"

"Remember that trip to the vet this morning…?"

EPILOGUE

Teresa

Six months later

I LEAN BACK against the polished chrome wall of the elevator, catching my reflection on the other side as I race to the forty-second floor. Red-soled stilettos and a shortie trench coat.

Subtle.

Smiling to myself, I slip off my wedding ring and tuck it into the inside pocket of my coat, reminding myself to keep my naked hand out of sight when walking through reception of Caruso Capital Management. I'm a regular fixture at the office, since that's where I can usually find the love of my life ruling the planet, but Will's employees are sharp as tacks. The boss's wife arriving without her walnut-sized rock wouldn't go unnoticed, and any negative speculation would piss off my husband.

Me? Not much pisses me off nowadays.

Still looking at my reflection, I turn sideways, laughing to myself at the incongruity of a woman on her way to a seduction…while wearing a backpack. But desperate times call for desperate measures. I've been paired up with another student filmmaker for a project in our Fantasy on Film class. We chose to analyze the movie *9 ½ Weeks* and so I've been watching a young, hot Mickey Rourke boff Kim Basinger all day. Sue me for not wanting to waste time stopping at home to drop off my books.

I arch an eyebrow at my reflection. Maybe I can even work *with* the backpack.

I'm supposed to meet Will for dinner in an hour—hence the stilettos and fancy coat—but I can't wait. He's been working around the clock this week on a deal, which isn't unusual and he always makes up for extended absences. But I haven't known him in the biblical sense for a week, and when that happens…I start to want the fantasy.

Something tells me Will knows that.

The elevator dings for the forty-second floor, sending a stampede of wild horses running through my belly, kicking up dust clouds of anticipation in their wake. *His mouth will be on me soon.* That simple truth turns my nipples to points, makes me shift in my heels. I tuck both hands into my pockets and prepare to exit, knowing eyes sweeping over me as I step out onto the black marble floors of CCM. But those knowing eyes are friendly, too. Most of Will's employees were at our wedding last month and don't hesitate to wave at me now from their modern, glass desks, the receptionist sending me toward the corner office with a smile.

The reminder of our Cipriani wedding, along with the incredible opulence of this place, forces me to perform a mental shake. CCM is a far cry from the casual halls of the Film Institute, but somehow I'm comfortable in both places. They're both important to me. Even Will's apartment, which is more like a palace, has become far less intimidating than the first time I stepped inside…and tried to run back out.

Only to be caught and carried back inside.

Now it's home. It's the place I do my homework. The place I wrestle with Southpaw, take turns cooking dinner with Will, watch the sun set. It's the place my husband takes me on all fours at the end of a hard day…and makes sweet, slow love to me when I'm tipsy or want to celebrate a good grade. Yes, it's huge and it has a concierge and a swimming pool—and we'll probably find something more suited to us someday. But for now, it's exactly where I want to be.

At first, I was concerned over not being able to contribute to household expenses. What I had saved for film school was laughable compared to Will's bank account. How could I just live in this enormous palace overlooking Manhattan, not having earned it? Will could see I was anxious, so he took me to his old neighborhood in New Jersey. He walked me down his block and past the boxing gym and through his high school. I know he was reminding me of who he is on the inside—a beast with a heart of gold and a fighter's soul—and then he proposed to me right there on the dirty sidewalk.

"I didn't know which man I was. Until you. Now I know I'm both. But I can only see them both clearly when you're looking at me. Teresa, never stop looking at me. Christ knows I never want to take my eyes off you." He'd opened the ring box, but I hadn't been able to tear my focus from his face. Good thing, too, because the size of the diamond might have knocked me on my butt. "None of it means anything without you. Share everything I've got. It's nothing compared to you sharing yourself with me. Marry me, woman."

After that day, I stopped complaining every time Will brought me home a gift or surprised me with a trip to Milan. Or Antigua. Or—

Point made. I'm spoiled and it's hard to care when it makes Will so happy. If I ever start to feel like the financial scales are imbalanced, I console myself with the future. When I'll be directing groundbreaking films and can afford to spoil Will, too.

If there's one thing in my life that isn't exactly easy to deal with, it's missing my brother. I haven't seen Nicky since the morning after Silas was arrested, when we dropped him off at

JFK. Will offered to let him stay with us for as long as he wanted, but my brother seemed…new, somehow. Less loveable screw-up, more determined young man. He was eager to return to Los Angeles and try living on his own. Which would be great. Really. If I didn't mourn his absence a little every time I saw an angel on television or a greeting card. Or siblings laughing together on the street. We talk on the phone, but he's busy with school and a new internship, so the calls are rushed. Or I can't see his expression to know if he's embellishing or teasing or—

Okay. Being sad is definitely not the way to arrive to a surprise romp with my overworked husband. Thinking of those hoarse sounds Will makes when he comes, I'm back in the mood by the time I arrive at his frosted glass office door. I give a light knock.

"Yeah," comes his muffled bark.

The employees closest to Will's office share a laugh with me. Will is never going to be the polished businessmen I now know his competitors to be. And I like that just fine. Love it, in fact.

Schooling my features, I open the office door and step inside.

Will

THANK GOD.

My head and chest echo those words when Teresa walks into my office. I've needed her for days—her taste, her smile, her touch—but I've been going home to grab a quick run and a shower before coming straight back to work, leaving her asleep in bed most of the time. She's working so damn hard herself at film school, which is the only reason I don't wake her up with my tongue, even when I'm dying for a lick. If I do that, though, I'll never leave. Quickies are never enough with Teresa, I always need more, whether we're going at it again or shit, talking. *Not* talking and just watching the city lights through the window. Making out in the pool. Everything I do with her is always the best thing I could be doing.

The night my father was arrested, I almost lost the woman I live for, which was horrific enough. But I also found out my mother went behind my back and made Silas her partner, giving him slight—although impactful—control of some of my company funds. It took a lot of cooperation with the SEC and law enforcement to keep those details unpublicized, but eventually it paid off and his name—along with his ill-gotten money—was quietly erased. Silas will be in jail for a long time. My mother is in her own type of prison, however, unsure how to proceed without the hope of a normal relationship. In a way, her signing on Silas as a partner brought Teresa into my life, so I don't hold it against her. How can I when I'm so fucking happy? Teresa insists on a visit to New Jersey every weekend. And things are starting to change for the better. Last time we went to my mother's house for Sunday brunch, Teresa taught my mother how to play poker—and pretended to lose. Just another reason I adore my wife like nobody's business.

Unfortunately, I still haven't quite made up for my impromptu leave of absence six months ago with my other investors, but I'm damn close. I'm so close to being back on top, and as soon as that happens, I'm going to spend a lot of time *on top* of my wife.

Fuck. Is this really my wife?

I'm on a conference call with Turkey, a translator chiming in every fifteen seconds to interpret, but I'm having a hard time paying attention now that the blood has drained from my head to behind my zipper. After setting down her backpack, she reaches up to let down her hair and I notice she's missing her wedding ring. I growl, causing the interpreter to stutter. My head knows Teresa came here to play, but I like having my mark of possession on her. Same way she likes having a gold band engraved with her name on my ring finger. Make no mistake, hers is going right back on as soon as we're finished.

She unties the trench coat and lets it fall.

There's a lock mechanism for my office door beneath my desk and I smack it now without looking, engaging the bolt. Because it will be a cold day in hell before anyone sees my wife in nothing but a red lace thong and high heels. My ass flexes without a command, pushing my hard cock up to grind it against the heavy desk drawer. There's no relief, though. Relief lies only with her—the woman who walked in wearing a backpack—and is standing in front of my desk with a dutiful expression. Waiting.

I'm the one who ordered her, after all.

I flick a glance toward the leather couch and she nods, tossing her hair and giving me a view of her beautiful ass as she clicks toward the furniture. She perches on the middle cushion and crosses her legs, looking nervous. Like a call girl about to learn the ropes. Goddamn.

We don't act out Teresa's fantasy every time we're intimate together. Not even close. But I've started to crave it like a motherfucker. Look, I crave anything that makes my wife look at me like I hung the moon. Which is why I'm glad she couldn't wait for dinner and came here early. I've got a surprise in store.

It takes me a few minutes to end the call, but I finally manage it, encouraged by Teresa's pouting pink nipples. "Pretty sure I just made a less than ideal business agreement so I could get inside your sexy little body sooner," I say, standing to loosen my tie. "How are you going to make it up to me?"

"Whatever the boss wants," she murmurs, watching me approach through her eyelashes, her ass shifting on the couch. "My job is to make you happy."

I stop in front of her and shed my tie, then my jacket. She's playing it a new way, sending longing looks at my erect dick before glancing away in embarrassment. "They sent me a curious girl, huh?" I reach down and fist myself through my pants. "You want to know what this is going to do to you?"

"Yes," she breathes, before shaking her head, sending hair falling around her shoulders and tits. "I-I mean, it doesn't matter. As long as you enjoy it."

Biting back a groan, I unbuckle my belt and lower my zipper, taking my cock out to stroke it right in front of her pinkening face. "Am I your first appointment, baby?"

Staring at my ready flesh, she nods slowly.

"Then it's a good thing we have three days together," I rasp, lowering to my knees in front of her, leaning in to lay a kiss on her stomach. "That should be enough time to teach you what I enjoy. And you're hiding what I enjoy inside those wet, red panties, hoping for a lick from its first man."

"Yes..." My wife peeks through the act, looking confused. "I—three days?"

I tug her thong away from her body, grunting at the slick flesh revealed. "That's right. I'm good for it."

"But don't you need to work?"

"I have some business in Los Angeles." Not wanting to miss her reaction, I press our foreheads together, noting she's stopped breathing. "You don't mind coming along, do you?"

"Will?" she whispers. "You don't really have business in Los Angeles, do you?" A little sob escapes her mouth, cutting me down the middle. "You're—are we going to see Nicky?"

"Yes." Her hands fly to her mouth, covering it. "But I didn't lie. I do have some business to handle." I run my hands up her smooth thighs, hooking my thumbs in her panties and dragging them to her knees. "There's a small matter of a gambling parlor I bought and shut down, just in case my woman ever tried to go back there. Turns out, it came part and parcel with a good-sized building. One being eyed by developers."

She shakes her head. "You're going into real estate now?"

I smile. "Never rule it out. But I owe a debt to someone and I'm signing over the building to her as payment."

Her lips part. "Who?"

"Mara, the patron saint of Lays potato chips." I toss aside her panties and move in to kiss her mouth once, twice, before laughing at her dumbfounded expression. "The one who stood up for you, before I knew you existed. The first piece of your work you showed me was about her—and I never forgot her. Never forgot that she looked out for you, Teresa."

"Neither did I." She lets out a hysterical laugh. "Oh my God, Will. You're—I can't believe you're doing this. When are we going?"

"Tonight. Southpaw is coming, too." I laugh at her squeal. "I only have the long weekend, but soon, baby, I won't have to work around the clock as often."

"Doesn't matter. Three days. Three days is more than I had this morning." She breathes a whimper. "I love you so much."

When she launches herself at me, I let her knock me back onto the floor, but quickly roll her beneath me. I clap a hand over her mouth and thrust my cock deep, pressing my own lips together to capture a guttural groan. And just like that, I'm in paradise, fucking my incredible wife on the floor of my office.

"Now, where were we?" I manage, capturing her wrists above her head and grinding myself into her tightness while she squirms. "Was I getting ready to put some work experience on your résumé before I burn it and keep you for myself?"

Her back arches on a shaky exhale. "Screw the fantasy." Our

eyes lock and the love shining back humbles me. Makes me ache and feel weightless at the same damn time. "*You're* my fantasy, Will."

"And you're mine, baby. One I'm going to keep having over and over again." I rear back and drive into her hard, the tide of my lust rising when her thighs spread wider, wider for me. "Christ, I love you, Teresa."

"I love you, too," she gasps into my kiss. "But...did I ever tell you I climbed the balcony and broke into your motel room the day we met?"

Only this woman could make me laugh when I'm ready to explode. "Why are you telling me this now?"

Her upper lip curls, reminding me of a naughty kitten. "A little pit stop in Dallas on the way home might be fun...just for old time's sake."

Imagining her screaming up against the door where I first kissed her, I press our heads together and ride her hard. "*Done.*"

THE END

ACKNOWLEDGMENTS

I am so grateful to everyone who picked up this book! Thank you! I have never self-published before and it's definitely an exercise in self-doubt sometimes. Luckily, I had the encouragement of some fantastic people to help me along the way. Thank you to Eagle at Aquila Editing for your mad editing skills and support. Thank you to Bailey's Babes for letting me tease you endlessly with Will, dirty talker extraordinaire. Thank you to my husband, Patrick, and daughter, Mackenzie, for your love, patience and uncanny ability to know when I need to zone out with a notebook and pen. Thank you to photographer Sara Eirew for the incredible cover. Thank you Trish Wrzosek for helping me with veterinary terminology and clarifying Southpaw's diagnosis. And last but not least, thank you to Rob Kugler whose real life journey with his dog Bella—documented on Instagram— inspired this book. Inspiration truly does come from everywhere.